Books By
Misha McKenzie

Burke Witches
Aria's Law
Anna's Knight
Evan's Pride
Ethan's Honor

The Magic of the Heart Series
Magic Found
Magic Hidden
Magic Lost
Magic Revealed

Single Titles
RavenStorm Witches

Tawny Justice
The Lost Creek Shifters

Misha McKenzie

ICASM PRESS

SAVANNAH

This book is a work of fiction. The characters, names, events and places are fictitious and products of the author's imagination or are used fictitiously. Any similarities to actual persons, living or dead, places or events is entirely coincidental.

Published by Icasm Publishing LLC
5710 Ogeechee Rd. Suite 200 #278, Savannah, GA 31405
www.icasmpress.com

Library of Congress Cataloging-in-Publication Data

McKenzie, Misha
Tawny Justice / Misha McKenzie
      p. cm.

ISBN-13:978-1-942318-43-9 (Trade Print)
ISBN-13:978-1-942318-44-6 (eBook)
I. Title

This book is dedicated to all of my family and friends I wanted to thank you all for sticking with me while I stepped away from witches and ventured into the world of shifters. Building an unfamiliar world can take some time, and you all have waited so patiently. I promise it's going to be worth it. I am super proud of this book, and hope to continue developing new characters we can all get to know and love.

To Kayla, thank you for letting me pick your brain. You were invaluable with everything horse training related. I hope you and Shorty enjoy your brief appearance. Lauren, your information on Double Merle Great Danes was amazing. And I hope the people reading this book will take notice and educate themselves a little more on these incredibly resilient and sweet dogs.

And a special thank you to David, Mandi, Sharyn, and all the others who got this book ready for publication. Without all of you, this new series probably wouldn't even exist. You all took a chance on that very first book without knowing where it would go. So, thank you.

1

The mountain lion stalked her prey with calculated stop-and-start movements the big cats had perfected millennia ago. At just under a hundred pounds, her long, sleek body stretched out to six feet. From her pink nose to the black tip of her thick, heavy tail, she was proof of nature's excellence.

Powerful muscle and sinewy swiftness let her reach speeds of up to forty-three miles an hour. She could jump forty feet from a standstill and leap vertically fifteen feet. Her coat was tawny, smooth, and gleamed when lit by the sun. Though she may not roar like the larger cats, her hiss and growl had the same effect and warned off anyone bent on messing with her.

Black shadowed her muzzle, the backs of her ears, and lined her eerie gray-green eyes.

And right now, those eyes were zeroed in on the man trespassing below her.

He'd come into *her* territory, a section of land in the Lost Creek State Park that encompassed about fifty square miles of western Montana. This was her backyard. This was her home, and she meant to protect it from the likes of him.

Poachers were always a danger to creatures such as her. Entitled humans who thought they could do whatever they pleased. Killing indiscriminately and answering to no one.

Well, not today. This one was going to answer to her.

She watched as he set his trap, pushing the great steel jaws wide and activating the trigger. When stepped on by some unsuspecting victim, that mouth would clamp onto a leg or body, where it would maim or kill in an instant.

The mountain lion waited until, satisfied with his work, the intruder backed away from the metal monster. Wide paws made her progress silent as she stalked closer, approaching from behind. When he finally turned to leave, she was there. Ten feet away, staring him down.

He went statue-still, eyes big and round as he realized his fate. Caught between the razor-sharp teeth of the cat that stood ready to pounce, and the ones of the instrument he'd set there himself.

The hunter glanced to the side where he'd propped his rifle against a boulder. Too bad it was just out of reach. When he made a move to retrieve it, she flattened her ears, lunging in that direction, and gave a warning growl.

He froze, watching her carefully.

Now that she had his undivided attention, she prowled forward one measured step. The lioness smiled inside when his foot mirrored hers, and he took one step in retreat. She went closer yet, one tormenting glide after another, prompting him to withdraw farther.

When she judged the distance as what she needed, the cougar screamed its signature yowl and swiped out with her massive paw—claws fully extended.

Just as she'd anticipated, he jerked backward away from her. His violent recoil had his weight tipping backward, stumbling over his own feet on the uneven ground. His arms wheeled wildly as he tried to reclaim his balance, and a look of abject terror twisted his features when he recognized nothing would stop his reverse momentum.

Gravity pulled him back, landing him directly onto the trap he'd just so cleverly planted.

The deadly fangs of the steel mouth clamped shut, biting

into his ass cheek and hip as he landed on the pressure plate. His screech of pain echoed off the hills and rocks surrounding them, startling numerous birds into flight from their roosts.

While she was sure the pain was significant, the injury would have been much worse if the trap had been larger...or its victim smaller. The wide round ass of the arrogant poacher would suffer no long-term damage, but had that been his foot...Well, then he might have gotten a taste of the torture he inflicted upon those he illegally hunted. The smaller the limb, the greater the destruction. His padded hind end had spared him greatly.

So, he would live. And he would know not to poach again. At least, not *here*.

The lioness stood over him for a moment, the threat implicit in her eyes as she stared down the cowering hunter. Satisfied that she'd made her point, she turned with a flick of her tail and faded back into the shadows.

She made her way through the forest until she neared where the woods gave way to a residential lawn. The cat slowed and then stopped. While still hidden within the tree line, she scanned the area to make sure she wouldn't be seen. The size of her eyes was proportionately larger than those of other carnivores—perfect for hunting and granting her extraordinary visual capabilities.

It was still early morning, just after dawn. Most day creatures, human and animal, were still tucked up in their dens, oblivious to the beautiful day already beginning.

Sensing all was clear, she allowed her body to shift and evolve, her frame slimming and shrinking as she reared up on her haunches. The metamorphosis was painless, and when it was complete, she stood upright on two strong legs.

In this form, she was a five-foot-eight-inch woman with skin the color of a creamy latte. Her long tawny hair curled into riotous waves as it hung down her back to brush against the curve of her waist. The eerie gray-green of her eyes remained the same—both in feline form and human. They were framed by full, dark lashes that swept across her cheeks every time she blinked. She'd been told by many a hopeful male that she had lips that fantasies were made of. Plump and dusky pink, they drew more attention than she cared for.

Her looks may capture the interest of men, but there wasn't much she could do about that. Thanks to genetics and a stunning mother, she'd been gifted more than most. She knew she was beautiful—more from how people reacted to her than because of her own vanity—but it wasn't something she considered important. Long-limbed and shapely, she could only imagine what someone might think if they saw her now, surrounded by the lush foliage of the forest. And completely naked.

With her nearest neighbor a half-mile away, Kaia Reid emerged from the shelter of the dense wood and strode, unabashedly nude, across her back lawn. Slim and toned, her long legs ate up the ground, just as her cat's had. Nearing the deck built onto the rear of her house, she made quick work of the three steps leading up.

Draped over a chair where she'd left it earlier was a thick sky-blue terrycloth robe. With a flip of her slender yet muscled arms, she had it wrapped around her body and belted tight.

Grasping the handle of the sliding glass door, Kaia pulled it open and stepped into the comfortable familiarity of her home.

She'd entered into the dining area of the house. Directly in front of her was the rectangular wood table that had seen so many family meals, arguments, and laughter. To the right was the kitchen, separated from the dining room by a waist-high counter lined with bar stools, where she'd sat for after-school snacks.

On the far side of the dining area was the living room where they'd all gathered to watch TV and play board games on Sunday nights. To the left was the hall that led to the bedrooms and bathroom.

It had once been her family's home, but now it was just hers—Kaia was the only one left. Her parents and brother had been taken senselessly and tragically, and she fought every day to put her life back together and go on. But she missed them terribly, and they were never far from her thoughts.

Shaking her head and pushing the grief and pain to the back of her mind, Kaia crossed to the one-cup brewing machine. She chose her usual black tea and set the pod into the receptacle. Pulling down her favorite mug that decreed her the Queen of Everything, she hit the brew button, and in less than a minute, she had steaming, fragrant tea.

Late-April mornings in Montana could still be quite frosty, and although, as a shifter, the cold didn't affect her the way it did most people, the thick robe and hot tea were a welcome balm to the chill and the lingering loneliness.

Taking her cup into the bathroom with her, Kaia went to shower. To keep her crazy hair from getting wet—and becoming even crazier—she bundled it on top of her head with a hair tie. The mass of curly brown and blonde-streaked hair took forever to dry, so she only washed it when she knew she had the time to take with it.

Today was not that day. She had something else she intended to do before going to work, and she needed to finish what she'd started out in the woods.

Half an hour later, she was climbing into her yellow four-door Jeep and setting off down the road towards Anaconda, the nearest city to where she lived. It was about a twenty-minute drive, and she made it uneventfully.

Pulling up to the Sheriff's Office, she parked next to the SUV cruiser the sheriff drove. He habitually came into work before anyone else, his only focus in life being his job. Well, that and making her life a living hell.

Sliding down from her seat, Kaia walked over and gave his

truck a kick. She hoped, by extension, he'd feel it.

Striding in, she walked past the empty reception desk and straight back to his office. Stepping into the doorway, she saw him lounging back in his chair as if he'd been expecting her.

Inhaling deeply, Kaia moved to stand directly in front of his desk.

His long, denim-clad legs were stretched out in front of him and disappeared under the desk. Kaia didn't have to see his booted feet to know they'd be crossed at the ankle. The uniform shirt he wore was pressed to a crisp, clean edge. His tanned arms were raised, and his hands were gripped behind a head that was full of ink-black hair. He kept it cut short, but the tousled locks showed the tell-tale signs of hands being run through it after taking off his black cowboy hat. Which she knew would be hanging on a hook by the door. If she bothered to glance back. Which she wouldn't.

Black suited him better than white ever could. He may be a lawman, but no way in hell was he a hero.

Lucas McNamara was the bane of her existence. He'd been her older brother's best friend, and when Jace had died, Mac had taken it upon himself to step into the role.

A role she really hadn't needed filled and, frankly, she resented the intrusion.

He was overprotective, overbearing, and an overall pain in her ass. And that was before he'd become Sheriff. He'd always looked down on her as if she were the gum he'd scraped off the bottom of his shoe. Obtaining the badge had only made those tendencies that much worse. She was twenty-eight now and didn't need the condescending bullshit he frequently heaped on her. Kaia figured at thirty-three, he'd have his own personal life to worry about and leave hers alone.

But, apparently, she'd been wrong.

She gave him a scathing glare just for form and tossed a slip of paper onto his desk.

He sat forward and picked it up, glancing down at it. "What's this?"

"Coordinates. I was out this morning and came across a poacher. This is the last place I saw him. If you're lucky, he may still be there."

Kaia turned to leave, but her name on a frustrated sigh made her stop.

When she turned back, his deep blue eyes were narrowed, and his thick black brows were drawn together, nearly meeting in the center of his forehead.

His tone was accusatory as he leaned forward and propped his weight on the edge of the desk. "What did you do?"

"If you hurry, you can probably catch him and throw the bastard in jail." She cocked her head at him. "Isn't that what you're supposed to do, *Sheriff*? Catch the bad guys?"

She swung around and headed for the exit again. But the scrape of chair legs on the tile floor said he'd gotten to his feet. She was pretty sure he thought his six-foot-two-inch frame was somehow intimidating, but Kaia was unafraid and couldn't care less.

"You can't keep doing this, Kaia." His gruff voice was firm but weary. "Putting yourself in danger isn't going to bring Jace back. He's been gone for three years."

Kaia whirled, the rage that never left her boiling to the surface over the injustice of her brother's death. At her sides, her hands fisted. "You don't have to remind me how long he's been gone, asshole. I know exactly, down to the minute," she ground out. "Just like I know the men who killed him are free to do as they fucking please. They should have been jailed for the rest of their miserable existences. But since they shot Jace while he was running in cat form, the worst they could get was a slap on the wrist for poaching. Six months, Mac. Six fucking months and a thousand-dollar fine."

She advanced on him until his desk stopped her forward

progression. "Or do you not care about that? Was Jace worth so little to you that you're okay with that? Well, he was *everything* to me." Her breath caught and her eyes burned, but she ignored it. "He was all I had left after our parents died, and he put his entire life on hold to raise me."

The tears threatened to choke off her words, but she swallowed them back as she fixed him with an icy glare. "Poachers stole the last piece of my family. So, I'll at least make sure that anyone stupid enough to come onto my land thinks twice before taking an innocent life. And unless you're planning to arrest me, Sheriff, there isn't a goddamned thing you can do to stop me."

Kaia stormed out of the office and into her vehicle. She held it together long enough to get out of town, but once past the city limits, the levee broke, and she had to pull over on the side of the road. She cried for the brother she'd lost. For the life he could have led, and for the time she would never have with him again.

He'd been such a large part of her life, she hadn't known what to do with him gone. It had been the two of them against the world. Clichéd, but true. They'd had no other relatives close by and had never even met any of their extended family. After their parents had died, he'd been the center of her universe. And it had been shattered three years ago by a single shot. She'd picked up the pieces, but she would never be the same again.

When the storm had finally blown itself out, Kaia wiped her face and blew her nose. Once she'd pulled herself together, she steered back onto the road. As eventful as her morning had been, she still had a full day of work ahead of her. And with Jace gone, her career was the most important part of her life. He'd always cheered her on, encouraging her to follow her dreams.

She'd been crazy about horses from the very first moment

she'd ever laid eyes on one in a book. Over time, that obsession had only grown stronger, and when she'd taken it further and told him she wanted to start her own training facility, he'd been behind her all the way. Jace never had any doubt that she would become the best at whatever she chose to do.

Only to die before he'd seen her dream realized.

After the tragic death of her brother, in an effort to distract her mind from the pain of his loss, Kaia had thrown herself into her business. She'd pushed herself to her limits and developed a successful training regimen, one that had gained her a reputation among equestrians as the most sought-after horse trainer in the west.

Three years later, and her clientele ranged from wealthy land owners to the filthy rich and famous, and she had a two-year waiting list of patrons who wanted only her. Kaia still couldn't believe it had happened. She had to pinch herself sometimes just to make sure it was real.

She'd done it for herself, of course, but more than that, she'd done it for Jace.

As repayment for his never-ending faith in her and what she could accomplish if only she believed in herself. Without his amazing support and influence in her life growing up, she would never have had the strength and courage to make it to where she was today.

Kaia also owed a huge debt to Helen. She wouldn't have made it as quickly as she had without her. The elderly woman, an old family friend who lived only a few short miles from her own home, had heard what she was trying to do. And one day had asked Kaia to come and see her. Over coffee and cakes, she'd made Kaia an offer she couldn't turn down.

Helen's family farm.

It had been over a decade since Helen had had use of anything other than the main house. The rest had been deteriorating from neglect. She had no children that could take over the property, so the rental arrangement Helen gave her would benefit them both.

While Kaia gained the use of acreage, barns, paddocks, round pens, and so much more, the money Helen charged her would enable her to keep the property that had been in her family for generations.

Kaia couldn't believe her luck and had jumped on it.

Those first eighteen months were non-stop work. Hard work that paid off when satisfied clients told friends. And they told their friends.

Word of mouth had spread, and soon Kaia's business was booming. She was able, with Helen's approval, to start making some significant renovations to the land and buildings.

Some couldn't understand why she would put her own hard-earned money into something that wasn't even hers. But as she saw it, everything she did here benefitted her. It brought in more clients, which in turn made it possible for her to further her career and grow her business.

And then there was the news Helen had shared with her only recently. With no family to pass the farm to, Helen had added a stipulation in her will: that when the time came, Kaia would have first rights to buy the farm, and at a significant discount than the price charged to an outsider.

Kaia couldn't believe the amazing generosity and kind heart of the gentle woman who'd become more like family than mere friend. But then Helen knew Kaia loved this place as much as she did. The land would always be taken care of and, someday, children would run free on it once again.

The improvements she'd made, and the ones she intended to make, took on a whole new meaning now.

She glanced at some of the progress now as she turned up the gravel drive. A new roof and fresh red paint on the main barn, sagging walls on a smaller outbuilding were shored up so she could use it as storage for extra tack. Fences throughout were replaced and upgraded. Larger areas were fenced off for when she turned the horses out for play time. She'd even added a washing station, so she could bathe and care for the animals in her charge.

Both she and Helen were extremely happy with the way things had turned out. Neither had any plans to ever change their arrangement.

As she drove past the house, the sweet lady was in her usual spot. No matter the weather, Helen would be on her front porch swing drinking her coffee. She smiled and raised a hand and waved at Kaia as she went by. Kaia returned the greeting as she continued to the barn.

Stepping out of her Jeep, someone was already calling to her. Kaia laughed and called back. "I hear you, Shorty. Keep your shoes on."

Shorty belonged to a friend of hers. She and Kayla had gone to school together, and being horse-crazy was something they'd had in common and still did. Kayla didn't currently have anywhere to board him, so Kaia had welcomed him with open arms. Kaia loved having Shorty, but it was more for selfish reasons that she'd offered to house him. The idea had been that with him here, she'd get to see her friend more often. Unfortunately, though, Kayla had been temporarily transferred out of state for her work. It was a yearlong transfer so, while they didn't get to do any trail riding right now, Kayla could rest easy knowing her boy was taken care of.

Which reminded her of how much she had to do today. Morning chores waited for no man...or woman, as the case may be. And being a one-woman show meant there was a never-ending list. There were horses to feed, stalls to clean, and manure to haul to name a few. And that had to be done before she even got to the training portion of her day.

Kaia should probably hire on some help, but she really liked doing it all herself. She was busy but not overwhelmingly so.

She had five horses in residence at her facility—Kayla's Shorty, her own mare Rayna, plus three more she was in the process of training. She walked into the barn to a chorus of hungry whinnies.

After pulling her hair up into a messy knot on top of her head, the next few hours passed in a blur of activity. Once her morning chores were done, Kaia moved to the stall of her newest addition.

"Well, Oscar, are you ready to get to work?"

The big bay shook his broad head and neighed loudly. Which didn't surprise Kaia at all. His name was Oscar for very good reason. He was the biggest grouch she'd ever seen. The client had bought this guy for his teenaged son, but the son hadn't been able to control the mount.

The horse did whatever he pleased with no regard to anyone's command. They'd brought him to Kaia, hoping she could straighten him out.

In the week she'd had him here, he'd made her earn every penny she was charging his owners. But no matter how obstinate he was or how much he tried her patience, Kaia never lost her temper with him. Or with any animal in her care. She loved them unconditionally. But at the same time, they all quickly came to realize she meant business.

"Now, we've been through this before, Oscar. You know exactly how this is going to work." Kaia, lunge line in hand, slid the gate back and stood in the doorway.

Oscar pranced and danced, shaking his head and swishing his tail. Through it all, Kaia just waited calmly. When he saw she wasn't going to react to his antics, Oscar eventually settled. With a big blow out of his large nostrils, he sauntered over to be hooked up.

"I don't know why you think you need to do that every time." Kaia rubbed her hand up and down his handsome face. From the tip of his velvety soft nose to the point between his ears was a favorite of his.

Leading him out to the round pen, Kaia continued to talk to him in a soothing voice. Once inside with the entry closed, she let out some line and got him moving.

She started out walking him, round and round. When he'd fight her or throw his head, she'd give a small tug on the line to get his attention and encourage him to keep moving forward. If he wasn't positioned just right, she'd point the whip in her right hand towards his hip to let him know what she wanted. As soon as he did as she requested, she released the pressure and softened her commands.

Kaia switched directions, clucked at him, and had him pick up his pace. He may be a stubborn ass sometimes, but when he moved, he was gorgeous—black mane and tail dancing in the breeze and glossy reddish-brown hide glinting in the sun. Legs that darkened to pitch black as the hoof rose and fell in a perfectly timed pace. This big beast was absolutely stunning, and he knew it.

As she took him through his paces, Kaia lost track of time.

It was getting late in the afternoon when she caught sight of Mac's cruiser pulling in. He was the last person she wanted to see. He brought out the worst in her, and they always ended up sniping at each other. Oscar, perceptive animal that he was, picked up on her anxiety and inattention and started acting up.

Kaia calmed herself and concentrated on the stallion. Once she had him settled, she got him moving around the pen again in a nice rhythm. After a few minutes, she called him in and ended the session on a good note. Happy with their progress, she took him in hand and led him back to the barn.

As Mac walked in one end of the barn, Kaia and Oscar came in the opposite. She hooked the horse up to the crossties, so she could wipe him down and brush him before turning him out into the pasture to graze with Shorty and Rayna.

Mac approached while she was grooming the bay.

"Don't they sense your cougar? I'd think they'd be skittish around you."

"They do." She ran the brush down over Oscar's neck. "And sometimes they are. At first. But they learn pretty quickly that nothing is going to harm them here."

Mac wasn't a shifter, and it had only been since Jace's death that he'd learned the truth. After Jace had been gunned down, Kaia had had no choice but to explain the true nature of their identities. She'd had to make him understand that it wasn't only a mountain lion those men had killed.

But a human.

He'd been disbelieving at first, but he'd been friends with Jace since they were little and had known there was something different about the Reid family. Until that day, he hadn't realized just how much.

Kaia pulled her thoughts back to the present. She'd need her wits about her to get through this. "What do you want, Sheriff?"

"Just thought you should know that the poacher is in the hospital."

"Is he?" Kaia steadily brushed Oscar. "Huh."

"I took his statement. His official story is that he was out there camping and came across the trap on a hike."

"Bullshit," Kaia muttered as she bent to run the brush down Oscar's leg.

"And then he said the damnedest thing. It seems a mountain lion came up on him and all but forced him back until he tripped and fell. Into the trap." His tone was as dry as the dust coating Kaia's boots. "His buttock and thigh took some damage."

"Wow." She rose and walked around Oscar, making sure to keep her face impassive. "Well, as they say, Karma's a bitch."

"Is that what we're calling your cat now?" he inquired, his midnight-blue eyes boring into hers.

Kaia spared him a quick glance. "I don't know what you're

talking about."

One black brow rose so far it got lost under the brim of his hat, but he said nothing. He eventually moved to stand on the other side of Oscar. Mac eyed her over the horse's wide back. "I'm pretty sure you do."

"Mmm," she hummed noncommittally. She wasn't a very good liar, so she didn't even try. "Well, at least he won't be breaking the law any time soon."

Finished, she unhooked Oscar and led him back out the way they'd come in. As she neared the gate for the pasture, hard footfalls told her Mac had followed. He reached past them and unlatched the gate for her.

Kaia removed Oscar's halter and sent him on his way with a light slap to the rump. He took off like a streak. She stood watching him as Mac closed and secured the fence.

They fell silent for a bit, both content to observe the exuberant greeting taking place between Oscar, Shorty, and Rayna.

"What you're doing is going to get you hurt, Kaia," Mac said into the sun-washed silence. "And he'd never forgive me if I let something happen to you."

"It's not your job to look out for me, Mac." There was a bite to her voice. "You're not my brother, and I definitely didn't ask for this."

"You're right. I'm definitely *not* your brother." He breathed in deep and released it. "Look. It's not fair how he was taken from us. It fucking sucks in a thousand different ways. But this isn't how to deal with it. Your luck at not getting caught has been holding, but it's going to fail one day. And what would Jace think if I stood by and let that happen?"

Thoughts of her brother had tears gathering in Kaia's eyes. She angled her head away to hide them.

They stood, neither saying anything else as they watched the three horses run and enjoy their freedom. Lost in her own thoughts, Kaia was startled when Mac spoke softly.

"I miss him every single day." His voice was low as he looked down and kicked idly at the bottom rung of the fence. "I *still* want to pick up the phone and call him to see what he thought of the game."

He took his hat off, staring at it as he held it in his hands, and brushed something from the rim. "I can't tell you how many times I wished for just one more beer with him." Mac paused. "He may not have been my blood, Kai," he replaced the hat on his head with practiced movements, "but he was damned sure my brother too."

He turned to face her now, but she still couldn't look at him. "You may not like it. Hell, you may not even like *me*. But I'm going to continue watching out for you. It's the least I can do for him."

Mac spun on his heel and left. Kaia didn't move until she heard the gravel flying out from beneath his tires as he sped away. Only then did she return to the barn.

2

Mac's intention had been to return to the station to finish the paperwork on the poacher Kaia had left for him. He didn't doubt for one minute that she'd had everything to do with him falling into his own trap. He just wished this vendetta of hers would end. She'd been lucky so far. Fortunately, they didn't get too many illegal hunters in these parts, and her machinations had so far gone undetected.

But he knew deep in his gut that what she was doing was going to bring trouble raining down on her head someday. Especially if stories spread of a rogue cat in the Lost Creek State Park. If that happened, they'd be flooded with lawless men on the hunt, looking for a once-in-a-lifetime trophy.

He hated like fuck that out of all the ways for his best friend to die, it had to be over something as senseless as poaching. But nothing she did was going to bring him back. Mac just needed to get a certain hard-headed kitty to understand that.

When he came to the end of the driveway, instead of making the right to go back to Anaconda, he turned left. About four miles up, there was an iron archway stretching over an old gravel two track. Pulling in, he followed the winding path around until he saw the tall oak.

Parking in its shadow, he got out. As he straightened, he dropped his hat on his head and looked out over the grave markers scattered in front of him. Stepping onto the grass,

Mac wound his way through. As he approached the section he needed, he removed his hat out of respect and made his greeting to the couple that had been second parents to him.

Tipping his head to the double headstone of his best friend's parents, Mac's voice was somber but filled with affection. "Hey, Nate. Cori." Mac had loved Corinne and Nathan Reid as much as he'd loved his own family. He and Jace had been inseparable from the moment they'd met in the first grade. If they weren't at his house, they were at Jace's, running and playing and getting into trouble as little boys were meant to do.

His gaze shifted to the right. To Jace's marble stone. Mac had been here when Jace had been laid to rest. He'd come back when the marker had been placed—reading the words that had been carved into it.

Jace Andrew Reid. Beloved Son, Brother, Friend. Under that were the dates of his birth and death. What it didn't say was that inside the coffin six feet under the green grass, lay the body of a mountain lion. Kaia had explained that because he'd been shot and killed in his animal form, that was how he would stay for the rest of eternity.

On top of what had already been a hard few days, Mac and Kaia had had to bury Jace in secret. Officially, he was listed as a missing person, but only Kaia and Mac knew the truth.

And that truth pissed him off just as much as it did Kaia. But he knew there was nothing that could be done. He couldn't go after those bastards for murder. There were no grounds. No way to prove they'd killed a human instead of a mountain lion.

Maybe it would have been feasible if they'd been in an area where shifters were more prevalent. Where more people knew and accepted. But in their little piece of Montana, that just wasn't the case. And it was futile to wish otherwise.

Staring down at the flowers Kaia had recently placed there, Mac ran his hands around the black felt of his hat.

"Hey buddy. How ya doing?" Mac squatted down. "We miss

you like crazy down here. We're all good, but I gotta tell ya, brother—that sister of yours is going to give me gray hair. She's still on this kick to rid Montana, and specifically Lost Creek, of any poacher dumb enough to trespass here." He went on to tell Jace of the latest stunt in Kaia's self-appointed mission.

"I have a really bad feeling about this, Jace. I just don't know what to say to her to make her stop. You know we've never really gotten along. You were the bridge that allowed us to even communicate civilly. Well, since you've been gone, it's gotten worse. I've tried to look out for her like you would have done, and it's like she resents me for making the effort. Like I'm purposely rubbing her nose in the fact that you're not here to do it yourself."

Mac took a bracing breath. "Hell. I want to do what you'd want, but she drives me completely bat-shit crazy. I just don't know what to do. If you have any ideas, feel free to let me know."

He smiled and took a moment to shake off his frustration over the whole mess. "Anyway..." Mac switched to other topics. Baseball, current events, anything he thought Jace would want to know.

When his news ran out, Mac brought it to a close.

"All right, friend. I gotta go. I still have to clean up the mess your sister made this morning. But I'll see you soon." Mac rose and fit his hat back onto his head. "Oh, and if you happen to have any special privileges up there, could you maybe use one to visit that sister of yours and talk her off the ledge? I'd really appreciate it. Later, bud."

Mac did finally get to that paperwork. By the time he finished it up, it was close to dinner time. He set it on Melissa's desk, his administrative assistant, for her to file in the morning. Locking up, Mac headed home.

~~~
~~~

Two mornings later, he was wading through yet more forms when Melissa blew into his office. She grabbed up the remote and pointed it at the small TV mounted up high in the corner.

"You need to see this." She hit the power button and then stepped back to wait.

What came on the screen had Mac swearing a blue streak. The poacher Kaia had ambushed in the woods was giving a press conference from his hospital bed.

"…came at me like it was crazy. I've never seen a cougar act that way. I was just out there camping, and it attacked me. It's going to kill someone; it needs to be put down."

Melissa turned frightened eyes towards him. "Do we have a man-eater in the park?"

"No. We most certainly do *not*." Melissa didn't know about shifters, so Mac had to tread carefully here. "Camping, my ass. I know for a fact that man is a poacher. And those wounds he suffered aren't from any mountain lion. They're from falling into his own goddamned trap."

Fuck! This is what Mac had been afraid would happen. And it was starting much sooner than he could have anticipated. Hunters were going to be swarming the hills looking for the rogue cat. Not only would that put everyone—resident and visitor—in danger, but it also put a target on the backs of all the native wildlife.

Most of the nitwits that would be tromping around out there didn't know their dicks from a hole in the ground. They'd shoot first and not think about the consequences. Anything or anyone could be caught in the crossfire.

He pictured wringing one tawny-haired hellion's neck as he put in a call to the TV station himself. He needed to try to put out this fire before it had a chance to flare up.

Jesus. He hated talking in front of crowds, he thought five minutes later as he hung up. If this worked, and it staved off a full-on free-for-all in his park, Kaia was going to owe him big for saving her hide.

Thirty minutes later, Mac rose and grabbed his hat on the way out the door. Within moments, he was stepping out onto the sidewalk in front of his office building. He took in those assembled and cringed internally. There were four news crews—cameras and microphones pointed at him like weapons. Citizens who had probably seen the earlier broadcast and were worried. And those who had seen a crowd gathered at the police station and were just curious as to what was happening.

He estimated about fifty people were waiting to hear what he had to say.

As Mac approached, the entire group came to attention. A murmur washed over the assembly, and some of the bolder reporters shouted out questions. Mac knew they were just hoping to get a jump on the rest, but he wasn't one to acknowledge that kind of behavior.

He stood tall, silent and imposing. His gaze raked over the gathered throng, the adamant questions becoming louder as they fought for his attention. When it became apparent he wouldn't speak until everyone was quiet, those few finally shut the hell up.

Once they had, Mac took a breath and began.

"I wanted to address a statement made earlier today regarding something that happened recently. It was *alleged* that a mountain lion in our own Lost Creek State Park stalked and subsequently injured someone. My office has investigated this incident extensively and has found no evidence to substantiate that claim. What we discovered instead, was that said individual had fallen onto a steel leg-trap. One, we have since concluded, was set by this person in an attempt to illegally obtain an animal."

He let that sink in. "Although we have no reason to believe that any such mountain lion exists, the Sheriff's Office and

Park Officials will be stepping up our presence to assure our good citizens that they are still safe in the park—whether that be from the wildlife, or from those with malicious intent."

Mac picked a camera at random and stared directly into it. "We also want to make it abundantly clear that if *anyone* is caught hunting with anything other than a camera in my jurisdiction, they will be arrested and prosecuted to the fullest extent of the law."

He took questions for the next fifteen minutes. Once they started repeating themselves, he shut it down and thanked them for coming. Mac took a deep breath and turned to walk back into his office. He hung his hat without even thinking about it, crossed to his desk, and dropped into his chair.

Son of a bitch.

He plowed his large hands through his short hair and gripped them together behind his neck. Leaning back, he stared at the ceiling, hoping that what he'd said would get through to those who'd been tempted to come looking for trouble.

~~~

Kaia pulled into Helen's driveway and was surprised to see her friend frantically waving her down from the yard. Kaia rolled her window down at the same time she slowed to a stop to see what had the older woman so agitated.

"Helen? Is something wrong?"

She hustled around the front end to Kaia's side of the jeep. "There was a man on TV. He's in the hospital. He was talking about a rogue mountain lion that targeted him. He said it was mad." Fear crept into Helen's voice. "That's very close to here, Kaia. Just in the park. You don't think it'll come this way, do you?"

Kaia's first thought was that she'd never hear the end of it from Mac. He'd warned her that this would happen, and here
~~~

it was. As if she didn't have to hear his bullshit often enough, now she'd be listening to him bitch about this. But she couldn't worry about that now. She had to convince Helen that they'd be okay.

"I really don't think there's a rogue cat anywhere near here." Aside from me, she thought grimly.

Helen was still fretting. "I just worry about you and your horses being out here alone. If something were to happen..." She let the words trail off. The anxiety was clear in her cornflower-blue eyes.

Kaia reached up and put her hand over Helen's where it rested on the doorsill. She held her gaze. "Nothing is going to happen. To you, me, or the horses. We're perfectly safe."

The surety in Kaia's tone must have soothed her, because her shoulders seemed to sag as her body relaxed. The smile on her face was almost sheepish. "Will you please be careful all the same?"

Kaia patted her wrinkled hand. "Of course I will. I promise."

Once Helen was back on the porch, Kaia drove on. She hated that she'd caused Helen's upset, even if the older woman didn't know. While she did her morning chores, her thoughts revolved around what she should do about the mess she'd made.

"You know what? I'm not going to feel guilty for doing what had to be done," she spoke aloud, her only witnesses the horses and the mice in the rafters. "Those poachers need to know this isn't the place for them." She pitched a load of soiled hay into the wheelbarrow.

"Let them come. Fill the woods with 'em. I'll take them all on, and they can either leave the easy way, or my way. When I'm done, hunters the world over will know not to fuck with Lost Creek."

She used her anger to bust through the rest of her duties. She'd burned most of it off when she heard, and then saw, a car coming up the drive. When she recognized it, her indignation returned full-force.

Long, determined strides carried her out the front door of the barn and onto the gravel. She pulled up short when Mac came to a screeching halt right in front of her.

Standing tall with her hands on her hips, she glared him down. "What the hell do you think you're doing, driving in here like that? Are you nuts? You could have hit someone."

He alighted from his truck and closed the door with enough muscle to rock the heavy SUV. "*I'm* nuts?" He bore down on her. "I guess you didn't happen to catch the news. According to an eyewitness account, we have a killer cat in the area."

Kaia crossed her arms over her chest and shifted her weight to one hip. "As it happens, I *didn't* see it. But Helen told me all about it as soon as I got here."

He seemed to be waiting for her to say something else. "And?" he finally prompted.

"And what?" she demanded with a defiant tilt of her head. The motion sent the hair that had escaped the hairband tumbling over her shoulder.

It drew Mac's gaze momentarily before he brought it back to her face. "Did she also happen to mention that I had to go on air right afterwards to try to dispel the panic and disprove everything he'd said? All because you felt like you could take the law into your own damned hands? Did it ever occur to you that the poacher you saw in the woods isn't the same one that killed Jace? You can't treat them all like they're murderers, Kaia! Yes, they're conducting illegal activities, but your vigilante revenge has got to stop!" Mac paused and drew a deep breath before continuing. "Regardless of everything I said on the news, you *do* realize that this is only going to draw in countless others just like him, right? I tried to deter them as best I could, but who knows if that will even work?"

"So? Let them come!" She threw her arms in the air. "I'll deal with anyone who decides to try it!" She could feel her cat stirring and getting restless in response to her anger. She held her off with a promise of a long run later. And maybe a hunt.

He stared at her as if she'd suddenly grown another head. His deep blue eyes were hard as they studied her. "You've lost your fucking mind, haven't you?" He spun on his heel away from her but only took two steps before he did an about-face. He stalked towards her again and didn't stop until they were inches apart and he was towering over her. "Do you have a death wish?" His glare drilled into her, and his voice was husky with emotion. "Is that it? Are you looking to join your parents and brother in that fucking cemetery?"

Mac reached out suddenly and gripped both of her upper arms. He pulled her up onto her toes and shook her. "Do you think that's what they would want? Do you think that's what *I* want?"

He looked almost offended that she didn't value her own life. Kaia didn't know what to make of his reaction. They weren't friends, even on a good day. Uncomfortable with the intensity of his emotions, she tried to break free of his hold, but his fingers only tightened.

She sent him a blistering scowl. "Let me go," Kaia ground out.

He held her for a moment longer, bodies and faces nearly pressed together. He looked like he either wanted to throttle her or...something. Still trying to interpret his expression, she was almost surprised when he released her, dropping her abruptly back down to her feet.

Kaia stumbled but caught herself quickly. "No. I don't have a death wish." She backed away a few steps, out of arms' reach. She brushed her hair back from her face with jerky movements. "I like my life just fine, and I don't plan on giving it up any time soon. But I won't stand idly by while a bunch of asshats overrun my home to hunt and kill unsuspecting animals."

"And you think your stupid stunts are *saving* those animals?"

His eyes glittered dangerously, the prior moment gone. "I hate to tell you this, little girl, but you've only endangered them more. Do you honestly think those men are going to miss out on bagging the prize you've presented them?" He didn't give her a chance to answer. "No, they're going to shoot anything that moves out there." Mac made a wide gesture to take in the surrounding area. "So, tell me. How is that helping one goddamned bit?"

Kaia bristled at the nickname he'd always used in their youth. But the indignation was quickly forgotten as his words struck home.

Shit. He was right. She'd put the animals, and the people too, at risk. Her stomach sank, but she couldn't let him see how deeply this upset her. She hid the worst of it, shielding the truth in a mask of self-righteousness.

"Well, you'll just have to do your job then, won't you?" Kaia made a move to walk away, but he caught her easily enough.

"Don't you dare walk away from me." His heated gaze pinned her to the spot. She'd never seen him this angry. "You're damned right I will, but just remember that *I* wasn't the one who went skipping through the woods on all fours, creating this shit-storm. I'll just be the only motherfucker left to clean it all up."

The hand on her arm squeezed harder but then suddenly, it was gone. One rough finger rose and pointed directly into her face. "You need to grow the fuck up and end this vendetta before you get yourself killed. Or worse, someone else."

With that, he left her standing there. Stunned speechless.

After he was gone, it took Kaia a second to make her legs work. Once she did, she numbly walked back into the barn and stopped. She stood there staring at nothing as Mac's words pounded in her head.

Endangered the animals. Get someone killed. End this vendetta.

Could she? In her grief over Jace, she'd been consumed with ridding her home of illegal hunters. The same kind that had taken her brother from her. It was the only thing that made her feel as if she were doing something about his death. The law couldn't do anything, so she'd taken it upon herself. She thought if she could stop just one poacher from killing needlessly, she'd have succeeded. And it had escalated from there.

She would never actually kill anyone, but she figured if she caused enough trouble for those who trespassed on her land, they'd leave and not come back. But if Mac was right, and her actions had brought even more danger for the ones she was trying to protect...

There was no way she could just stand back and let this happen. She had to do something to repair and prevent the situation from snowballing any further.

Kaia thought about nothing else for the rest of the day. She thought she'd come up with a possible solution, but she would need Mac's help. And that chapped her ass just a little.

The following morning, Kaia threw some equipment in her Jeep and was on the road to Anaconda bright and early. If she had to swallow this bitter pill, she'd get it over with quickly.

When she stepped into his office, he didn't bother to look up. It wasn't hard to see he was still angry, but she didn't let that sway her.

"I think I know how we can keep more poachers from coming here."

He sat back and finally looked up at her. "Oh yeah? And how is that?"

"If the temptation of taking the rogue cat is what's going to bring them, I say we give them one. A dead one. One shot by our own capable Sheriff. If there's no longer a threat, or a trophy to bag, there's no longer a draw to this area."

When he didn't say anything, she went on.

"We'll take a picture of you standing over a dead mountain

lion. After what that man said yesterday, all the news channels will run it, and Lost Creek will be safe again."

Mac sat silent, and Kaia wondered what he was thinking. She couldn't read anything in his face.

"I take it you're to be the dead cat?"

"Yes," she stated simply.

He nodded once. "While it might feel good to have you dead at my feet," there was a bit of smugness in his eyes, "I think we'll hold that option in reserve. My whole press conference yesterday was geared towards assuring everyone that there *is* no man-killing cat. Suddenly showing up with one would either give the impression that I lied to everyone, or that I don't know what the hell I'm talking about. Neither is good for this office. Let's hope the warning I gave will be enough to discourage them from coming."

She nodded, feeling slightly chastened. "What exactly did you say to them?"

"The truth." He shrugged and sat back in his seat. "And I reminded the entire viewing audience that anyone caught hunting illegally would be prosecuted. Severely. I also advised them that the Sheriff's Department and the Park Rangers would show a bigger presence throughout the area to make sure everyone stays safe."

"Well, it sounds like you have it all covered." Feeling a little let down, Kaia turned to go. "I guess I'll let you get back to work then."

She was almost to the door when he said her name. Kaia glanced over her shoulder at him.

"Steer clear of the woods for a while. My explanation may dissuade most of our would-be criminals, but it won't keep them all away. I'd hate to see you get caught up in something more than you can handle."

Kaia said nothing as she left. What he'd asked was more than she could deliver. Those acres were her home. He didn't understand that her cat needed the daily runs to stay strong and healthy. Both in mind and body.

She promised herself she'd abstain from actively searching out those up to no good, but there was no way she could stay out of the forest altogether. That was impossible.

3

On a fair, pre-dawn morning, a week after her talk with Mac, Kaia stood at the sliding door that overlooked her backyard and park beyond. Reaching out, she slid it open and stepped onto the wooden decking. The boards were a little chilly on her bare feet.

She soaked in the briskness of the air, breathing it deep into her lungs and letting it soothe and strengthen her. This was her home, the only one she'd ever known. Probably the only one she'd ever have.

Her hand went to her waist as she untied the belt of her robe. The garment slid down her arms, and with practiced ease, she caught it by the collar and draped it over a nearby chair.

Creamy skin gleamed in the last light of the moon.

Kaia called to her cat, and it greeted her with love and affection. Each one half of the other. She was the lioness, and the lioness was her. Separate creatures yet bound for all time.

The shift washed over her, and Kaia dropped to her hands and knees as honey-colored fur sprouted all along her body. Bones and muscle transformed, becoming something new. A long tail growing and flicking in eagerness. Suddenly, her senses came alive with infinite new stimuli. Her eyes saw farther, and images were crisper. Her ears picked up the scurry of tiny feet and the rustle of feathered wings coming from the nearby forest. Scents came to her so much stronger now. As the faint odor of death wafted towards her, she knew that some poor animal hadn't made it through the night.

She took a moment to revel in the feel of her new, more powerful body. The cat stretched languidly, extending her claws and digging them into the boards of the deck. Muscles limber and ready, she launched herself off the porch in one bounding leap.

She streaked for the tree line and ran full-out just for the pure joy of it. It was quite a while before the cougar slowed, sides heaving, to tour her domain.

Despite Mac's warning, Kaia had continued her daily runs. She needed this—her feline half hungered for the freedom and the physical outlet—the urge to keep her instincts honed and her body at peak performance. Not to mention, the exhilaration and the power that came with her animal companion were heady stuff, and she enjoyed every minute.

But she also wasn't as reckless as Mac seemed to think. While she explored, she kept a wary eye out for any signs of humans. She stayed to the higher elevations, hoping to avoid any unwanted interactions.

That wasn't to say she still didn't keep watch over what was happening within her range. But so far, there were no indications that anyone else was hunting these lands. She'd seen no evidence of traps, snares, nets, or any other kind of device that poachers routinely used to capture or kill their prey.

Mac had been true to his word, she'd noticed that week. As the sun had risen each day, she'd seen a visible increase in the number of patrols in the park and surrounding areas, both human and animal. The dogs bearing the K9 vests were a nice addition, she thought. She'd even seen *him* a time or two out driving the back roads where cars and trucks could be easily hidden from sight.

All was looking good. The shitstorm, as Mac had called it, looked like it had blown over without ever dropping any actual shit on them.

Hours later, Kaia made her way back home, her large pads silent as she traversed the dead foliage that littered the ground. As always, her cat was alert to any sound, movement, or smell. So, when a particularly spicy, woodsy scent reached her cat's nose, Kaia knew exactly who waited for her.

Fuck.

She was still about twenty-five yards from where the trees ended and her lawn began when she spotted him. He was lounging against one of the larger trunks just within the shadows. His shoulder was pressed into the rough bark, his arms were folded over his chest, and his booted feet were crossed. The black cowboy hat was perched perfectly on his head, and a flash of blue told her the robe she'd left on the deck was slung over one shoulder.

The feline halted and stared at him, her tail swishing and twitching as Kaia decided how best to handle this. She knew she should shift so they could hash this out, but there was no way in hell she was going to leave the woods in just her birthday suit. While she was completely comfortable with her own nudity, she wasn't about to go strutting around in front of Mac that way.

It had been three years since he'd learned the truth, and she'd thought she may have to literally let her cat out of the bag in order to prove it to him. But he'd surprised her by believing her every word without proof. So, while he knew what she was, he'd never seen her shift or the cat she turned into.

Kaia was kind of curious as to how he'd react if he did see it happen.

She pulled her thoughts back when he pushed off the tree to stroll closer. For his first face-to-face meeting with her large cougar form, he seemed rather calm. She knew her feisty feline would never hurt him, but did he?

"What are you doing, Kaia? I thought we'd agreed you'd stay

out of the park. Did you think I wouldn't know it was you?"

How *had* he known? The park and surrounding areas were huge—giving home to a few other mountain lions. To most, it was difficult to differentiate between one cougar and the next. How had he?

As if reading her mind, Mac answered the unspoken question.

"I've been seeing a cat prowling through the forest all week. And I told myself that you wouldn't be out there after the talk we'd had. But I was wrong, wasn't I? You see, I got a good look at her today with my binoculars." He paused a moment, his deep blue eyes serious. "She has your eyes." His brows knit with indecision. "Or you have hers; I'm not sure how that works." Mac shook his head. "Whichever, that unique green doesn't change. As soon as I saw them, I knew it was you."

As he drew nearer, and a stray breeze brought his scent to her again, her cat suddenly lost her mind. She gracefully stretched—front legs out, hind-end in the air—before dropping fully to the ground to lay and roll in the dirt and grass.

"What the hell are you doing? Get your ass up."

As if Kaia didn't have enough to worry about, she now had the cougar's behavior to add to her list. Kaia was appalled by the driving need she sensed in her cat to rub herself up against him. To put his scent all over her. And transfer hers to him.

"Back the hell off, kitty. He's not even our type. We don't go for domineering, know-it-all, pains-in-the-ass."

For the first time in her life, her cat didn't pay any attention to her. Until this moment, they had always been of the same mind. Not one mind, but they'd always agreed at a basic level. She and her cat were two separate creatures sharing the same body. As a human, Kaia was fully in charge but could sense what her cat felt or thought. When in cat form, the animal was wholly present. Kaia could talk to her and interact, and— normally—they had an accord as to what was best for them.

But not now. Not in this instance. Instead, she rose and

crossed half the space between them on long, slow, sensuous strides. She stopped again, sat, and stared up at him, the tip of her tail waving back and forth in short movements.

"Are you freaking kidding me? You're flirting with him? You need to knock this shit off. Right now."

The cat stood and edged closer. Only to drop at his feet and gaze up at him.

Un-fucking-believable.

Shock softened some of the hard planes of Mac's face. "Well. Okay, then." he muttered, clearly confused and forgetting for a moment he was mad at her. He knelt and tentatively reached out to touch her.

Kaia was completely mortified when her cat started to purr under Mac's ministrations.

"What the hell is wrong with you? You should be ashamed of yourself! Get your ass up and behave!"

The mountain lion gave a soft growl in response to Kaia's order, which in turn startled Mac. He jerked his hand away quickly and stood.

He gathered himself and the stern expression returned. "Come inside, Kaia. We need to talk." He folded her robe over a low branch, turned, and walked away. She watched as he strode right up to her house and let himself in.

Well shit.

Kaia was tempted to take off into the trees again, but she wasn't a coward. She kept telling herself that, even as the need to run nearly overpowered her.

And besides, she had to shift back before her other half did something Kaia couldn't take back. Like chase after him and hump his leg, or some other such disgusting nonsense. Kaia would be beyond humiliated.

As she took her human form and her cat receded back, Kaia breathed a sigh of relief. She didn't know why her inner feline had reacted to him like that. On the whole, the mountain lion side of her didn't care for people much. Especially upon their first meeting. She was very untrusting.

So why, in all that was holy, out of all the people on the planet, did she seem to be so infatuated with Mac? Kaia didn't know. What she did know was that it had to stop.

Angry now over how the last few minutes had gone, Kaia cinched the belt tight. She stalked across her yard and into the house.

Only to see he'd made himself at home and had brewed himself a cup of coffee.

"Just help yourself," she grumbled as she skirted around where he was leaning against the counter to get her own cup of tea.

As the coffeemaker spit and sputtered, Kaia thought it might be smart to get out in front of this situation. She turned to face him, resting one hand on her hip and the other on the edge of the cabinet. "I never agreed I'd stay out of the park. My cat needs to run. But I was careful and stayed well off the beaten path to avoid any human contact."

Her tea finished, but Mac had yet to say anything. Frustrated with him and shaking her head, she took her cup to the table and sat.

Mac gave it a moment, took a sip of his coffee, and then pushed off the counter and followed. He sat down across from her. But a heavy sigh stopped anything she'd been about to say.

It sounded so defeated. And that was strange coming from Mac. He didn't give up. On anything. Ever.

Now she was worried. Had something happened that she hadn't heard about? Had he found evidence that poachers had come after all? Had they killed already?

"Mac?" Uncertainty laced her tone. "What is it?"

"Do you hate me? For being alive while Jace is dead? Is that why you make a point to go against everything I say? Even if it means putting yourself in grave danger? I'm only trying to protect you, Kaia. Just like Jace would have wanted me to." His hands wrapped around his mug as he stared down into its black depths. "I can't tell you how many times he told me that you were the most important person in his life. That if anything happened to you, he didn't know how he'd make it up to your parents. You may not know this, but he stood over their graves and promised them that he would take care of you. At nineteen, he stepped up, so you wouldn't have to go into foster care, or be shipped off to some long-lost relative you didn't know. Most guys his age wouldn't have. But he did, even while suffering his own grief. He was barely old enough to take care of himself. Yet he took on a thirteen-year-old girl who'd been devastated by the loss of her parents. And he made it work. Somehow, he made it all work. And he never complained—not even to me—that it was too much for him. He just did as he'd promised to do."

His words were shattering her indignation.

"I was there with him when he made that vow. And right then, I swore to myself that if, God forbid, anything ever happened to Jace, I'd pick up wherever he left off. You were important to him, so you became important to me. I feel the same way he did that day at the cemetery. If anything were to happen to you on my watch, there would be no way I could ever make up for that."

Mac finally looked over at her, his eyes a stormy blue and emotions roiling behind them. Some she shared. The pain, the loss, the missing him. But others, she couldn't define and didn't try to discern.

This whole conversation was ripping at her heart. And for some reason, it was also making her nervous.

Mac finished his thoughts. "So, while you may resent me, I'm not going anywhere. I made a vow to my best friend, and I'll damned well keep it."

Kaia had never heard him talk like this. He was usually a

man of few words and never one to explain himself. This was the most she'd ever heard him say at one time. And to hear such sentiment behind it…

She was feeling a little off-balance and confused. "I don't hate you, Mac. And I don't resent you."

He sent her a mocking look.

"Okay." She huffed out a breath. "I don't resent you, *much*."

Mac nodded as he looked back down at his coffee.

"But it has absolutely nothing to do with you being alive in Jace's place." It actually hurt her heart that he would think their disagreements stemmed from that. "I'm so sorry if I gave you that impression. But if we're being honest, Mac, you have to admit you were Jace's friend, not mine. After he died, the last thing I expected was to see you in my face every time I turned around—telling me what I could and couldn't do like you'd suddenly become my parent. It pissed me off to say the least. I was twenty-five, and you were treating me like I was ten."

He opened his mouth to speak, but she continued. "I understand why now, but you could have told me. Or went about it in a different way."

"Would it have changed anything?"

"Probably not." She sent him a grin, but he didn't return it. Kaia took a breath. "Look, you and I will probably never be besties, but we need to work together right now. I should have tried to explain my need to run," Kaia conceded.

"Explain now." Mac leaned forward and rested his arms on the table in front of him. "You said the cougar needs it."

Kaia took a sip of her tea and then nodded as she set the cup down. "She does. She gets restless and agitated if she can't run and hunt every day." Before he could ask, she clarified. "By hunt, I mean finding and stalking prey, but not necessarily killing. She does sometimes, but usually just small game. It keeps her sharp and in shape."

She recalled the fun she and her brother used to have on their outings. "Jace and I would track each other." A sad smile touched her lips. "When I was little, we'd all go out. While Mom and Dad sat up high in a tree and watched, Jace would let me practice my stalking skills on him." Kaia laughed at the memory. "I probably sounded like an elephant crashing through a china shop, but he'd always pretend that I'd snuck up on him. Then we'd wrestle and roll around until our parents called us back. After they died," her smiled faded again, "Jace and I would go out, but it was never the same. Instead, he had to teach me everything they hadn't gotten a chance to."

"There was no one who could have helped?" The weight of Mac's full focus was on her. "After?"

"There were lots—on both sides," she shared. "But they're hours away. There was an incident when Mom and Dad were dating, and because of that, they decided to move away soon after they got married."

Mac nodded. "Jace said something about that, but he was always kind of vague. In hindsight, I'm guessing there was more to the story than just some simple family squabbles."

Kaia gave a knowing laugh but elaborated. "From what I was told, there was someone else who was interested in Mom. He was the son of another mountain lion clan's leader. It seems he didn't care that Mom loved Dad and had chosen him. This guy wanted her for himself, and he meant to have her, at any cost. He and Dad fought, and I'm guessing it was pretty brutal. Dad kicked his ass, but because of who his father was, this asshole thought the rules didn't apply to him. He actually kidnapped my mom once and tried to rape her. Thankfully, he was caught before anything could happen, but as a result, Mom and Dad were married in a quick, quiet ceremony, kissed their families goodbye, and left Colorado. They never told anyone where they were going, and they never looked back."

"And you've been cut off from the rest of your family for all these years?"

Kaia took a sip and nodded. "Mostly. Phone calls here and there when I was young. But I think they had to be extremely careful in case that man found out where they'd gone. All their sacrifice and diligence must have worked, because to my knowledge, he never found us."

"Do your families know your parents died?"

Kaia furrowed her brow and thought back for a minute. "I think I remember Jace saying he would get word to them. But I never heard anything else after that."

"I take it you didn't contact them about what happened to your brother then."

"No." Kaia shook her head. "I have no idea how to reach them."

"Do you want me to do some digging? I could find them for you. They might like to see you."

It would be nice to see who was still out there. "Sure. Why not?"

Mac looked at his watch and noted the time. "I'd better get back to the office." He rose to stand next to his chair. "I understand now that I can't keep you out of the park, but will you please be careful?"

Kaia could easily agree to that. "I will. I promise."

She walked him to the door and opened it. He paused at the threshold and turned back to her. "She's beautiful, by the way—your cat. I would have thought she'd be more prickly and grumpy, though." Mac grinned for the first time. "Kind of like you."

"Ha ha," she countered sardonically. There was no way she was going to explain that, even if she knew. "I guess you caught her on a good day."

"Well, tell her I enjoyed meeting her."

Feeling slightly embarrassed for some unknown reason, Kaia watched Mac walk away. That was the longest, most civilized conversation they'd ever had. Maybe they could find a way to get along after all. She'd just have to make sure the frisky kitty inside of her minded her manners from here on out.

~~~

Two days later, Kaia was taking her usual morning run before going to work. Her cat was tracking a rabbit just for the fun of it when she picked up a smell that told her all wasn't right with her home. Prey forgotten, she slowed her stride and scented the air.

Blood. But old. Off to the left.

Carefully picking her way through, Kaia tested each step before shifting her weight to that paw. It was a good thing too, because she felt the cold, flat plate of a trap just beneath the leaf-litter.

This is what she'd smelled. It still carried the stench of the poor animals that had suffered in its jaws.

Pulling her foot back, she scanned the surrounding area. If the poacher who'd set it was still here, she couldn't see or smell him. And, in her experience, they usually didn't stick around, instead choosing to wait elsewhere before coming back to check their success.

She needed to get word to Mac, but she couldn't just leave the leg trap there to injure or kill some other unsuspecting animal.

Kaia knew what she had to do. Something she'd done more than once.

After a quick search, she found what she needed. She bent to pick up a heavy stick. Through trial and error, she'd figured out she needed to grasp it more to one end to accomplish her goal.

Carrying it back to the trap, she tilted her head to the side and pushed one end onto the pressure plate. It took a few attempts, but she triggered the jaws to snap closed, rendering
~~~

it ineffective until the ass-wipe who set it returned.

Bounding away, Kaia set a quick pace. It would be faster to just find Mac in the park than to run all the way home and call him. And since she'd watched the cops and rangers patrol for over a week, she was pretty familiar with where everyone would be. Including Mac.

She found him about two miles away. He was driving down an old overgrown path. Judging his speed so she didn't leap out in front of him, she planted herself in the road, giving him a long lead to stop. Large greenish eyes stared straight at him through the windshield.

He slammed on the brakes and got out.

"I take it since this is the first time you've ever searched me out, you've found something."

The cat lifted her head and then lowered it.

Mac shook his own, then rubbed the back of his neck. "Talking to a cougar. This is the craziest conversation I've ever had." It was said more to himself than to her, but she completely agreed.

"Are you going to shift so you can tell me?"

Kaia looked to the trees, and then back at Mac.

"You can't just do it here?"

Her tawny head tilted to the side, and she rolled her eyes.

Knowledge dawned. "Oh, shit. Clothes. Yeah, go. I'll wait here."

In three leaps, she was deep into the shadows. She let the change take her and stood on two long, very naked legs. She slowly made her way back to the edge of the forest but stopped behind a large tree.

She saw Mac leaning against his truck. Kaia raised her voice so he could hear her. "I found a trap set about two miles from here. I triggered it, but who knows how long it'll be before the hunter comes back to check it."

"Where was this?"

Kaia gave him directions, detailing the exact location where she'd left it.

"All right, I'll head on up there and check it out."

"Good." Kaia felt better having told him. "I gotta go. I've still got a full day at the barn today."

"I'll come by later to let you know what I found."

"Thanks."

Kaia shifted back and ran off before her animal instincts could win out and get any closer to Mac. As it was, she could barely resist the insatiable need to go weave in and out of his legs like an amorous housecat.

4

From the safety of his camp, the hunter opened the app on his smart phone. The one that gave him access to the feed from the trail-cam he'd carefully hidden in the trees. It wouldn't do to have someone find it. Especially not so near where he'd left his little surprise.

He was very good at what he did, and it wasn't often he came away empty-handed. He grinned, thinking of the money this animal would bring him.

Once the video was loaded, he sat and watched a lot of nothing until he saw a mountain lion slowly make her way into frame. When she placed a large paw directly over the top of the trigger, he held his breath in anticipation of it snapping closed.

That breath whooshed out in disbelief when she carefully drew her leg back as if she knew what awaited her.

"What the hell?" He sat up straighter and brought the small screen closer to better witness what she'd do next.

He couldn't believe what he was seeing. After backing away from the trap, she seemed to be searching for something. Pacing around briefly, she evidently found what she'd been looking for. He blinked when she came up with a thick stick about two feet long.

She held it in her mouth—positioned where her bite was closer to one end. Carrying it back to the middle of the frame, she turned her head and jammed the opposite end into the center of the plate. When nothing happened, she readjusted and poked at it again and again until the steel jaws slammed closed on the wood, breaking the end off.

The hunter had to rewind the footage. He watched it over and over to make sure he'd really seen what was clearly visible on the display.

Hitting pause, he sat and pondered. This had to be the one. The one Ted had been talking about. He'd seen him on the news release, but it sounded farfetched, even for him. Cougars just didn't act the way he'd described. He thought he'd either been embellishing like fuck or higher than a kite. Everyone knew they didn't target people. And they sure as hell didn't maneuver them into hurting themselves.

But after seeing the cat himself, he had to conclude that his buddy had been right. And she was going to make him a hell of a lot richer than he'd ever imagined.

~~~

Mac found the site Kaia had told him about. The offending device was right where she'd left it. Before removing it though, Mac took pictures and scoured the area for any evidence the perpetrator may have left behind. Chances were slim there'd be any. Men who did this routinely were experts at hiding their presence. But he had to look.

Once he'd done what he could to no avail, he carefully picked up the trap and lowered it into the evidence bag he'd laid out. Once it was sealed up tight to protect any trace that might be present, he took it to the rear of his SUV and set it in the cargo area. He'd take care of it when he got back to the station. Might be a long shot, but maybe he could pull some prints from it. If this were a repeat poacher, he might be in the system already. In the meantime, Mac needed to check in with his deputies and the park rangers to let them know it was starting.
~~~

It was several hours later when he was finally able to get a free moment to update Kaia. It was getting fairly late in the afternoon, but he knew she'd still be working, so he headed over to Helen's place.

Pulling in, he parked in front of the barn where the horses were housed. Stepping into the shadowed interior, he glanced around but didn't see her. He checked each stall as he passed, but she wasn't in any of them. Walking to the other end, Mac exited out the open doors there. And that's when he found her.

She was in the round pen working with the same big bay stallion she'd been training the last time he'd come out. Her long curly hair was somehow secured on top of her head again. Errant strands had slipped loose and were now damp with sweat and stuck to her face and neck.

The faded blue shirt she wore clung to her, molded to her body like a second skin. Despite still being early spring, the darker patches told him she'd been at this for quite some time, and the horse had been giving her a workout as much as she was him.

Mac slowly approached the fence so as not to spook Kaia or her student. He braced one foot on the bottom rung and reached out to rest his arms on the top. As she ran her charge through different commands, Mac studied her.

The soft denim hugging her lower body and the brown leather boots molded to her feet were covered in dust. The steps she took to follow the mustang around the training arena kicked up a small cloud that settled on every inch of her.

Her hands were gentle on the longline, her voice smoothly coaxing as she ran the horse through his paces. Mac reflected on how that was so far removed from what he knew about her. She was tough, smart, mouthy, and enormously driven. She'd had to be to survive so much loss in her life. And not only had she overcome that, but she'd also made a success of herself in a very short amount of time.

As Mac admired her and watched how she handled her stubborn companion, it suddenly struck him. He'd always thought of her simply as Jace's little sister—a cute kid who could sometimes be annoying—and even more so in her adult years. But now…now he was truly seeing her for the first time, for who she really was. Independent, ambitious, and determined to live life on her own terms. The woman in front of him moved with an agile grace and had become, much like her cat, absolutely stunning. All that wild tawny hair, creamy skin, soft curves, and those haunting eyes…

Mac shook himself out of his musings before they could get him into trouble. To let his mind even wander in that direction would have gotten him a good old-fashioned ass-whooping by her big brother. But even with Jace gone, it felt disrespectful to be seeing her this way. He'd promised Jace he'd watch out for her, and damn it! That's *all* he'd do.

While he'd been absorbed in his crisis of conscience, Kaia had finished up her session. After cooling the horse down, she turned him out into the paddock.

"Thanks for waiting. Oscar is one I really need to keep my eye on."

"Oscar?" Mac asked, still not quite back on an even keel as he walked with her back into the barn.

Kaia chuckled lightly. "Yeah. As in the kids' show character."

Her easy laugh did something strange to him, but he fought it back. "Handful, huh?"

She nodded. "If you're not careful. He knows I won't put up with his shenanigans, but if I'm at all preoccupied, he'll try to take advantage. And that's never good."

"No, it's not." He watched her stretch up to return the line she'd used to the hook on the wall. As she did, the hem of her shirt slipped free of her waistband. Before Mac could avert his gaze, he caught a peek of smooth, tanned skin underneath.

Desperate for a distraction, he rattled off the first thing he could think of. "I found the trap." He shifted his eyes away, veering his focus back to business. "There wasn't any sign of the person who'd set it. But that's only par for the course."

Mac rocked his weight back on his heels, sliding his hands into the pockets of his jeans. He had the strongest urge to touch her. To feel the warmth of her body. Smell the scent of sweat on her skin.

His hands fisted.

"I let everyone who's working out there know we have a poacher in the vicinity. They'll all be keeping their eyes open."

"Good." She crossed to a minifridge, unaware of the fight he was waging with himself. When the door swung wide, Mac saw that it was loaded with bottles of water. She took two out and offered him one.

"Thanks." He twisted off the top and took a long drink in an attempt to cool off.

"I'll keep mine open too." She'd circled it back around and eyed him over her upturned bottle. The speculative look in her eyes all but dared him to demand she stay out of it. As much as Mac's gut was telling him to do just that, he also knew it would be pointless.

"I just ask that you watch your back." He recapped his water deliberately. "We'll hope this is an unrelated incident, and that he's not here for you."

"I know how to be careful, Mac. I've been running in those woods for a long time."

Mac was about to press his point when Kaia's cell phone rang. She slid it from her pocket and looked at the screen.

"Are we done here? I need to take this."

"Yeah. We're good." Mac had just started to turn away when she answered.

"Oh, my God! Bri!" Her voice was excited and animated. "It's been so long...Wait. What? You're coming home? When?"

Wonderful. Mac rolled his eyes as he spun and walked back

to his truck.

He knew exactly who Bri was. She'd been Kaia's best friend all through high school. Abrianna Elizabetta Calladega. A pretentious name for a pretentious girl. Mac hadn't cared for her then, and he was pretty sure that would hold true now as well. She'd been one of the shallowest people he'd ever met. He'd never understood how Kaia could be such good friends with someone like her. Everything had to be all about Bri. All she seemed to care about was her looks and what everyone else could do for her.

Her parents were well-off and had lavished their only child—fulfilling her every whim. She'd wanted for nothing and hadn't been shy about who knew it. She and Kaia couldn't have been more opposite, but somehow, a friendship had been forged between them and was apparently still ongoing.

Bri had gone off to college, her parents had moved away, and Mac hadn't given her another thought. If she were coming back though, he'd better start bracing for the whirlwind now.

~~~

Kaia floated through her evening chores and went home excited.

It didn't even bother her that she'd seen the disgusted look on Mac's face. Kaia knew he didn't like Bri—he never had. But then again, he only saw what Bri wanted him to see. The self-absorbed, spoiled, rich kid.

But Kaia knew the façade Bri showed the world was just a way to protect herself. She'd learned early that, because of who and what her parents were, people expected her to be a certain way. So that's what she gave them. In spades.

Very few knew the real Bri, and Kaia counted herself as one of the lucky ones. They'd felt a kinship towards each other as soon as they'd met in fifth grade math class. Both had a part
~~~

of themselves that had to be kept hidden from those around them, for fear they would be taken advantage of.

Bri for her money and prestige, and Kaia for her abilities.

Soon after they'd become friends, they'd shared their deepest and darkest secrets, knowing that the other would keep them safe for the rest of their lives.

And they had. Neither had broken the other's confidence. Not once. So, while Kaia recognized that most would not be happy for Bri's return, she was ecstatic.

Kaia missed her so much it hurt. Infrequent phone calls or emails just weren't enough. She hadn't seen her in person since Jace's funeral, and even then, Bri had only been able to stay for that single day.

Because she'd had to leave so early the next morning, they'd had a sleepover as they'd done when they were kids. They'd talked and cried and laughed all night long, just like they used to. Only this time, there was no one to yell at them to quiet down and go to sleep. When morning had come, they'd been exhausted but happy for the time they'd had together.

After that night, another two months had passed before they'd been able to catch each other again. And then only by phone. Three weeks later, and a couple of emails. Three months after that, there was a quick text to assure Kaia she was still alive.

And that's how it went with them. But through it all, it didn't matter how much time passed. As with all devoted friends, they picked up right where they'd left off when they were able to reconnect.

Bri was a photographer who went into some dangerous situations to get the shots she needed. Bri loved her job, and she was fantastic at it. So much so, that she'd won award after award for the gripping and unique photos she'd taken.

Kaia could never be jealous of what Bri had accomplished. She was so proud of everything her friend had achieved in her career. But she could hate that it took her away for such long stretches of time.

But no more. In another week, Bri would be home—for good.

The reason for the call had not only been to share that tidbit, but to reveal some unbelievable and exciting news. A few months ago, Bri had adopted a little girl. Her name was Min, and she came from an orphanage in one of those war-torn foreign countries she often traveled to for work. Kaia had peppered her with questions, but Bri had promised to explain how it had all come about when she got home. To tide Kaia over and to show off her new daughter, Bri had sent a picture of Min via text while they'd talked.

Kaia fell instantly in love. The thin two-year-old with ruler-straight black hair and almond-shaped dark eyes was small for her age, but she smiled shyly into Bri's camera lens.

Kaia laughed fondly as she looked at the photo again. "Get used to it, little one. You're going to have a camera in your face for a very long time." Kaia studied the image more and could see a brightness, a shining light, hiding behind the guarded gaze.

She couldn't wait to see Bri again and meet the precious little girl that had changed her friend's life for the better.

Kaia went to bed that night full of plans and ideas for when Bri and Min finally came. When she awoke the next morning, she was still grinning. Her happy mood lasted about an hour into her morning romp. Because that's when she began to sense that she was the target of someone's focused attention.

Once the feeling had hit her, she started to take more notice of her surroundings—a rookie mistake that she'd be keeping under wraps. It had been stupid to get so carried away and not be vigilant with her safety. She'd sworn to Mac that she could take care of herself, and here she was, acting like a kitten with a ball of yarn while a poacher could be eyeing her through a rifle scope this very minute.

Kaia immediately changed course and headed up. Higher ground would give her a better vantage point to survey the landscape below.

Crouched low on an outcropping of rock, she relied on her superior feline vision to scan the surrounding terrain. But try as she might, she couldn't seem to pinpoint the origin of the threat. She had no doubt that what she'd felt was real. Something she'd learned early on as a cub was that her instincts were rarely wrong. Someone was definitely on her trail.

Kaia needed to find out who this was and what he was doing here. Preferably, without him being aware that he'd become the prey. Strategy in mind, she went on the hunt.

She wound her way down and around, watching for any signs of the intruder and careful not to give herself away. There were moments when she sensed she was getting close, but then, whatever trace she'd been following would be gone. She'd tracked him for a good hour before hearing the faint sound of an engine revving to life. Kaia took off in the direction of the nearest road, her long, sinewy body and powerful legs eating up the ground. But by the time she reached the source of the sound, all she saw were taillights glinting through the dust kicked up by tires speeding away.

Shit!

With no other recourse, and knowing what she had to do, Kaia headed back towards home. When she shifted back to her human form, she took more precautions than normal. If people were stalking her woods, she'd make damned sure no one was nearby when she transformed. And while she was at it, she'd make a few changes to her routine until this problem was taken care of.

Kaia jogged for the house and got inside quickly.

Once there, she took a moment to throw some clothes on before taking her phone off the charger and calling Mac. He would want to know what had happened this morning. She'd leave out the part about being preoccupied though. He'd never let her live it down if he knew she'd been so careless.

Phone in hand, Kaia went back into the kitchen. As she stood looking out over her backyard, she started to dial. Only to exit out of the screen before she finished.

"I don't even know if this was the same guy who set that trap. It could have been some hiker fascinated by the sight of a mountain lion."

She shook her head. "No. It's better to find out what we're dealing with before calling Mac in."

Though deep down, she knew it was exactly what it seemed. The poacher was now hunting her.

Over the next few days, Kaia took different routes through her territory. On every occasion, she eventually felt him watching her. But he was extremely skilled at obscuring his trail and keeping his position hidden. No matter how she wound around or doubled back, she could never come upon him.

As soon as she'd think she had his location, he'd be gone by the time she got there. It was really starting to piss her off, and her cougar was getting frustrated. Between her brain and her cat's skill, they'd never not been able to track and hunt prey. This one was proving to be an exception.

By the fourth day, Kaia was certain he was fixated only on her. She'd not found any traps though. Was he trying to find a pattern to her travels? Determine the best place to enact his capture based on where she went every day?

Yeah, good luck with that.

Kaia had been sure to vary her activities—keep him from guessing her next move and putting something in place. She had even started to shift farther away from her home in the hopes that he wouldn't be able to follow her right to her door.

She couldn't risk her secret being discovered.

He was definitely stalking her, but she couldn't figure out his motive for not actively trying to trap her. That had her completely bewildered.

Taking a breath, Kaia called Mac.

He answered on the second ring. "McNamara." His voice was gruff and clipped.

It took her by surprise a little, hearing him address himself by his last name. She didn't often think of him as McNamara. Or even Lucas. He'd always just been Mac.

"Uh, yeah, it's Kaia."

"Is something wrong?"

"Not exactly. I just wanted to let you know that I'm pretty sure our poacher has been tracking me."

There was a pause. "Human-you, or animal-you?"

"Animal-me." Kaia filled him in on all their games of cat-and-mouse over the past week.

"You've been playing hide-and-seek with this fucker?"

Kaia ignored the censure in his voice. "Well, I tried to. But he's good. He was able to make it back to his vehicle before I ever got a chance to see him. I thought if I could ID him, we'd at least know who we're dealing with."

"Kaia—"

"Mac." She cut him off sharply. "Do you want to catch this guy, or not? He's obviously here because of me. About which I feel horrible. But, on the up-side, we can use the fact that he's zeroed in on me to set our own trap."

"No. Absolutely not." His voice was adamant. "I refuse to endanger you even further by using you as bait."

"Mac. Think about it. This could work."

"Damn it, Kaia. I said *no*."

"It's perfect." She ignored him and plowed on. "Where else are you going to get a mountain lion you can work with? One who can follow instructions and draw him in?"

He barked out a humorless laugh. "That's fucking hilarious. You can't follow instructions as a *human*. Why the hell should I think that cat of yours would be any different?" He paused a moment. She heard him heave a frustrated sigh. "Look. I'm swamped right now. I don't have the time to get into this with you. I said no, and I don't want to hear any more about it."

Kaia was taken aback by his imperious attitude. Who the hell did he think he was talking to? She'd called him in the spirit of cooperation and offered a sound strategy to get this guy out of Lost Creek.

And he'd dismissed it, and her, out of hand. Well, screw him.

"Oh, don't worry. You definitely won't be hearing any more from me." She jerked the phone away from her face and slapped her thumb to the red end button in a huff. He'd already launched into his next round of arguments—practically yelling—and Kaia had had enough. She had nothing more to say to him. He had no right to boss her around like that and expect her to come to heel. She was a cunning, intelligent cat. Not some slobbering, oafish dog. And she sure as hell didn't need his permission. Or his goddamned protection.

The cell buzzed in her hand. Glancing down, she saw his name light up across the screen. She knew her temper was still running too high, so before she could do something stupid, like throw her phone across the room, she deliberately set it down on the table and walked away.

She needed to push this aside and deal with everything else still left on her agenda for the day. Which was getting to her horses and fulfilling the promises she'd made to their owners. And to be the person the animals needed her to be, she had to lock the rage away. Horses were very perceptive animals. If she were off in any way, they would feel it, and any lessons she taught would be for nothing. Not only that, but it could potentially cause harm if they felt they couldn't trust her any longer.

Ten minutes later, she was ready to walk out the door. As an afterthought, she picked up her phone and slid it into her pocket without looking at it. She didn't have to see it to know

Mac had already called multiple times. His overbearing and controlling nature would insist he lecture her more. She just wasn't in the mood to listen to it. He'd said enough, and she'd heard plenty.

She should have known he wouldn't treat her as an equal partner. To him, she'd always and forever be just his best friend's bratty kid sister.

Kaia waited all day for him to show up and give her a piece of his mind. But he never did, and she got through the rest of the day in peace.

And as she'd worked, she came up with a game plan of her own.

5

The hunter sat in his camp and thought about what he'd seen over the past week.

He'd come across the female the first time, quite literally, by accident. Making his way to where he'd set out some traps, he'd caught sight of her running and leaping as if...happy. He'd never seen anything like it, so he'd followed at a distance to observe her frolicking antics.

Until she caught a scent or sensed his presence. Then her whole demeanor had changed. It was more guarded, more aware. And then she'd changed direction and gone up to the rock ledge overlooking the park. The hunter had made sure to stay downwind and remain hidden as she'd scanned the area. What was she doing?

This cougar was unlike anything he had ever seen. He'd tracked and killed countless animals, and none of them behaved as this one did. As he'd contemplated that, she'd turned and descended. He'd kept a careful eye on her to see what she'd do next.

Astonishment had coursed through him as she'd begun to sniff and search. Not stalk like she had prey in sight, but almost like a hound would when it was on the scent of something.

Holy shit. It had struck him like a bat to the face as she drew nearer and nearer. Wild game, even predators like mountain lions, didn't seek out danger if they found it. They ran like hell to escape and elude the threat. But this one was actively in pursuit, drawing in closer as the hunted became the hunter. It had taken all of his skill to evade her. He'd never been so relieved as when he'd finally made it back to his truck.

His heart had been pounding in his chest as air had sawed in and out of his lungs in great gasps. As he tore out of there, he wondered what would have happened is she'd found him. If the guy from the news was any indication, probably nothing good.

Over the following days, he'd pitted his talents against hers. She'd nearly bested him more than a few times, but he'd managed to slip past her. Barely. This extraordinary cougar had the most complex, problem-solving mind he'd ever seen.

So here he sat. Coming up with a strategy to outwit this amazing creature.

~~~

When Kaia awoke the next morning, she was all set to put her plan into motion. She'd already told Helen that she'd be late in getting to the farm and not to worry when she didn't see her first thing.

In the pre-dawn darkness, Kaia left her house with a sense of anticipation. If this worked, one more poacher would be on his way out of her woods.

Her cat could feel her excitement and pushed to be let out. She would be. Soon. But instead of beginning her run from any of her usual locations, Kaia drove deep into the park. She'd shift there, and once the hunter was on her trail, she'd lead him on a merry chase. One that would parade him right past the cameras she'd set up the evening before.

She'd get a record of this bastard's face. Chances were, he was in the system, and it shouldn't take long to get a match through some handy facial recognition software. Once identified, they'd have him. All of his information would be at their fingertips—
~~~

the most important being his name, vehicle, and plate number. Every cop and ranger in the park would be on the lookout for him. This whole area would become a hot zone, and they'd either catch him, or he'd go back to where he'd come from.

Any way it happened, he'd be gone.

She pulled into a clearing just off an old logging road. Taking her time, she let her senses search the area. Her human sight, hearing, and smell were no match to the cougar's, but they far surpassed those of normal humans. A benefit of sharing a body with a predator.

It was clear.

Getting out of her Jeep, she walked around to the rear, keeping alert to any sound. Stripping out of her clothes, Kaia folded them and tucked them into the bag she'd brought. Once she was naked, she locked her car and hid the keys.

The mountain lion inside of her was ready to come out and play. She knew what their task was today and was eager to start the game.

What cat didn't like to toy with its prey a little?

With just a thought, the transformation process washed over her. Kaia never took her gift for granted. Her parents had filled her with stories and legends for as long as she could remember, up until the day they'd died. And then Jace had taken over to teach her how important and extraordinary being a mountain lion shifter was.

They could date their family back hundreds of years. Strong, fierce, determined, unfaltering—her heritage was filled with bravery and cunning. And Kaia refused to not live up to their example.

Resolve strengthened, she started off into the surrounding woods, her large, wide paws almost soundless on the forest floor. Tracking in this region of the forest was as familiar to the lioness as breathing. This was her playground, her sanctuary. Her home.

She broke into a lope, and as soon as she was far enough away from her Jeep, she started the hunt.

It wasn't long before Kaia got her first inkling that he was watching her. She hadn't actually seen him, but her instincts, honed to a razor's edge, told her he was there. As she started to make her way near where she'd laid her own trap, she kept to the more heavily wooded areas. She didn't think he'd chance drawing attention to himself by shooting her, but better to be safe among the natural cover of the dense trees.

Seemingly strolling for another half an hour, she was still about twenty yards from her destination when she felt it.

A quick, sharp pinch to her hip.

Out of instinct, the cat screamed in panic and instantly bolted.

Fuck. What the hell was that?

She'd obviously been hit with something, but she didn't notice any pain. She took a few precious moments to glance at her backside. And there, sticking out of the large muscle of her hind leg, was a feathered dart.

A tranquilizer. Shit.

She needed to haul ass out of there before she lost consciousness. Get somewhere safe and wait out the inevitable oblivion.

But before Kaia could fully escape the vicinity, she stumbled. Her vision wavered. Oh, God. She wasn't going to make it.

The adrenalin pumping through her system carried with it the sedative he'd shot her with. Her vision waned, and her legs faltered again. She screamed out in frustration, anger, and most of all, fear.

Son of a bitch! She had to keep going. Had to find someplace to hide.

He couldn't find her.

That was her last thought as the drug rushed through her body, taking her down.

~~~

Mac hadn't had a chance to track Kaia down yesterday. He'd tried calling her back several times, but when it became apparent she wasn't going to answer, he'd given up. And now, he was worried about what she might be doing.

He'd handled the situation completely wrong—had known it the moment the words had come out of his mouth. But by that point, it had been too late to take them back. So, now he had to find her and make sure she wasn't doing anything stupid. Or dangerous.

Considering the source, leaping before she thought would be par for the course.

Dawn was painting brilliant colors across the sky when he went by her house expecting to catch her. But when her bright yellow Jeep was nowhere to be seen, he could only hope that she was already at the farm.

However, as soon as he pulled in at Helen's place, he knew she wasn't there either. He saw the kind woman sitting on the porch, and she gave him a wave as he slowed to a stop.

Mac opened his door and stood in the opening. "Morning, Miss Helen," he called out.

"What can I do for you this beautiful morning, Lucas?" She was one of the few who still called him by his first name.

"I was looking for Kaia, but I see she's not here yet."

"Did you try her cell?"

"Yes, ma'am. She's not picking up." For him anyway.

"Well, she did say she would be late coming over today. Must have had some errands she needed to get done."

"That could be." But he highly doubted it. "Well, if you see her, please tell her I came by."

"I sure will."

"Thank you, ma'am." Mac got back into the cruiser and backed out.
~~~

Pulling out onto the road, he knew where he had to try next. Where he probably should have thought to go first. The park.

Finding her there would be no easy task though. And if she ventured into the Deerlodge National Forest, which backed up to Lost Creek, all bets were off—Deerlodge consisted of millions of acres.

Although it was a possibility, Mac didn't really expect that to be the case. The closer he got to those five hundred acres of Lost Creek, the worse the dread in the pit of his stomach became. She was in there somewhere. He didn't understand why or how he knew, but he could tell she was in trouble. Right here in their park.

Pressing harder on the accelerator, the powerful motor set him back in his seat.

He knew he couldn't wander aimlessly looking for her. He needed a starting point. And the first place they'd found the poacher's trap would be as good as any. He'd begin there and fan out, looking for any sign. He just hoped that, regardless of whatever harebrained scheme she'd concocted, he'd find her before it was too late.

Turning up the road that would lead him nearest his destination, Mac fought back the nearly overwhelming urgency pushing at him to go faster. He had to find her. He had to make sure she was safe.

Before he'd gone a mile, a voice came over the radio hooked at his belt. "Becky here. Sheriff, are you there?"

Snatching it up, Mac hit the key to talk. "Yeah, Becky, whatcha' got?" He released the button.

"You told us to keep a lookout for vehicles that seem suspicious. I'm on the old logging road, right where it levels off for a stretch, and there's a newer yellow Jeep tucked back into the trees. It appears to be empty."

Mac rubbed the back of his neck. *What the hell are you doing way out there, Kaia?*

"I know who that Jeep belongs to, Becky. I'll be there in five. Thanks."

True to his word, he skidded to a stop behind the ranger's drab green pickup a few minutes later. Becky was leaning against the hood, waiting for him. Getting out, he settled his hat on his head and crossed to her.

"Where is it?" Mac asked her.

Becky pointed up the road a little farther. "Right in there." She pushed off the grill. "Do you need me to show you?"

Mac glanced to where she'd indicated and then back to the patrol. "No, I'll take it from here. Thanks."

"No problem, Sheriff."

He watched as she drove off before spinning around and hurrying to where Kaia had left her vehicle. A quick inspection told him it was locked up tight. Through the side window he saw a duffle bag resting on the back seat. If he had to hazard a guess, he'd say it likely contained her clothes.

A brief image of her stripping down naked flashed in his mind. He swore and pushed the inappropriate thought away.

He turned and started studying the ground. He saw a partial bare footprint and followed the direction she had to have taken. He watched the floor of the forest closely, hunting for when... There.

He squatted close to the track, reaching down to lift a dry leaf that was partially concealing it. A distinct paw print. He glanced back to where he'd found the human print and again down at the cat's.

He shook his head in wonder.

From one step to the next, Kaia had gone from human to mountain lion. It still stunned him that something like that was even possible.

Up until three years ago, he hadn't known anything like her existed. He'd spent the whole of his adolescent life in the presence of shifters and never had a clue what they were. Even his own best friend had never thought fit to share that secret with him. As inseparable as they'd been, Jace hadn't trusted him enough to tell him.

At first, he'd been hurt by the news. Pissed off, actually, that he'd never truly known the man that Jace really was. And although he sometimes wished things could have been different, Mac had also come to understand the need for his secrecy.

While being a shifter may be incredible on the surface, it also had to bring a whole slew of issues that Mac had no way of comprehending.

What happened if the general populous found out?

If being Sheriff had taught Mac one thing, it's that people most often weren't receptive to things that were out of the ordinary. And someone who could morph from human to animal would certainly draw a lot of attention.

Especially from those meaning to harm. Like this poacher that was, right now, stalking Kaia. If he ever found out her true nature... It didn't bear thinking about.

Bringing his mind back on track, Mac stood. Casting his focus all around him, he searched in all directions for any other indication of which way she'd gone. But after that single indentation, she'd disappeared.

Staring off into the distance, trying to decide which way to go, he heard the echo of an eerily human scream. He recognized the sound instantly. It was the distress call of a cougar, and he knew exactly who had made it.

"Kaia." His whole body clenched at the thought of what could be happening to her.

But the way sound bounced through these mountains, tracking where it had come from would be damned near impossible.

What other choice did he have, though? He had to try.

Listening to his gut, Mac broke into a run.

Visions of her lying dead somewhere tormented him as he flew through the trees. And then he remembered the extra patrols. He grabbed the radio off his belt without losing a stride.

"This is Sheriff McNamara," he panted out. "Tell me *someone* heard that and knows where it came from," he demanded from anyone listening. They were all on high alert after having found evidence of a poacher in the area. Someone had to have been out patrolling near where it happened.

He heard a click, static, and finally a voice. "Sheriff, this is Troy Jones. I'm riding the ridge up above the falls. I'm pretty sure it came from just south of me."

He knew exactly where that was. That area was between his current position and Troy's.

"Copy that." It was only muscle memory that had the radio clipped to his belt again as he poured on more speed. He ducked and dodged the low-hanging branches that tried to take him off his feet and stop him from getting to her.

Her second cry had him veering to the left. She was still alive, but he didn't know for how long. He had no way of knowing what he'd be rushing into, and without even thinking about it, had his gun drawn. Both of their lives could depend on what happened in the next few minutes.

Mac ran, ignoring everything but his need to find her. When he burst through the trees, he saw a man carrying her limp, fur-covered body draped over his shoulders. The poacher startled at the commotion and swung his head around. Most of his face was obscured by the mound of Kaia's midsection and the stocking cap pulled low over his brow. But there was a moment when Mac's eyes met those of his enemy.

Sensing his defeat, and almost certain death if he stayed, the hunter suddenly dumped the cat to the ground and took off running.

There was a heartbeat of time that Mac thought about going after him. But the sight of Kaia—lying so still and lifeless—

changed his mind. Instead, he plucked the radio off his hip again.

He pressed the button as he hurried to Kaia's side. "Troy! Suspect headed your way! White male, average build, dark camo hoodie, jeans, dark vest, black knit cap. Find him and hold him!"

"Roger, Sheriff. I'm on it!"

Mac dropped the walkie and fell to his knees beside her. His breath shuddered out in relief when he saw the rise and fall of her chest.

"Oh, thank God." He scrubbed his hands over his face and back through his hair, knocking his black cowboy hat to the ground, unnoticed.

With shaking hands, he checked her all over, looking for signs of a gunshot wound. But her tawny, gleaming fur was soft and unblemished. She hadn't been shot, so why...? A closer inspection revealed a dot of blood about the size of a dime on her rear flank.

What the fuck? He'd darted her? That seemed odd, but Mac was too thankful she hadn't been more badly hurt to think about why. His most pressing issue now was getting her out of here before someone else who'd heard that shot showed up. They'd want a vet called in to get her examined, but given Kaia's unique abilities, he didn't know if that was such a good idea.

And because he wasn't sure how long the drug would keep her under, he'd also prefer to move her before she woke up. Mac could imagine she was going to be one grumpy kitty, and then one pissed-off human when she did.

If he could get her home, she could come around in the familiarity and privacy of her own room. Hopefully, that would keep her from tearing him up.

But if he didn't get moving quickly, that might just happen here.

As he stood, he spotted his radio and reattached it to his belt. Next, he bent back down to heft the unconscious cougar up and around his shoulders. Her belly was warm and soft against the back of his neck. He gripped her front and rear legs, so she wouldn't slip from his grasp.

Turning, his foot connected with his hat still lying on the ground. Squatting carefully, Mac picked it up and secured it on his head.

He glanced over to where her head lay on his arm. Those gray-green eyes of hers were still closed.

"We'll all be happier if you just stay asleep for a bit longer, okay?"

Thankfully, there was no response.

He'd taken a few steps when Troy's voice came from his waist. "Sheriff? You there?"

Letting go of her front legs, Mac unclipped the walkie. "Yeah. I'm here. Did you get him?"

"No. Sorry, Sheriff, but I never saw him. He didn't come this way. Was it the poacher we've been looking for?"

"Fuck!" Mac shouted before calming himself and pressing the button to speak again. "Yeah, it was. He was close to taking a mountain lion, but she got away."

"Is she all right?"

Mac peeked at the black-lined face so close to his own. "Yeah. She ran past me, and I checked, but there was no blood trail. She should be fine."

"I'll let everyone know. We'll step up our patrols."

"Thanks, Troy. I didn't see much of his face, but I'll get a description of what I did see written up and over to you all as soon as I get back to my office."

He started off again.

Careful of his burden, it took him a lot longer to navigate back to their vehicles. With a hundred pounds of dead weight added, the return trip was more tiring than the mad dash he'd made uphill in his efforts to find her.

By the time he reached his truck, he was sweating and panting. He laid her gently in the cargo area of his SUV and, with one last look, closed the door.

The ride to her house was nerve-wracking but uneventful. His eyes were glued to the rearview mirror and her sleeping form as much as it was to the road.

Scanning the area when he exited his truck, Mac made sure no one was there to witness what he was doing. With the coast clear, he opened the rear doors. Checking closely that she was still doped up, he slid his hands underneath her. And nearly pissed himself when the disturbance caused a soft growl to escape from the comatose cougar. He stilled, his whole body breaking out in a cold sweat. But she remained gloriously unconscious.

Gathering her close to his own body, he carried her inside. He swiftly made his way down the hall. Remembering there were three bedrooms, and assuming she'd taken over the master, that's where he headed.

When he walked into the bright and airy room, he knew he'd chosen correctly. His trained eye took note of her personal items littered throughout. And it smelled like her. Soft, floral, and a little wild.

Shaking those thoughts out of his mind, Mac crossed to the bed and laid her down.

She looked so vulnerable, he almost hated to leave her. But smarter heads prevailed when his gaze landed on the size of her paws. This may be Kaia, but she'd likely be groggy and disoriented when she woke. And just in case the angry predator surfaced before the logical human mind, he thought it safest for everyone if he just left her alone.

With one last look, he closed the door behind him. Mac breathed out a sigh and went to the kitchen for a cup of coffee, and to wait.

6

From one heartbeat to the next, the darkness released Kaia. And her cat.

As it evaporated, the danger she'd been in came back in a breath-stealing rush. The cat leapt to her feet, ears flat to her head, and gave a scream of rage, ready to strike out at the one who threatened her.

It took her a moment before she realized where she was. Safe at home.

What the hell? How did I get here?

Kaia's last memory was of falling to the forest floor, vision fading. Had she managed to get herself back to the house somehow? With that thought, another more sobering one followed. Had she, in her drug-induced flight to safety, led that bastard right to her door?

The need to scout around, to make sure her home was still secure, made Kaia call to her human form. As she shifted from feline to human, she pushed up from her hands and knees to kneel naked on her bed. The movement pulled at her sore hip where the dart had hit her and injected the sedative. She ignored it as she scanned her bedroom for any indication that someone else had been there.

That was when she noticed the door and windows were closed.

If she'd gotten here under her own steam, how had she

gained access to her room? There was no way her cat could have opened and closed either the door or the windows.

As she tried to find a suitable answer, the scent of coffee reached her nose. *Who the…?* Suddenly, it dawned on her how she'd gotten home. Only one person would have known to bring the mountain lion here.

Great. Now she'd never hear the end of it.

Kaia got off the bed and went to her closet to throw some clothes on. As she reached for the doorknob, she paused to fortify herself for the confrontation to come.

Making her way down the short hall was like walking to her own execution. As she emerged into the dining room, she saw Mac sitting at her table. He was leaned forward, forearms on the table, holding a cup of coffee gripped in both hands. His complete attention had been on what was inside that mug until he sensed her. He slowly looked up. His barely-held-in-check anger was easy to read. And the way his blue eyes sparked and lit told Kaia she was in for one hell of a lecture.

Before he got started, there was something she needed to know. "Did you see him?" Kaia lowered into the chair adjacent to him, copying his posture. "Were you able to catch him?"

Mac's gaze drilled into hers. "Yes, I saw him, but no. He got away."

"What? Why didn't you go after him?" Her tone was sharper than she'd intended.

"Because…I was a little preoccupied with getting to *you*. And making sure you weren't dead. Or bleeding to death from being caught in a trap." His voice was low and gruff, as if just thinking about it brought renewed pain.

The anger was foremost, but there was also an undercurrent of fear in his tone now. She'd never heard that from him, and it caused her a moment of guilt. As much as she wanted to shift her focus away from his steely gaze, she didn't.

She kept her voice gentle, trying to ease his mind about the danger she'd been in. "It was only a tranq, Mac."

Except his blue eyes heated. "Only a tranq," he scoffed. "Unbelievable." On a humorless laugh, he pushed away from the table. She tracked his path as he went to stand in front of the coffeemaker.

She sensed he was trying to gather himself as he carefully put one of her tea pods into the machine. He closed it with a snap that seemed loud in the tense kitchen. After setting her favorite cup under the spout, he stabbed the brew button.

As it noisily went about its business, Mac leaned heavily on the counter. His head was dropped forward, and his hands gripped the edge with such ferocity that it turned his knuckles bloodless.

Kaia eyed him warily, but he didn't move or say anything else until the last drip of water had plopped into her mug. Then he slowly, deliberately, picked it up and returned to the table. Setting the steaming tea in front of her, Mac resumed his seat. When his gaze met hers again, Kaia saw so many emotions swirling there, it nearly took her breath away.

She opened her mouth to plead her case, but one scorching look from him had her biting her tongue.

"Do you have any idea…" He trailed off, drew air into his lungs, and released it cautiously. Visibly trying to control himself.

"What, *exactly*, was your plan out there this morning?" he finally got out, obviously diverting from what he'd been going to say.

As much as his derisive tone sparked her own temper, Kaia choked back her snarky response. She hated to admit it, but she owed him for saving her life. And for hauling her drugged ass all the way back home.

"I have cameras set up near where he sh—" She stopped when the muscles in his jaw flexed, his teeth grinding together in agitation. "I was going to lead him past them, so we'd have a picture of his face. I figured once I had that, you could run it through your databases. I guarantee he's in there somewhere. Anyway, when we got a hit, we'd know who we were looking for. Then we could put some pressure on him."

Mac absorbed her words for a moment. "At any point in your plotting, did you think about the fact that all he had to do was shoot you? And not with...*only a tranq*?" He threw her own words back at her.

Kaia held tight to her temper. But it was hard, because this was as much his fault as hers. She'd called him to discuss a plan. He'd wanted nothing to do with it—had told her he didn't have time to deal with it. Or her.

"I did consider it." After playing cat-and-mouse with this guy for over a week, Kaia had thought she'd had his number. She'd thought she could out-maneuver him. "I honestly didn't think he'd take a chance of making that much noise when there were so many uniforms and search dogs in the area. He'd have to be deaf and blind to not have seen everyone out there. I figured he'd play it safe and stick to the more traditional traps and snares. And *those* I was on the lookout for."

"But he *did* shoot you, Kaia. If I hadn't found you when I did..." Mac's voice broke just ever so slightly.

That small sound did something to her heart. And it dissolved whatever anger she'd been holding on to. He was truly hurt by what had happened out there today. She opened her mouth to speak, but he went on.

"You would have been gone. Without a trace. You'd be decorating his wall or floor somewhere before I'd even known what had happened to you."

He wound down, and they stared at each other for a beat. His deep blue eyes were dark again, and something that resembled despair clouded their depths.

Seeing it, and knowing she'd caused that pain, made her stomach twist into knots. Her gaze dropped to her hands. "I know." Kaia forced herself to look up and meet his eyes. "Thank you. For finding me and bringing me home."

He rose up and crossed to the sliding glass door. He stood there, hands in his front pockets, and stared out over her yard.

Studying his back, Kaia didn't know what to do or think. Something had changed. She was used to him being a pain in her ass—telling her what to do, butting in where he had no right. But there was another element to it now. Something... more. She wasn't sure how to talk to him right now. Sensing this shift in him, it had made her vaguely uncomfortable.

As weird as it was to even think it, she wished things could just go back to the way they were before. When he was just a thorn in her side.

She slowly got up and went to him. "Mac—"

That was as far as she got before he swung around with a speed that shocked her. He compounded that surprise by grabbing her face in his rough hands and slamming his lips to hers. Which were parted on a gasp.

This was like no other kiss Kaia had ever received. This was possession and anger and grinding need. There was nothing soft or gentle about the way his tongue plundered her mouth or the crushing weight of his body pressing into hers. In spite of herself, she got lost in the heat and intensity of it, returning it with some of her own pent-up angst.

His mouth was incredible, and the hard edge of his teeth as he bit and nibbled at her sent her system into complete meltdown. All the while, her inner kitty purred and stretched, rubbing her soft body along the inside of hers. The dual assault from both sides was almost more than she could bear.

Until it hit her, like a hammer to the gut. This was Mac. *Mac.* Her tormentor, her ridiculer, her...dare she say it? Friend.

They couldn't do this. *She* couldn't do this.

Her hands found their way to his chest. And after a brief and pitched struggle with her conscience, gave him a push. He didn't fight her. He slowly released her and took a step back.

Her mouth still burned from his utter domination. She wanted to rub at the tender skin with her fingertips but kept her hands down.

"What was that?" Kaia's voice was gruff and raspy as she stepped out of arms' reach. With an iron will, she ignored the demanding feline inside of her that hissed and growled at being denied.

Mac's shoulders rose and fell, heaving with the exertion. His face was set with knife-sharp edges and gave away nothing of what he was feeling.

She began to think the moment of madness had affected him as much as it had her. But he drew himself up and spoke in words made of ice.

"That won't ever happen again."

He skirted around her, but Kaia remained where she was, struck dumb as he stalked out her front door, and flinching slightly when it closed soundly.

Her cat gave her a nudge as if to say, "Go after him." Kaia scowled. "Pipe down, Missy. You have no say in this."

Kaia was confused and stunned at the sudden turn of events. What the hell had just happened? She couldn't wrap her mind around it.

She forced herself to move a few minutes later. She had work to do and couldn't stand around all day wondering. And really, why would she? Like he'd said, it was a one-time thing, so she could put it out of her mind and forget about the last ten minutes altogether.

Hopefully.

~~~

Mac swore ripely as he got into his truck and slammed the door. Giving the key a vicious twist, he set the vehicle into
~~~

motion, spraying rock and dirt out behind him as he sped off away from her.

"What the fuck were you thinking?" he demanded of himself.

He hadn't been, and that's what had gotten him to where he was now. Craving the taste and feel of her again.

The rage over what could have happened, and the tearing fear over almost losing her, had filled him to the point of nearly losing his mind. The longer he'd had to wait for her to come around from the drug that bastard had pumped into her, the closer to the edge he'd come.

He never would have guessed when he blew, it would manifest in the way it had. He'd been just as stunned as she when it happened. That had quickly faded though, to reveal a need in him he hadn't known was there. A need for her. The sexy hellion that had driven him mad for so many years.

As soon as his lips had touched hers, Mac had felt his world shift. It had been knocked completely off its axis. He had a sinking feeling it would never right itself again, and in turn, *he* would never be the same. Not after tasting the unique, fierce, and overwhelming flavor that now called to him like morphine.

And she had kissed him back, he remembered. That's almost what made it worse. She'd been just as invested in it as he. She'd poured everything she was into that kiss, and his blood had sizzled in his veins in response. If she had just slapped him, maybe he could have recovered and walked away with nothing but his wounded pride. But she hadn't, and now he knew just what being with her would feel like.

Until something had spooked her, and she'd pushed him away. She may have been rejecting whatever this was between them, but he'd seen the truth—the need lingering in her heated green eyes.

Mac ruthlessly shook off the effects of the kiss. It didn't matter. That single, mesmerizing, soul-stealing embrace would have to last him, because it was the only one he would ever share with her. She was Jace's baby sister, for Christ's sake.

And Mac could already feel the betrayal to his best friend burning deep in his gut.

Somehow, some way, he would have to ignore his body's demand to claim her as his own. He knew it wouldn't be easy, but it had to be done. There was no other choice.

Mac drove back to the office and buried himself in his work. If he had a shorter fuse than usual, no one said anything to him about it. And by the time he'd finished for the day, Mac had successfully beaten it down to a manageable level.

~~~

In an abandoned, forgotten cottage deep in the woods, someone else was also raging. He'd been so close. He'd had her in his arms, nearly walking out of the woods with his prize.

If not for that nosy, goddamned sheriff...

A string of expletives exploded from his mouth as he kicked savagely at the wall. He watched with grim satisfaction as his foot went through the old wood. Pulling it out again, dust and decaying bug carcasses rained down to the filthy floor.

He'd been holed up in this dump for over a week, and he needed to get the hell out. But not before he got his hands on that cougar. She would be his ticket to riches, and he had no intention of leaving without her.

Alive.

Because she was like nothing he'd ever seen before. He wanted to know what made her so different. To know how that brain of hers worked. It was impossible to believe, but she seemed to think and deduce almost as a human would.

The right people would pay top dollar when they found out what he had. If they wanted to see her, to test her, his price would have to be met.

He'd have to step up his game now though. He'd been lucky
~~~

so far, dodging the authorities that littered the forest. But they had his scent now. They knew he was here and what he was after. He'd have to be even more careful in his hunting from here on out.

Because he *would* have her. It was only a matter of time.

7

Kaia awoke well before dawn the following morning feeling pretty good, considering. Which was a gift, because she had a lot to get done in a short amount of time. She put her confusion over Mac, and her determination where the poacher was concerned, out of her mind and prepared for the day.

She was going to the barn early. She wanted the horses fed, the stalls cleaned, and any other things that needed to be done finished as soon as possible.

Today was the day that Bri came home. She'd gotten a text from her late last night saying they were stopping for the night. Once back on the road, they would probably make it into town around ten. Bri had asked about hotels, but Kaia had cut her off and told her to come straight to her place. That she and Min could stay with her as long as they liked.

Bri had sent back a line of smiling emojis, and one of the kissy-faces.

After getting dressed, Kaia brewed a tea to go and was in her Jeep within fifteen minutes of waking. A few minutes later, she pulled into the parking area in front of the barn. The world was still dark and sleeping. So early, that Helen hadn't even been out to greet her.

The horses wouldn't appreciate getting started at this ungodly hour, but Kaia wanted them taken care of, so she could get back home.

She kept careful track of the time, and at eight, Kaia turned the last horse out and headed for home. She still had a few preparations left to make for her best friend.

At nine forty-five, Kaia was loading more juice boxes into the refrigerator when she heard a car crunching over gravel in her driveway. She grinned broadly and ran for the front door. Giddy like a kid on Christmas morning, she waited for Bri to unbuckle her daughter and come in.

Kaia barely let them cross the threshold before she had Bri in her arms hugging her tight. "Oh, I've missed you," Kaia whispered to her friend.

"Me too." Bri squeezed her a little harder.

Kaia released her to squat down in front of the beautiful little girl holding on to Bri's hand.

Her picture hadn't done her justice at all. The tiny toddler was absolutely gorgeous. Her almond-shaped eyes were big and dark, and the left she saw had a dark spec—just on the edge of the iris. When Kaia had seen it in the photo, she'd assumed the picture had a blemish. But she saw now that Min had what appeared to be a birthmark on her eye. She'd heard of that before, but until now, had never actually seen anything like it up close.

It drew notice, but it didn't detract from the overall beauty of the child in the least.

Her hair was straight and black and sprouted in every direction at once, despite the fact that Bri had tried to tame it into short, stubby pigtails. She was small and thin and had a guarded look about her.

Kaia couldn't blame her. She'd gone through a lot in her short life.

There was also something she sensed in Bri's new daughter that hadn't been evident in the portrait the proud momma had sent her. Min had a cat of her own. It was impossible to tell which one yet, but it would be interesting to see when she got a few years older. The part of the world where she came from was home to some amazing felines. Multiple species of leopards, tigers, lions, and other smaller breeds were all native to Asia and the surrounding areas. She could be any one of those.

Her gaze shot up to Bri. Did she know? Most likely not. This little girl probably didn't know herself, as she wouldn't be able to shift for a few more years. That usually didn't happen for the first time until around five years of age, when the child could be taught to call to that other piece of themselves and give their whole self over to the shift.

Kaia was pretty sure that if Bri had known, she would have mentioned it before now.

She and Bri were going to have to sit down and have a serious talk about how she'd come to adopt *this* particular child. Had Bri been drawn to her because of her friendship with Kaia? Had knowing about and accepting Kaia's differences allowed her to somehow detect the same in Min?

Bri sent her a curious look when she caught Kaia staring at her too long. "What?"

Kaia smiled. "Nothing." She'd give it a bit—figure out how best to approach Bri with this life-altering information. In the meantime, Kaia wanted to get to know this little beauty.

She turned back to Min. "Hi. I'm Kaia. It is so nice to finally meet you."

Min stared back at her silently, those large eyes taking her measure. She looked up at Bri, uncertain.

Bri gave the hand she was holding a little shake. "Do you remember? I told you all about my friend Kaia. We're going to stay with her for a few days."

Kaia grinned at Min. "Or more. You guys can stay here forever if you'd like. I know I'd like it."

Bri laughed. "We'll see how it goes."

Standing, Kaia pointed down the hall. "I've got your room all set up. Would you like to see it?"

"I sure would." Bri sent an animated smile to Min. "What do you say?"

The tiny dark head nodded slightly.

"I really hope you like it." Kaia turned and guided them to the room directly across the hall from her old one. It used to be Jace's. Aside from the master—which was now hers—it was the larger of the remaining two. And perfect for what she'd had in mind.

When she pushed the door open, Bri gasped. "Oh, Kai! It's lovely!"

It had taken Kaia a while to even step into this room after Jace had died. All of his things had stayed just the way he'd left them until she'd felt strong enough to deal with them. She'd eventually packed his belongings away, but she hadn't changed the room itself until Bri had told her she was coming home.

That had been the impetus Kaia had needed to finish it. Now, instead of being dark and masculine, it was light and feminine, but not overly so. The walls were a light gray, the carpet a shade darker. Trim and molding were now a crisp, clean white.

She'd found a bedding set in gray, black, and bright sunny yellow that tied in well with the yellow accents she'd chosen.

And then there was the far corner of the room. She'd curtained it off to make an area for the white toddler bed she had bought for Min. The lacey panels she'd hung from the ceiling for the makeshift room had a white background with bright, multi-hued flowers stitched all over them. They were tied back at the moment to reveal the bedding she'd found. It was a rainbow of colors that matched the flowers.

She'd raided the store for all the girly wall appliques and had spent over an hour arranging them to cover the walls around the bed. There were fairies, butterflies, hearts, flowers, unicorns, and ladybugs. Everywhere Min looked, Kaia wanted her to see happy and pretty things.

There was a small shelf higher up on the wall that held books and little trinkets she thought a two-year-old would like.

Kaia held her breath as Min cautiously explored her new room. She crawled up on the bed and ran her fingers over the almost transparent wings of one of the fairies.

"What do you think, Min?" Bri asked her. "Do you like it?"

Min turned and gave a small timid smile. "Yike it. Aank oo." Her words were hesitant and accented, but Kaia had no trouble understanding them.

Kaia's heart melted, and she felt the burn of tears in her eyes. "Oh, you're welcome, sweetie." She looked at Bri. "I thought she'd be more comfortable closer to you."

"It's perfect," Bri whispered. "I yike it too. Thank you."

Kaia gave her a hug. "Welcome home."

Over the next hour, Kaia helped them unpack and get settled.

"Is anyone hungry?" she asked them. "I have sandwiches, and I also bought a watermelon."

Out of the corner of Kaia's eye, she saw Min's head pivot to look up at her.

Kaia bit back a grin. She'd known that Min loved the sweet, juicy fruit. Bri had filled her in on some of her favorites to make this move somewhat easier. She glanced down to where Min was standing almost behind Bri's legs and saw those big eyes sparkling with anticipation.

"You don't happen to like watermelon, do you, Min?" she asked of the little girl.

Pigtails bobbed as she nodded her head.

Kaia made a show of gasping in surprise. "Me too." She had to hold back a laugh at the little girl's wondrous expression. "Why don't we go get some, and you can help me eat it?"

Min looked up at Bri, her touchstone in this unfamiliar time, to make sure it was all right. Bri ran a hand over the coal-black hair.

"I think that sounds wonderful." Bri held her hand out for Min. "Come on, baby girl."

Kaia led the way. Reaching the kitchen, she crossed to the fridge to retrieve the large bowl of wedges she'd cut earlier. As Bri and Min took their seats at the dining room table, she brought the bowl over and placed it between them.

While Min sat happily munching, Kaia returned to the counter to put together three sandwiches. A handful of chips went on each plate, and when she was done, she handed out plates and sat to join them for lunch.

As they ate, they chatted of anything and everything and caught up. When Bri saw that Min's eyes were starting to droop, she excused herself to put her little one down for a nap. Kaia cleaned up and refilled their water glasses while Bri took care of her daughter.

Kaia was just sitting again when Bri came back and sat down with a contented sigh. "She had to touch all the fairies and ladybugs before she'd lay down. She's out for the count now, though."

"Sooo, spill." Kaia grinned at Bri. "I want to know everything. Where have you been? And most important of all, where did Min come from?"

"I was bouncing around Asia, mostly. But you already knew that."

"And that's where you found Min?"

"Yeah." Bri smiled softly, remembering. "I'd been traveling from city to city, gathering the shots I needed for a new project I was working on." Bri shook her head a little. "I ended up in this little village at the base of some mountains. As I was walking around, I found this stunning park area with tiered levels of grassy sections to sit and enjoy the scenery. There was a waterfall cascading down from one of the mountains, flowing into this tranquil, rock-lined pond. The trees and flowers were blooming, and I think it might be the most peaceful place I've ever been. It took my breath away, Kai."

Bri paused a moment, obviously seeing the setting in her mind.

"Anyway, I'd been taking pictures there for over an hour when I noticed this small two-story building that was separated from the park by a low wooden fence. Children were outside running and playing. I knew right away it was an orphanage, I'd seen so many in my travels. They always make me sad, but I stood and watched them for a minute before I went back to what I was there for. What I didn't realize until I sat down to look through my camera later, was that one child in particular had caught my eye.

"I hadn't noticed it at the time, but after getting her on film that first time, I must've subconsciously started looking for her. According to the series of pictures I had taken, I obviously couldn't stay away from her. Once I realized what I'd done, I made myself go back to my hotel. I tried to block her from my mind and forget her. I love my job. I love the travel. And besides, what do *I* know about kids? There was no way I'd make anyone a good mother."

She went on before Kaia could object to that erroneous conclusion.

"But she was never far from my thoughts. She began to haunt me. I looked at those damned photos so many times, I wore holes in them." Bri took a breath before going on. "I'd dream about her calling out to me. Crying for me." Kaia noticed Bri's hands were shaking slightly as she took a sip of water. It clearly still moved her to think about it.

"Why that one face out of so many drew me, I don't know. She looked much the same as all the others." Bri smiled. "But something in that little face called to me.

"I held out for about a week before I couldn't take it any longer. I had to go back. I had to see her and make sure she was okay." Bri pushed a stray lock of hair back from her face.

"After that, I was lost. I visited her every chance I got, even extending my stay, just so I wouldn't have to tell her goodbye. And then suddenly, I was talking with officials about what it would take to adopt her. It wasn't easy, but I used every bit of clout my family and I had. I even called in some favors I never thought I'd revisit."

She held Kaia's gaze. "You know I've resented that money and prestige most of my life. But I wielded it to pave the way. And because I did, a process that usually takes years to complete was pushed through in only a few short months."

Bri laughed. "I gotta tell you Kai—I was never so afraid as when I walked into that place, papers legal and binding, making me her mother. When they put her in my arms, I was scared boneless." A warm smile broke over her face, and her honey-colored eyes sparkled. "And so in love I couldn't even breathe. We hung out at the hotel for a few weeks getting to know each other before making our way stateside."

Kaia reached out and took Bri's hands. "If any of the things your parents covet brought you happiness, then it was worth it. I can see how much Min has brought to your life. And it's all good."

Tears shimmered in Bri's eyes. "She's amazing, Kaia. She really is. Wait until you get to know her."

"I can't wait." Kaia thought now would be as good a time as any. She kept her voice light and casual. "What do you know about her birth parents? Or even the extended family?"

"Next to nothing. They told me she'd been dropped at their door one night when she was about a year old."

"That's terrible! And no one ever came back for her?"

"No."

She should have known Bri's brilliant brain would kick in. Her eyes narrowed. "What is it? Do you know something?" Her voice lowered to a whisper. "Is it a cat thing? Did you sense something?"

Kaia had to grin at Bri's conspiratorial tone, even when no one was around. "You might say that. It *is* a cat thing...but it has nothing to do with mine. Your new daughter is a shifter too."

"*What?*" Bri sat back in her seat, and her eyes darted to the hall. "No. That's not possible. She's never..."

"And she wouldn't have. Not until she's about five."

Bri was still disbelieving. "How can you know this?"

"I can feel her. As I imagine Min can feel mine. She just doesn't know what it means yet."

"This is unbelievable." Bri ran a hand over her face and tucked the loose blonde strands behind her ears. "How, out of all the children in all the orphanages, did I choose that one?"

"I was going to ask *you* that. It's definitely interesting, but I don't know." Kaia shrugged. "It could be because you and I are so close. You may have sensed a...*familiarity* with her that didn't exist with the other children. Or maybe shifters are just more prevalent in those parts, and your odds were higher of finding one." Kaia waved a hand in dismissal. "To be honest, I have no clue how or why this happened, or if there's even an explanation. But it doesn't matter. The important thing here is that you've found each other."

Kaia watched her friend for a moment as she tried to process this news.

Suddenly, Bri's demeanor changed. Whatever had crossed her mind had put a heavy dose of fear into her. "Oh crap. How am I going to teach her what she needs to know? I can't show her how to transform or how to be a shifter." Bri's eyes were wide when she pinned Kaia with a look of panic. "What if she does it while we're out in public? And I unexpectedly have a wild animal on my hands? Will she change into a full-grown cat or a cub? How am I going to handle all that?"

Kaia tried to hide a grin while she talked Bri down. "Don't get so worked up. It's not that bad. All shifters know instinctively to be careful of where and how we change. Whichever breed of cat she is, she'll start out as a cub and remain so until she gets older. Her cat will grow as she does. And as for the rest, I'll help with all of that."

Wonder lit Bri's gaze. "Could she be like you? A mountain lion?"

"It's possible, I guess, but I doubt it. She would be something indigenous to the area of Asia she's from, and there are a lot of cats native to that region. We'll just have to wait and see."

"I have so much more to learn now. Not just about raising a child, but specifically a shifter child." Bri rubbed a hand over her forehead. She looked over at Kaia expectantly. "I'll have approximately three more years to wrap my head around all of this, right? To get ready?"

"Yeah." Kaia nodded with a smile at her friend's apparent trepidation.

Bri sat quietly while she digested all the information. Kaia took a drink of her water and waited.

"Will you show her what you are?" Bri finally asked.

Kaia set her glass aside. "It would probably be a good idea, just to let her know that the feelings she'll start having are normal, and not to be afraid of them—that it's actually a very beautiful thing."

Bri reached out and touched her hand. "Thank you. I don't know what I'd do without you."

Kaia rolled her hand over to grasp Bri's. She squeezed it once. "You are so welcome."

A frown washed over Bri's face. "Wait. *Should* I worry about where she came from and who her family is? I can't imagine how she ended up alone. When you mentioned the size of the clan...what if someone is out there trying to find her? Do I have to worry that she'll be taken from me? I'm not like them. I can't give her everything she needs."

"Bri. *Yes, you can.* And I believe with all my heart that

Fate put her exactly where she's meant to be. Plus, you said she'd been in that orphanage for a year. If anyone had been looking for her, I'm sure they would have taken her back by now. Maybe she was part of a smaller group like mine. They may have separated from the rest of the family for some reason. Whatever the case may be, if she'd had *any* other blood relatives, she never would have ended up abandoned. Shifters are very protective of their clans."

Kaia paused while her friend thought that over.

Bri breathed out a sigh and visibly relaxed. "Okay." She paused for a beat. "You really think she was meant to be mine?"

Kaia's smile beamed. "I do. Like you said, of all the children in all the orphanages…"

They talked for a while longer until Kaia knew she needed to get back to the barn. She hated to leave, but there were more chores to be done. Training, feeding, grooming—and it all waited for her.

~~~

Chores weren't the only thing that waited for her when she pulled into the driveway ten minutes later. A familiar police cruiser was sitting in front of the barn.

"Well, shit." She'd successfully pushed all thoughts of one annoying and puzzling sheriff out of her mind. And now, here he was. Along with all the unsettling feelings he stirred in her.

Great.

With a resigned sigh, Kaia parked next to him and got out. He followed suit and exited his own vehicle.

"Running a little late today, aren't you?"

She so wasn't ready for his snarky attitude today. She was still off-balance by what he'd done the day before, and she had yet to reconcile what it all meant.

"Not that it's any of your business, but I've already been here
~~~

once today. Bri got in this morning." She didn't miss his wince at that news but chose to ignore it. "I didn't want to miss her arrival, so I finished what I could early and then spent a few hours at home. Now, I'm back for the rest."

"Brianna is in town." His dry tone told her just how excited he was to hear that.

"Yes, she is." Kaia folded her arms under her breasts and met his bland stare. "What can I do for you, Sheriff?"

He seemed to get himself back on track. "I needed to talk to you, but more than that, I wanted to see how you were doing."

"Well, as you can see, I'm fine." She spread her arms wide before letting them drop. "Back at work and out of the woods. Now, if you don't mind, I'd like to get on with it."

He reached out and caught her arm as she tried to move past him. "Wait."

"For what?" She jerked her arm to pull it free and faced off against him. "For you to lecture me again? Tell me how reckless I am? I don't want to hear it, Mac. I've had about all the sermons I can take."

His blue eyes held a hint of anger and annoyance. "I had no intention of lecturing you—it only falls on deaf ears. What I came here to tell you is that I found your parents' families. They're all still living in Colorado, and I have their phone numbers if you want them."

Kaia felt somewhat embarrassed at having reacted so harshly. "Uh, yeah. That would be great. Thank you."

"No problem." He clipped the words off as he dug a slip of paper out of his pocket. He all but tossed it at her before turning to leave.

Kaia caught it and just stood there with it clutched in her hand, watching as his truck drove off.

"Well, that sucked," she muttered, slipping the numbers into her own pocket.

8

It wasn't until nearly six that Kaia had a chance to take a break. As she sat on a bale of hay drinking some water, she took her grandparents' numbers out of her pocket. Before she lost her nerve, Kaia unlocked her phone and dialed the first one on the list.

She'd never met any of these people, but they were her family. The only family she had left. With her mom dead, the issue that had driven them away from their homes was moot. Nothing was stopping her from having a relationship with her relatives now.

The call was answered on the second ring. "Hello?" A woman's voice answered, strong and clear.

This didn't sound like a woman in her late sixties. "Um, yes, I'm looking for," she took another glance at the paper, "Jackie Logan."

"This is Jackie," she returned.

Kaia couldn't quite believe she was speaking with her grandmother. Her mom's mom. They'd had to stay away from everyone for fear that her mom's stalker would find out and somehow find them. Neither Kaia, nor Jace, had ever met either set of grandparents. It seemed surreal now to hear her voice.

"Hello?" Jackie broke into her thoughts. "Are you still there?"

"Yes, I'm sorry. I was calling to…um, that is…" Kaia didn't

know what to say to her. "This is Kaia," she finally blurted out.

She heard a quick intake of breath. "Oh, my…Kaia? My Corinne's Kaia?" A shuddering sigh came through the phone lines and Kaia knew the older woman was crying.

Her own eyes stung. "Yes, ma'am."

"I need to see you," Jackie suddenly demanded. "Do you have a video calling app?"

"I do." Kaia and Bri had used it a lot to bridge the miles between them. But she was somewhat surprised that the older woman would have one too. Or would be tech savvy enough to know how to use it.

"Call me back on that. I need to see my granddaughter's face."

Kaia laughed as she disconnected the call. Taking a deep breath, she found the app with the green background and tapped on it. She entered the number and hit the icon that would let her come face-to-face with her grandmother for the first time.

There was only one ring this time before it was answered. What Kaia saw surprised her. This woman had stamped her features on Kaia's mother, and also on Kaia herself. Jackie's hair was a darker shade of brown than Kaia's, and the eyes weren't quite the same startling green, but there were definite similarities.

Moisture sparkled in the faded green eyes that took Kaia in, and a huge smile radiated from her lips.

"You grew up to be just as beautiful as I thought you would. So much like your mom." Jackie's hand rested on her chest as if holding her heart in place. Kaia understood as her own pounded erratically. "Cori sent me pictures up until she and Nate passed. But after that, I never received anymore." Sadness gave away how much the elder woman had missed them.

"I'm sorry," Kaia felt obliged to say. "We didn't know she'd been in contact with you, or we would have continued. Jace said he'd gotten word to you about their deaths, but after that, I think he was just worried about *us*. We never meant to lose touch for so long."

"That's completely understandable, sweetie. So, how is Jace?"

Kaia's stomach clenched. "He, uh... There was an accident, and he was killed. About three years ago."

"Oh, no. Not Jace too." Jackie quietly cried over losing the grandson she'd only ever known in pictures. When she collected herself again, she turned still-shimmering eyes to Kaia. "So much loss for you. I am so sorry, sweetheart. How are you holding up? Are you okay?"

"It's hard. But I'm doing all right. I'm sorry you're just learning of this now. I didn't have a way to contact any of you at the time. I searched through Mom and Dad's things, and then Jace's, but I never found any way to call you. And then, I guess life just went on. A friend, who is in law enforcement, recently offered to search for you. I thought with Mom and Dad gone now, it would be safe. Just today, he was able to get me your contact information."

"Well, whoever this friend is, I am forever grateful that he found us."

"Me too." Shame washed over Kaia again for how she'd treated Mac earlier, but she set it aside as curiosity got the better of her. "Mom didn't talk much about growing up with the clan in Colorado. I think she felt bad that we were missing out on what she'd had. We understood—safety had to come first—but we always wondered. When we could get her to share with us, she made it sound like the families were huge."

Jackie laughed. "Oh, honey, too many to count. And we have all missed you dearly. Especially us and your daddy's parents. Elva and Victor are going to flip out when I tell them about this. Would you mind if I gave them your number? They're going to want to talk to you as soon as they find out you've been in touch."

"No, that's fine. I'm anxious to speak with them too."

They spoke for a bit longer before saying goodbye. But not before each promised to talk again very soon. Kaia was so happy, but at the same time, a little sad. There were so many people out there who shared her blood and her abilities, but she'd been denied knowing them because of the actions of one man.

She wondered what she would do if she ever met up with the bastard who'd driven her parents away from their homes and loved ones. No, it was better to just leave that alone. And for all she knew, he could be dead as well.

She hoped he was.

~~~

When she got home that evening, Bri was sitting on the couch. Her legs were folded underneath her, and her laptop was propped on top of them.

"Hi, honey, I'm home." Kaia grinned.

Bri looked up and laughed. "How was your day at the office, dear?"

Kaia plopped down next to her. The smile slipped a bit. "I spoke with my grandmother today."

"What?" Bri turned more to face her. "How?"

"Mac got me her phone number. I called her."

"Wow. How'd that go? She had to have been shocked."

"To say the least," Kaia agreed. "And then I had to tell her that Jace has been dead for three years."

"Oh no. I'm sorry, Kai. How'd she take it?"

"Not well, of course. She told me that Mom used to send them pictures of us. And now that's all she'll ever have of him. She'll never get to meet him. To know what a terrific guy he was." Kaia's eyes filled with tears. "God, I miss him."
~~~

Bri set her computer aside, reached an arm around Kaia shoulders, and pulled her in close. She said nothing as Kaia gave in to the grief she still felt.

When the worst of it had passed, Kaia sniffled. "You know, I always dreamed that you and Jace would get together. And then we could be actual sisters."

"I know." Bri tipped her head to the side and rested in on top of Kaia's. "You weren't very subtle about it, my friend. But me and your brother would never have been a good match." She paused a beat. "Speaking of matches…are you going to tell me what's up with you and Mac?"

Kaia wiped the last of the tears away and sat up. "What do you mean?"

"You usually regale me, in great detail I might add, with every way that man drives you nuts. You all but demonize him every time we talk. But then…not one word since I've been here. Something is up there, babe."

"It's only been a day," she protested, but she couldn't look at Bri. "I wanted to enjoy some time with you and that precious little girl." Kaia knew she'd bitched to Bri about him, but had it been that bad? "Give it time. There's still plenty I can tell you."

"Yeah…" She peeked up to see Bri studying her skeptically. "I don't think that's all there is to it. Don't forget, I'm an expert at picking up on subtleties and what's behind the eyes." Bri pointed a finger at her. Then circled it between them before letting it drop to her lap. "And I can guarantee there's something you're not telling me."

Kaia waited barely a heartbeat. She knew she'd tell Bri; it had only been a matter of time before she couldn't hold it in any longer. "He kissed me." She felt a blush heat her cheeks. "And I kissed him back."

Blonde brows shot upward. "Well. Okay. That's not what I expected."

"You're not the only one." Kaia laid her head back on the

couch and closed her eyes. Which was a mistake, because talking about it brought back the memory of it, along with all the feelings she'd been trying to understand.

"What happened exactly?" Bri ventured.

The words came out on a sigh. "We'd been arguing—"

That drew a short laugh from Bri. "Now *that* doesn't surprise me."

"Yeah." Kaia straightened. "Well, this one was a doozy. He'd just rescued me from a poacher I'd been tracking. And he'd had to haul my unconscious cat all the way home and put us to bed."

That news wiped all humor from Bri's face, and she sat straight up, waving her hands. "Wait. What poacher? And why were you unconscious? What the hell is going on, Kai?"

Kaia recounted everything that had taken place over the last few weeks. When she caught up to present day, Bri hauled off and punched her in the arm.

"Are you fucking crazy?"

Kaia rubbed her bicep. "Ow. What did you do that for?"

"Mac was right to be pissed off at you. You put yourself in danger out of pride and stubbornness."

"No." Kaia felt a little hurt. "I did it so these assholes who think they can come here and do whatever they want, won't take another innocent life."

"What happened to Jace was tragic and horrifying. But do you honestly think you can stop all poachers singlehandedly? You're risking your life for something that's not even possible."

"You'll think differently when it's Min out there running the forest," Kaia snapped out. And then instantly regretted it when Bri recoiled as if she'd been slapped.

She was worried enough about her daughter now that she knew she was a shifter. Shame clung to Kaia in all its oily blackness as her words echoed in her mind. What she'd said was inexcusable, putting that kind of idea into Bri's head just to defend her actions and make a point.

Bri's gaze flew to the hall and beyond, where her little girl was sleeping peacefully. Kaia's heart broke when terror further drained the color from Bri's face.

Tears gathered in Kaia's eyes. "Oh, God, Bri. I am so sorry." She reached out to hold Bri's hands. They were cold. "That was completely uncalled for. I am so, so sorry," she repeated.

Bri slowly brought her anxious gaze back to Kaia's. "That was cruel of you." Her voice was whisper soft.

Kaia dropped her gaze to their clasped hands and nodded. "I don't know why I said it. It was beyond wrong. Please forgive me."

The other woman was silent for a long moment. "Just the thought of anyone hurting Min that way..." Bri's words trailed off as she shook her head. When she raised her eyes to Kaia's, there was steely determination in them again. "I get it now, though—why you're doing what you're doing. I still don't like it and I think it's dangerous, but I can understand why you think you need to."

She squeezed Kaia's hands. "Nevertheless, there has to be a better way to go about it. Something that doesn't mean using yourself as bait. Because this protective streak I have for my daughter, is the same one I have for you. And if his reaction is any indication, it sounds like Mac feels the same way. Neither of us want to lose you to this, Kai. You have to be more careful. We love you."

Kaia pulled Bri in for a hug. "I love you too."

"Now," Bri released her and sat back, "how do I protect my daughter? How do I keep Min safe from what happened to your brother?"

There was still fear in Bri's gaze, but the kick-ass attitude she normally wore like a cozy robe was returning. "By being smart and teaching her. Showing her what to watch out for and what to do if she's ever in a situation like that." Kaia grinned at Bri. "She'll grow, and she'll run, and she'll learn what it is to be a shifter. She'll revel in the power it gives her to thrive. She'll be strong and confident and beautiful. You and I will make sure of that."

"Okay." Bri's eyes shimmered with moisture. "I'm still scared—probably always will be when it comes to her—but knowing you'll have our backs helps."

She took a breath. Let it out. "Now. Back to easier topics. The kiss."

"Easier for who?" Kaia muttered under her breath.

Bri ignored her. "How did an argument with Mac turn into him kissing you?"

"I'm not sure." Kaia thought back on it. "He'd seemed... *off* somehow. Different after that poacher shot me with the tranquilizer. When I came out of my room, he was sitting at my table, silently drinking a cup of coffee. I knew he was mad, but there seemed to be more to it, and I couldn't define what it was. He walked away from me at one point and stood looking out the window. When I followed him and tried to reassure him that I was fine, he spun around, grabbed my face, and kissed me. I was so dazed, I couldn't do anything for a moment. But then I lost my mind too. Once I had my wits back and realized what was happening, I pushed him away. It's been kind of strained ever since."

"I can imagine. You two aren't the best of friends on a good day. And now that hot, sexy kiss is between you."

"I never said it was hot or sexy," Kaia denied.

"Oh, honey, you didn't have to. I can see it in those cat eyes of yours." Bri smirked. "He blew your panties off, didn't he?"

Kaia thought about deflecting, but like Bri said, she knew her too well. She slumped back against the couch. "Damn it, yes," she said, defeated. "And it didn't help that my cat was purring and urging me to take more. She actually threw a tantrum when I broke it off," Kaia groused, and then blistered

Bri with a dirty look when she busted out laughing.

"Oh, my." Bri tried to catch her breath. "You poor thing."

"I really don't find this funny."

"I know, sweetie." Bri cleared her throat and made a visible effort to control her mirth. "So, what are you going to do?"

"Continue to train horses and hunt poachers."

"I meant about Mac?"

"I know. But there's nothing to be done. Like you said, we're barely civil to each other. Plus, he made it clear it was a mistake and said it would never happen again. Since I don't have any desire to repeat it either, how about we forget it, and move on?"

"Can *you*?" Bri's tone was serious. "You said yourself your cat has a thing for him."

Kaia lifted her hair up off her neck and let it drop again. "She'll just have to get over herself then, because she is shit out of luck."

Bri gave her a look she would rather not examine. A cry from the other room saved Kaia from having to protest further. While Bri was attending to her daughter, Kaia retired to her own room to start getting ready for bed.

She let out a sigh as she fell back against her pillows. Tugging the blanket with her, Kaia rolled to her side, closed her eyes, and eventually drifted into sleep.

9

The morning sun was bright and warm. As Kaia worked in the round pen, she enjoyed the sounds of the farm, the smell of the horses, and the friction of worn leather in her hands.

She kept her student moving in circles, studying her form and gait and checking for anything she needed to correct or work on more. So far, the mare was responding beautifully. She listened and followed Kaia's commands like a proper, well-behaved lady.

Kaia took her time and gave her star pupil a thorough workout. Very pleased with the lesson, they returned to the barn where Kaia began to groom the mare. Once her coat was gleaming, Kaia unhooked her and turned her out.

She paused a moment to enjoy the sight of the horse streaking across the pasture in a joyous gallop, her head and tail held high, long hair fluttering in the breeze. She really was a gorgeous creature.

Kaia still had a soft smile on her face when she turned to walk back into the barn. It was then she saw Mac's cruiser pull in and park.

I knew my luck wouldn't last. She cringed inwardly.

Resigned to the uncomfortable meeting, Kaia went about her business. Putting away the tack she'd used, she didn't even look over at him as he stalked in the opposite end. He said nothing as he came directly towards her. His booted feet struck the hard-packed ground with solid thuds. When she turned her head, she saw that his face was set and hard.

He looked pissed, and she wondered what had set him off. Probably something she'd done, she thought grimly.

Bracing, she turned towards him fully as he drew even with her. Her morning had been going so delightfully. Why should she let him ruin it for her with his sour mood?

Breathing out on a sigh, Kaia hoped she could talk him down. She opened her mouth to speak, but she never got the words out. He suddenly grabbed her by both upper arms and pushed her back into the door of a stall.

Luckily, there wasn't a horse in it right now. Otherwise, it would have been frightened by the loud bang as her body slammed into it. He pressed fully into her, his hard body holding her trapped against the wood at her back.

She was shocked by his actions but couldn't draw air to rail at him. His mouth was sealed tightly to hers, stealing not only every word, but every breath and brain cell.

As Kaia's world narrowed down to only him, all she could do was hold on. In desperation, her hands clutched at his waist, fisting in the stiff cotton of his uniform shirt. Beneath her fingers, his skin felt like it was on fire. The heat radiated from him like solar flares, and with nowhere else to go, burned into her. His entire body branded itself onto hers as his mouth scorched a path over her lips, across her chin, down her neck, and then back again.

His broad hands slid from her arms to her breasts, cupping and molding them as a moan ripped from deep within her throat. Before she knew what was happening, he found the front of her shirt and yanked it wide. Her bra went next, the small strip of material in the middle no match for Mac's urgency.

Her breasts swelled in response, their weight heavy as they fell from their bindings. But only for an instant as he took a rounded mound in each hand. Kaia's head spun as he squeezed and fondled them while he continued to devour her mouth.

She whimpered helplessly when he rolled both nipples between his fingers and thumbs, the dual assault arrowing straight to her core. Everything inside of her clenched with driving need, leaving her breathless and shaky.

It seemed like hours that he ravaged her before those maddeningly talented fingers released her and found their way to her hair. They unerringly located the band holding it up off her neck. Kaia felt the tug on her head, and then all of her riotous curls were falling down around her shoulders.

Mac took two fistfuls of it and pulled her head back, exposing her neck. He lowered his mouth and bit down on the cord there, sucking the skin into his molten mouth. Kaia nearly purred at the onslaught of pleasure and pain. There'd be a mark when he was done, but she didn't care.

As long as he didn't stop, she was beyond caring what he did.

He was driving her to utter madness. She wanted him. She had to have him, but he wasn't through having his way with her yet. His lips and tongue found her puckered, overly-sensitive nipples. His teeth pulling against the taut buds made her knees buckle.

When she began to slide down the wall, he ruthlessly hauled her back up. Bringing one leg forward, he braced it between her thighs, his goal to hold her in place. But the sudden pressure at her center served a dual purpose, and her hips rocked against him in desperate pursuit of release. Kaia rode his denim-clad thigh, thrusting and jerking as she tried to find some relief to the torment.

She was so close. And cried out in frustration when he stepped back away from her. Panting and trembling and needing him badly, Kaia could only watch as he stripped out of his shirt. She drank in the sight of his powerful chest, shoulders, and arms—darkly tanned skin stretched taut over them. The flat plane of his stomach was rippled with muscle, each one clearly defined and begging for her mouth to taste and savor.

When he reached for his belt, she licked her dry lips. His eyes flared, and his jaw flexed in answer. Anticipating her first glimpse of him, Kaia's heart pounded and the walls of her sex spasmed. A flood of moisture soaked her already-wet panties.

After unclasping his belt, he popped the button, his long, strong fingers lowering the tab of the zipper. The rasping sound seemed loud and triggered a shudder of desire racing through her.

Now, she thought. He'd fill her and end this torture.

Except, instead of revealing anything more, his hands fell away, leaving his jeans hanging open and barely holding on to his lean hips. The black waistband and dark gray cotton of his underwear stood out against his bronzed skin, as did the head of his shaft, the elastic failing to keep it contained.

Another wave of arousal shook her and had Kaia pressing her thighs together.

"Mac..." she begged, her voice urgent.

His hands fisted and released where they hung at his sides. She got the impression he only barely had himself under control. So, she wasn't the only one moving beyond sanity.

Just when Kaia began to wonder how long he'd make her wait, he prowled back towards her.

He took both of her arms and raised them over her head. Closing her fingers around the horseshoe hook on the crossmember overhanging the stall door, Mac quickly had them bound to it. Kaia tipped her head back to see a leather lead securing her hands. She gave them a gentle tug, but they held fast.

She was still processing how she felt about that when she felt his fingers unfastening the closure of her own jeans.

Once released, Mac stepped in close and slid his hands into the back of her panties, running them over the globes of her ass and down, taking her clothing with them.

Crouching, he pushed them to below her knees where they caught on her boots. He lifted one foot, and in one smooth motion, slipped both boot and clothing from that leg. Turning, he repeated the process, and when he'd slung the barriers across the barn, he looked back up and met her gaze. As he rose from a squat, he trailed his hand up her skin from ankle to thigh. When he paused at the heated juncture he found there, Kaia's breath caught in her throat. His eyes blazed into hers as his fingers slid easily through her folds and up into her core.

Her breath came out in a rush, the touch so intimate but firm as he hooked his fingers forward to stroke her inner walls. Her legs started to quiver as he worked his fingers in and out, and just when she thought she'd explode, he withdrew.

She nearly screamed in frustration, but in an expert move, he grasped each of her legs behind the knee and lifted, pulling them apart and fitting himself between them.

The bindings and the mass of his body pinned her against the wall as he shoved his own clothes down out of the way. She felt him adjust his stance, and then he was there—at the entrance to her body. He held her for several loud, thumping heartbeats as he stared deep into her eyes, studying her face.

He leaned in to kiss her, and just before their lips met, he whispered, "You drive me so crazy."

As his mouth took hers, he thrust.

"Fuck," Mac groaned, once he was seated fully inside her. "So. Fucking. Good."

Kaia had to agree on all counts. She'd never had anyone like Mac. He filled her to the point of pain, but it was freaking glorious. There wasn't a hidden place inside of her that he didn't touch in the most carnal way. When he ground his pelvis against hers and included her little pleasure nub in the action, all thought left her. After that, he set a hard and demanding pace. All that could be heard was their panting and gasping and skin slapping skin.

Kaia's orgasm tore through her with a force she thought might knock her out, but he didn't stop. He didn't give her a chance to recover—he just sent her up and over, again and again. She lost count of how many climaxes he'd pounded out of her when she felt him reach his own peak.

With a grunt and a curse, Mac buried himself deep and gave in.

Kaia came awake violently, shooting upright in bed, and still pulsating from an orgasm so intense, it robbed her of breath.

When she gradually gained it back, she ran her hands over her face. "Holy fucking shit." A delicious shiver coursed through her as her body continued to convulse in aftershocks for several minutes.

She was still shaky as she rolled to the side of the bed and stood up. On weak legs, Kaia made her way to the bathroom. The woman who greeted her in the mirror had been completely and utterly ravished. Her eyes were wide and glassy, and strands of hair that had escaped the hair-tie were curling crazily around her face. Her creamy skin was dewy with sweat, and a lingering arousal vibrated her insides. Just the brush of her t-shirt over her nipples sent need shooting to her center.

Turning away, Kaia went to the shower and spun the handle on the faucet. She kept it on the cooler side in hopes of dousing the flames still wreaking havoc within her.

Stripping out of her damp pajamas, she stepped right into the spray. Holding her breath, she let the lukewarm water rinse away the most erotic dream she'd ever experienced. That it starred Mac was something she didn't want to think about right now.

Putting her back to the tepid fall of water, Kaia tipped her head and soaked her hair. It would be impossible to tame later, but at this point, she just didn't care.

Try as she might though, she couldn't stop the replay. For every nerve the shower soothed, the memory fired them up again.

After the severity of her orgasm, she would have expected to feel sated and relaxed. So the persistent craving, the insatiable need to have this man inside her, left her irritable with longing. She had a feeling she would be haunted by this hot, twitchy need all day.

She groaned, scrubbing her hands over her face.

Her cat, thankfully, remained quiet. She hadn't taken the opportunity to make this harder than it already was. But then again, she was probably ecstatic to have finally gotten her way. Even if it was only part of a dream.

By the time Kaia finished, she was a little steadier. At least enough to face the day.

Dressed for work and damp hair braided in a thick tail down her back, she headed for the kitchen. She found Bri and Min seated at the table, munching away on some toast. If Kaia wasn't mistaken, it had cinnamon and sugar sprinkled on it.

"Oh, man, that was always my favorite." Kaia grinned at Min. "You've got a pretty good momma if she's making you cinnamon toast. Do you mind if I join you?"

Min, sugar granules all over her mouth, smiled and nodded.

Bri studied Kaia carefully, but all she said was, "I'll get your toast started." Bri rose as Kaia went to the coffeemaker.

She didn't miss the covert looks her friend was sending her.

"Are you okay?" Bri finally asked, keeping her voice low. "You look...flushed."

She knew she should share. Bri would want all the details. And Kaia normally would have—with relish. But for some reason, she couldn't bring herself to give it voice just yet.

"I'm fine." And she really hoped it was the truth.

~~~

Mac had spent his night poring over maps, strategizing. But,
~~~

when not even coffee could keep his brain focused any longer, he had to take a couple of hours down. He was up again well before dawn, readying himself for what was to come.

He was going hunting.

He'd run this bastard to ground if it was the last thing he did. He wouldn't get away with what he'd done to Kaia. Or with endangering everyone else in the park.

And if, in the process, his pursuit kept the need for her at bay, Mac was all for it. He'd discovered that no matter how hard he tried, he couldn't get the taste of her out of his mind. It lingered and punched him in the gut if he didn't keep his brain distracted. As he saw it, dogging this poacher was a win-win.

As the sun began its assent, Mac drove into Lost Creek. Behind him in the trailer he was towing was his best horse, Maverick.

What could he say? He'd been a fifteen-year-old kid who had liked to think of himself as the lead character in Top Gun. Jace had been his Goose, and they'd "flown" countless missions, taking out the bad guys. Which may have led to Mac becoming a cop, now that he thought about it.

And as a cop, he and Maverick had worked together for years doing search and rescues of hikers or day-trippers. The horse could always sense the lost soul, and if anyone were hiding nearby, Maverick would know and signal to Mac.

He'd been retired for a while now, but Mac had pulled him out just for this job. Maverick was a sturdy and stable mount on any trail. Nothing spooked him, and he would alert Mac when someone, or something, was amiss.

Parking near where Kaia had the other day, Mac walked to the rear of the trailer and opened the doors.

"Hey, old friend. Are you ready to do this?"

Maverick looked back over his shoulder at Mac and swished his long white-blond tail. His large white and brown speckled rump shifted as he stomped restlessly.

Mac stepped up into the rig and ran his hand over the patterned hide. Maverick was an Appaloosa, and his coloring resembled the dappled spots sun gave the ground as it shone through a heavy canopy of trees.

Still strongly muscled, the gelding stood almost seventeen hands. Which was several inches over the average Appaloosa. His robust appearance and powerful frame belied the fact that he was eighteen years old.

As much as it had hurt Mac, he'd had to scale back on the workload he assigned to Maverick. Most of his days were now spent running around the pasture with the rest of the herd.

Mac's parents ran a riding stable and vacation resort off their two-hundred-acre ranch. To give the guests the full ranch-life experience, there were a number of different livestock, along with bunkhouses, pens, and paddocks.

They could work like a cowhand or trail ride, help with round-ups or just relax. There was plenty for the guests to do.

At last count, Mac's parents ran a herd of about fifty horses. Depending on how many lodgers they had, they'd rotate the stock in and out so they all had a chance to work and to rest. Square M belonged to his parents, himself, and his grandmother.

His paternal grandparents, Luke and Stella McNamara, had taken the land over from *his* family. And seeing a way to keep it prosperous, had built it into what it was today. Mac's dad, John Luke, had been their only child. Just as he, Lucas John, was. The McNamaras weren't a prolific bunch, but they knew horses, and they knew the land.

Now his mom, dad, and grandma Stella ran the business, allowing him to follow his own dream of being Sheriff. He still did what he could to help out, but most days he was busy keeping law and order in their small slice of Montana.

And that's what he was setting out to do here today.

Bringing his thoughts back around, Mac guided Maverick

out. He'd saddled him before they left, leaving the cinch strap loose for comfort on the ride. He tightened it and double-checked that he had everything he needed.

Placing his foot in the stirrup, Mac mounted smoothly and easily. Once settled in the saddle, he consulted the map one more time. Direction clear in his mind, he turned Maverick and started off into the trees.

He'd only been able to clear a few hours this morning, so he had to make the most of the time he did have. He'd already worked out which areas he wanted to cover first, based on where the poacher had shown his face prior. Mac had the sections of the park marked that could be where he'd set up his base.

Two hours later, he'd covered about a quarter of it when he caught a glimpse of something through the trees. It looked to be a building of some kind. A slight tug on the reins had Maverick slowing, and then stopping. This far into the park, a trail map was the only way to navigate. Hikers and rangers used it, because it accurately showed trails and landmarks not seen on any of the satellite maps. Mac pulled it from his back pocket and noted his position.

It indicated a structure here, but it was labeled as a hazard. Anyone looking at this would know to steer clear of this area.

What better place for a poacher to hide out?

Dismounting, Mac left the reins draped over Maverick's neck. The well-trained horse would stay there until Mac either came back or whistled for him.

Mac eased closer for a better look. If someone were in there, he didn't need to announce his presence. Making sure to remain in the shadows, Mac peered through the leaves. It wasn't much more than four barely-there walls and a half-caved-in roof. No one in their right mind would go anywhere near it.

But Mac had to check it out. He glanced over at Maverick and saw his nostrils flared, scenting the air.

Not one of Maverick's more urgent alarms, Mac wasn't

overly concerned. All the same, he paused to take another long look at the old cabin.

Not knowing what he'd find when he stepped out of the shelter of the trees, Mac drew his weapon and thumbed off the safety. The Kimber 1911 fit as perfectly in his palm as his ass fit the saddle. And just as he became a part of his horse, the pistol became a part of him.

He held it at the ready as he bent low and, as quickly and quietly as possible, approached the dilapidated structure.

There was no movement from inside that he could detect. As he flattened himself against one outer wall, Mac eased his head around the opening to what had once been a window. His eyes scanned but found no sign of anyone.

The cabin consisted of one large room approximately twenty by twenty. It was easy to see it had been abandoned a long time ago.

Conscious of everything around him, he made his way to the door. The old wooden door still hung on its worn hinges, but he didn't know how well. Would it still swing free, or would it break loose and crash to the floor at the slightest touch?

Keeping his pistol in hand, Mac grasped the door knob with the other. Bracing his shoulder against it, he leaned into it.

Surprisingly, the old door swung inward without an issue. Mac stepped in and surveyed the area.

In the corner where the roof still existed, fast food bags, plastic drink cups, and other debris littered the floor.

He approached slowly and examined the scene. Not too far away from the pile of garbage, the grime on the scarred wood floor had been disturbed it two places.

One was large, about man-sized. Probably a bed-roll. Mac squatted down for a better look at the second. Four distinct spots formed a perfect rectangular shape—legs of some kind, he figured. Too small to be a table or chair. Next to that, a dark stain on the worn flooring gained his attention. It was about three inches in diameter and looked like something had dripped there repeatedly.

There were thousands of possibilities of what this could be. But Mac needed to know which one. Tipping his hat back out of the way, he braced his hands on either side of it and bent forward.

One sniff was all it took. Kerosene. And if the strength of the lingering odor was any indication, it hadn't been there long. That explained the leg marks.

Mac straightened and adjusted his hat. Someone had definitely made camp here, laying out a sleeping bag or mat with a portable heater close by to fight the chilly mountain nights.

To him, this looked like someone holed up and hiding out.

He kicked one of the crumpled bags aside. The sudden disturbance had a mouse skittering out from under it and several napkins fluttering around.

To his surprise, Mac saw one of them had writing and what looked like a drawing on it. He picked it up to get a better look, and the air left his lungs.

It was a crude pencil sketch of a mountain lion. Doodled all around the cat was one single word—*mine*—printed again and again. One in particular had been written over so many times and so heavily, there were gaping holes ripped through the several layers of napkin, nearly obliterating the word altogether.

Mac's heart clenched. "No, you crazy son-of-a-bitch. She's *not*." He wanted to shred this fucked up shit into a thousand tiny pieces, but he held the urge in check. Barely. It took grinding his teeth together until he thought they'd shatter, but he did it. Once he had his raging fury under some semblance of control, he slid the napkin into an evidence bag to be processed and examined later.

Intuition told him he'd find nothing more—that the bastard

had pulled up stakes and moved to a different location. Maybe after the close call with Kaia. But Mac still scoured the site, looking for anything that might lead him to the identity of his poacher.

It didn't take long to know he'd been right. He'd not left anything else of himself behind. Returning to where Maverick patiently waited, Mac had already switched his mind to the next section of woods. He rode for another two hours, marking off where he'd searched on the map.

Conscious of the time, Mac had to cut the rest of his recon short to get back to the office. The remainder of his day was swamped.

Frustrated, Mac loaded Maverick. And after dropping him off at the ranch, Mac headed into town.

10

The hunter followed the progress of the man on horseback through the scope on his rifle. Even from this distance, the magnification brought the sheriff into clear view. He wanted to drop the meddling little bitch where he sat. If it weren't for him, he'd have that gorgeous cougar right now, and he'd be on his way to making a shit-ton of money.

His finger resting on the trigger tightened by a hair. He should just take him out and be done with it. No one else would stand in his way.

All it would take was another fraction of an inch, and a lead round would find its way into the fucker's head.

But that would be stupid. On a sigh, the hunter lowered the weapon. While it would make him feel good, killing a sheriff would only rain hell down on his hunting ground. The last thing he needed was even more cops tromping through these woods, scaring off his cougar.

With a final curse, the hunter backed out of his position and returned to his new camp to plan.

~~~

Kaia had just gotten in from working a full day when her cell rang. She sat down at the dining room table and spent the next hour talking to her dad's parents. There were tears and
~~~

laughter, lots of words of love, and a whirlwind of who's who in the family. The longer her grandmother talked, the more Kaia's head spun. There was no way she'd ever remember the names of all her aunts, uncles, and cousins.

Her grandparents were beyond excited to spread the word that Kaia had come back to them. Her grandmother jokingly said she'd shout it from the rooftop if she could get up there. Kaia promised to visit as soon as possible, but in the meantime, they would call and text and get to know each other.

She also promised to send lots of recent pictures, and to keep up via email so they could still stay in touch during all their busy lives.

Bri had emerged from the hall while Kaia had been on the phone. Not wanting to interrupt, Bri had gone to work, preparing dinner for the three of them. When Kaia hung up, Bri joined her at the table, bringing two bottles of water from the fridge. Kaia vaguely wondered if she looked as dazed as she felt.

At her friend's questioning glance, Kaia grimaced. "It seems I have approximately fifteen thousand family members waiting to meet me in Colorado."

"I'm sure it's not that bad," Bri said on a laugh.

Kaia twisted the cap off her water and took a quick drink. "I'm going to need cue cards when I meet all these people."

"You'll be fine," Bri said dismissively with a smirk.

"Just so you know, you're going with me when I do go." She grinned in satisfaction when Bri choked a little on the water she'd just sipped.

Not much phased her for long though, and she recovered quickly. "Say the word. I'm there."

Kaia needed a change of subject. After growing up with just her parents and brother, so much family out of the blue felt overwhelming.

"Where's Min?"

Bri nodded down the hall. "She's in there, talking with the fairies on her walls."

"I'm glad she likes them. How is she? Is she settling in okay?"

Bri smiled easily. "She's great. Such a little trooper. So much has changed for her in the last six months. I'm so happy I can offer her a home of stability and love."

"She's one lucky girl." An idea struck Kaia. "Do you think she'd like to meet the horses? The two of you could meet me at the barn tomorrow morning and hang out for a bit. I'd love the company."

"I don't know that she's ever seen a horse." Bri frowned a little. "I wouldn't want to do anything that would scare her."

"You know Rayna. She's super gentle." But Kaia understood Bri's new-momma nerves. She reached out and grasped Bri's hand. "I'll leave that up to you. Now," Kaia sat back in her chair, "what smells so good? I'm starving."

"I made dinner for you." Bri grinned and rose.

"You did? Since when do you cook?" Kaia followed her to the stove.

"Since I now have a daughter who needs to eat more than orange pasta."

Bri removed the lid on the pot. Kaia looked in and then burst out laughing. "Red pasta."

"Baby steps, my dear friend. Baby steps. I also made some garlic bread to go with the spaghetti. It's warming in the oven."

Kaia threw her arms around Bri. "I love it. Thank you."

Having dinner with a two-year-old was an experience for Kaia. Bri had set aside a bowl of plain noodles for Min, but when she saw that they both had sauce on theirs, she had to have the same.

Bri served her up a small bowl, but then the little girl changed her mind again and wanted the plain ones back. It ended up that she had both bowls set in front of her. She ate a little out of each one before deciding all she wanted was, "Arly bwed."

It was the best meal Kaia had had in a long time. They laughed at Min trying to slurp the noodles as they'd shown her. And when she'd finally gotten it, they all cheered. Kaia went to bed that night feeling happy and relaxed.

The mood lingered into the next morning. She woke up early and headed to the kitchen for tea. Standing at the sliding door with her steaming mug, she looked out at the park where it met her yard.

Her cat was ready for a run, but did she dare? It had only been a day since she'd been shot. And he was still out there, waiting for her to show back up.

What he didn't know though, was that the cougar he was hunting wasn't the average feline. She was all wild animal in a lot of ways, but her human side gave her an edge in any situation.

And she'd use that to her advantage.

She'd hold off for today. But she wouldn't be denied the land she had grown up on and loved.

Mind made up, Kaia turned to go dress for the day. Bri and Min were still sleeping when she left a few minutes later.

Having not made her usual run, she was early getting to the barn. But Helen was still in her usual spot. Kaia waved and smiled as she drove on by. Morning chores were seen to, and Kaia went to get Daisy, the little mare she'd be working with today.

She was about fifteen minutes into her training when it struck her like a bolt. This was the way the dream she'd had the other night had begun.

Her mind was instantly right back there. Tied to the stall door, being ravished by Mac. She shivered in the warm morning air. Just thinking about what he'd done to her had moisture pooling. Her channel clenched as arousal washed over her.

Kaia had to stop the mare mid-trot to take a couple of deep

breaths. Except it was doing nothing to calm the urge now clawing at her. Her inner kitty only made it worse, purring and rolling and brushing up against the inside of her skin.

The sound of a car approaching snapped her out of the passion-haze.

Oh, God. Was it him?

Kaia stood frozen until she heard Bri's voice calling to her.

"Yeah—" She had to clear her throat. "Yeah," she said more clearly. "I'm out back. Come through the barn."

She was standing at the fence holding the mare when Bri, carrying Min, came out into the bright sun.

"You came. I'm so glad." Kaia smiled. "Hey, Min. Did you come to see some horses?"

Big dark eyes stared at the gleaming white animal next to her.

"This is Daisy. She's named that, because she's all white like the flower. Would you like to pet her?"

Min curled her hand in tight between her body and Bri's.

"She's very nice and super sweet. Here, I'll show you how." With one hand holding the bridle under Daisy's chin, she brought the other up to rub up and down the mare's nose and forehead. She looked back at Min.

"Do you want to try it?"

The small, tentative nod didn't surprise Kaia all that much. Min's cat may be dormant, but she'd still give the little girl the strength and courage she needed.

Bri shot Kaia a quick look. Kaia nodded in assurance that it would be okay. With a silent breath, she led Daisy forward so Min could pet her first horse, as Bri readied her cell phone with one hand to capture the moment.

The tiny hand reached out and patted Daisy's velvet nose. "Orsey," Kaia heard her whisper.

"Come on into the barn, and I'll introduce you to the rest."

Min was in love. She had to meet every single one. And

even Oscar fell under the spell of the sweet, gentle toddler. He behaved like the perfect gentleman, throwing none of his tantrums and standing still and tame as Min's small palm stroked the length of his nose.

"You have the special touch with him," Kaia told Min. "He's usually pretty grumpy."

"Orsey. Orsey." Min bounced in Bri's arms, beaming.

Kaia pulled Rayna from her stall and led her out to the round pen. Min's fascinated eyes followed the progress of the Palomino as Bri carried her out. Once inside, Kaia mounted bareback and guided Rayna to the side.

"How about a ride?" Kaia held her arms out to Min.

"Wide. Wide." Min looked up at her mom.

Bri laughed. "Who am I to say no?" She handed her daughter over to Kaia and deposited her phone into her back pocket. "But hold on just a second. Don't start yet. I want to run back to my car and get my good camera to catch her first reaction."

"Sure thing. We'll be here."

Bri took off running and was back in a less than a minute. She positioned herself across the arena to get a full face shot of Min as Kaia gave Rayna the command to walk.

She felt her passenger tighten up for a moment, but then she relaxed into it. They went around and around, Bri snapping pictures the entire time.

Kaia gathered a handful of Rayna's blonde mane into her hands. "Min, can you grab onto this right here? We're going to go a little faster." Kaia helped her get a good grip and then gave Rayna a nudge to prompt her to pick up the pace.

Min screeched in delight.

They rode for about half an hour before Kaia slowed her mount to a stop.

"Wide," Min demanded.

"Rayna needs her lunch. But before that, we need to brush her. Do you want to help me?"

Min nodded excitedly. "Help."

"All right. Let's go."

Even with crates to stand on, Min could barely reach above Rayna's belly. But she did what she could under their watchful eyes.

When Min kept rubbing her eyes and yawning, Kaia knew the fun was almost over. It was naptime. She walked with them to the car and waited until Bri had strapped Min in.

Kaia grinned. "I think that went well."

"I'd say so. And I got some amazing shots."

"I can't wait to see them."

"I'll get some printed for you to look at when you get home."

"Awesome. Thanks."

"No. Thank *you*. You made my daughter's day. But you know she'll want to come back every day now," Bri laughed.

"She's more than welcome. I'll put her to work."

"If there's anything I've learned in my short time as a parent to a toddler, it's that they leave more chaos in their wake than anything else. I can just imagine what your barn would look like when she got done."

Kaia laughed. "Okay, maybe we'll wait until she's a little older."

"Given what you told me of her abilities, I might just insist you take her anyway. That way, Momma can have a break from the madness every now and then," Bri said with a wink.

They hugged and said goodbye. Kaia returned to the barn and got back to work.

When she got home that evening, there was a note from Bri, saying that they'd run into town and would be back in a bit. But she had left about a dozen photos lying on the table. Kaia picked them up and laughed as she thumbed through them.

In all of them, Min had the biggest, brightest smile on her face. They were amazing photographs of a beautiful child on the happiest day of her life. Kaia would have to frame a couple and hang them up. She thought they'd be great on her website too, but she'd ask Bri if that was okay first. There were some strange people out in the world, and they couldn't be too careful.

Moving through the empty house, Kaia made her way to her bedroom. Gathering up her pajamas, she walked back out into the hall and into the bathroom. She'd draw a hot bath and soak for a while.

Being submerged in a tub full of water wasn't one of her cat's favorite pastimes. Which is why she normally stuck with showers. Her cat didn't care for those either, but at least they didn't take as long. For tonight though, the little troublemaker could suck it up.

Bundling her hair on top of her head, Kaia stripped and sank down into the warm depths. Resting back against the slope, she took stock of her life.

She was twenty-eight years old, and aside from her horse training—which she was unbelievably proud of—she didn't have a whole lot to show for it. Seeing Bri with Min was starting to make her think about a family of her own. It had been so long since she'd been able to share her life with someone.

At thirteen, her parents had been killed in a car accident, leaving just her and her brother. And now even he was gone, and she was alone. She had friends, but no husband, no boyfriend… Hell, she didn't even have a prospect on the horizon.

A quick flash of Mac blazed in her mind. And with it, that kiss. Her body heated, and her nipples puckered in response to the memory. Her mind took it further and seamlessly transitioned into the dream.

Just under her skin, she could feel her cat coming to life. Stretching, rolling, purring.

She closed her eyes and pictured Mac's hands skimming up her torso, cupping her breasts. She let her own hands follow the path of his, mimicking his movements.

Even though it had only been a dream, her body remembered

what it felt like to be filled with him. Stroked by him. The power of him was breathtaking. His lips on hers, his blistering skin scorching her all over.

Kaia was needy and restless now. Below the water, her hand moved down her body, over her mound, and between her legs. Thoughts filled with Mac, she brought herself to climax.

Panting, Kaia swore. "God, I can't go on like this."

What was it about him that made her and her cat lose their minds? He wasn't even a shifter. He had no inner animal to tempt and call to hers. She wasn't too sure how it all worked, but shouldn't she be attracted to someone more like herself?

Both of her parents had been shifters. Kaia, having never been told otherwise, figured that's the way it was. She'd had a few boyfriends—some she'd even slept with—but she'd never had deep feelings for any of them, and her cat showed no interest in them whatsoever. She'd just assumed it was because none of them had been like her. The only shifters she'd ever known had been family, so she'd had no way of finding out.

But now there was Mac.

Her lioness definitely had feelings for him. She'd made that clear in no uncertain terms. But why now? Kaia had known him all her life, and at best, her inner feline had tolerated him the same way she did. So why, suddenly, had it changed?

Something her mom had once told her whispered into her mind. She'd been trying to have "the talk" with Kaia since she'd recently started her period. Kaia could remember only half-listening, because she'd been so embarrassed by the topic. She'd been eleven at the time and hadn't wanted to think about that kind of stuff. And to have her mom talking about it—that was just gross.

Thinking back on it now, Kaia wished she had paid more attention. It had something to do with her cat and how it matured.

What had she said?

Kaia concentrated on bringing the memory back.

They'd been in her room, sitting on the bed. Her mom was explaining how nature worked, and how it was different for her human side and her feline side. Though she'd become a woman herself, the shifter side of her wouldn't reach maturity until much later.

Was that what this was? Was her cat coming into heat for the first time?

Would she be lusting after every man that came around, shifter or not? Was her horny mountain lion side affecting how she felt? Was that why she'd had that damned dream? Did that mean this would be happening more and more until her cat finally got laid or finished her cycle?

She had no answers and wished she had someone to talk to about all of this. Her newfound grandmothers would probably tell her whatever she wanted to know, but she just didn't feel right talking to them about it.

About Mac.

She didn't even know how *she* felt about him. There'd never been any feelings between them at all, other than animosity. The only thing they'd ever had in common was their love of Jace.

But now, thanks to her lioness, that seemed to be changing. She thought about him at odd moments, and her mind would replay parts of that dream, leaving her all twitchy and aroused for hours.

Finishing her bath, Kaia dried off and dressed. Stepping up to the sink, she went through her nightly cleansing routine. She'd just come out of the bathroom when she heard Bri and Min coming in the front door. She went to greet them.

"Hey. Pick up anything good?"

"As a matter of fact..." Bri grinned and reached into the bag she was carrying. When her hand emerged, she was holding a DVD case. Kaia recognized it instantly.

"No way!"

"Way!" Bri returned, falling back on a teenaged habit.

They had watched this movie hundreds of times in high school. Roadhouse, starring Patrick Swayze. He had been the thing of adolescent dreams, for both of them. They'd swooned when he'd found love and cheered him on when he'd fought against the town bully. They'd cringed when he'd ripped that guy's throat out and laughed like loons when the polar bear had fallen on Tiny.

Kaia's mother had introduced her to the wonder that was Patrick Swayze as soon as she'd started taking an interest in boys. Even though in real life, he was old enough to be her dad, in these older movies, he was just an extremely hot guy with ninja-type skills.

And don't get her started on Dirty Dancing. Oh, man.

That had been the first of his movies she had watched with her mom. Ever since her childhood, they'd have girl's night once a month. They'd binge on over-buttered and over-salted popcorn, and the movies her mom had grown up with. It was a special time she'd shared with her, and she would always treasure them.

Eventually, Bri had joined them on a few of those nights and had developed the same crush for the handsome actor. After her mom had passed, she and Bri had continued the tradition, but as they'd gotten older, their busy schedules had interfered with the beloved pastime, and it had been years since the last one.

"Oh, yeah," Kaia whooped. "Movie night." She paused and frowned. "Crap. I don't have any popcorn."

But Bri saved the day when she produced a box of extra-buttered microwave popcorn from the bag.

"I love you," Kaia crooned.

Bri smiled sweetly. "I know."

They made a quick dinner and together, gave Min a bath and

got her ready for bed. Two stories later, after saying goodnight to each and every fairy on her walls, she was sleeping peacefully.

While Bri changed into pajamas, Kaia popped two bags of popcorn and filled two glasses with ice water. Carrying it all to the living room, she set it down on the coffee table. She had just hit the start button on the DVD player when Bri joined her.

They snuggled in together on the couch with their drinks, munchies, and a hot guy.

11

Mac dragged ass into his house, crossed the room, and dropped down onto his couch. His booted feet came up, one at a time, to land on the low table with a thud. He let his head fall back as he closed his eyes. A jaw-cracking yawn had him scrubbing his hands over his face, the heels of his palms digging into his gritty eyes.

Nails clicking on the hardwood floor gave away Moose's approach. Not that a dog his size could be stealthy. Moose was a Great Dane and shared the house with Mac. Lifting his giant paw, he simply walked up on the couch next to Mac. No circling for this beast—he just let his large hind end drop to the cushion. He draped his front feet over Mac's legs and rested his head on them.

Mac could barely raise a hand to give Moose a scratch. He was beyond exhausted. But how could he be otherwise when he couldn't fucking sleep? Whenever his head hit the pillow, his cock came to life. Because that was when his brain tormented him with images of Kaia stretched out naked in every position possible. Some he knew for a fact weren't even anatomically possible.

He'd jacked off so many times, his dick was getting raw. But the joke of it was, he never got any peace. He was beginning to think only *she* could do that. Only her body. And since that wasn't going to happen, he was screwed.

Well no, actually he wasn't. And therein lay the root of his problem.

After suffering for two long nights, he'd learned not to let his mind veer in her direction. So, over the next three days, he kept it busy by charting maps all night, and searching those damned woods every other minute. He'd spent so much time there, he could describe every fucking inch down to the last pile of raccoon shit.

But through all of his hunting, he'd found no trace of the poacher he was looking for. He'd never faced anyone who could conceal themselves the way this guy could. He knew the motherfucker was still there, but he could find no other evidence to where he'd been holing up.

He hated to even contemplate it, but he may have to revisit Kaia's plan. If she, as her mountain lion, could draw him out, they may have a chance of taking him down.

He'd have to give it some serious thought. Come up with a fool-proof plan that wouldn't get either of them killed. For now, though, he had to get ready for another night of tracking.

In a minute, he thought as he yawned again.

Before he knew what had happened, the bottom dropped out and Mac fell with it. He was asleep between one breath and the next.

But instead of the sex dreams he'd been having, this time he found himself in the middle of a nightmare.

The poacher had Kaia again. Her cat was draped around his neck as it had been before. Except this time, Mac couldn't get to them. He ran but couldn't make up the distance. As he watched, she shifted to her human form and called out for him.

Her arms and legs were bound where they rested over the hunter's shoulders. Her long curly hair hung and swayed as her captor ran.

Mac screamed out his frustration as he fought to rescue her.

And then she was gone, and he stood alone in the forest. He

knew he needed to go after them, but he couldn't move.

Suddenly, he felt a presence and turned to come face-to-face with Jace.

"You let him take her away," Jace accused.

"No. I don't know what happened. This wasn't—"

"You didn't protect her." There was censure in Jace's hazel eyes. Nothing of their decades-long friendship remained. "You promised me you'd protect her. You promised me you'd take care of her. You lied!"

Mac came awake on a gasp. Sitting straight up, his feet hit the floor, wobbling Moose from his position. Mac sat there, breathing away the fear and sorrow that had swamped him. That wasn't the way it had taken place. He *had* saved her that day. But what about since then, his conscience asked.

He'd left her alone. To run, and maybe be taken by the poacher he couldn't seem to find. Was that why he hadn't been able to locate him? Had that asshole already gotten his hands on her again and skipped town? Had he killed her while Mac was wallowing in self-pity?

Suddenly, he had to know if she was okay. Reaching into his pocket, Mac pulled up her number and hit send.

One ring. Two. Three. Four.

Mac was starting to sweat. Had his selfishness cost her her life?

Finally, he heard the phone connect. "Hello?" Her voice was husky and sexy as hell with sleep. The sultry sound distracted him a moment, but the relief he felt pushed it aside.

Thank God. Mac breathed out a silent sigh.

"Mac?" her drowsy voice asked. "Why are you calling me in the middle of the night?"

"I...ah..." He didn't know what to say. Now that the panic was gone, he kind of felt like an ass. "I wanted to, uh, check in and see if you'd seen any more of that poacher. We've been searching, but we haven't been able to locate him."

"And you needed to know this at two a.m.?"

"I'm sorry. I didn't notice the time before I called. I'll let you get back to sleep."

"Mac," she paused, "are you okay? You sound...like something's bothering you."

He couldn't tell her that thoughts of her had been haunting him endlessly. That he craved the taste of her every minute of every day. That he wanted his hands on her and his body buried inside her. That he dreamed of her mouth on him, licking, biting, kissing him. That he was going insane with wanting her.

Since Mac could tell her none of that, instead he said, "I'm just tired. I haven't been getting much sleep lately."

"Well, I don't know if this will help you sleep or not, but I haven't even been out to the woods. My cat is going crazy. But maybe there's nothing to worry about. Maybe the close call with you scared him off."

"Possibly." But he didn't think so.

"Mac, is everything okay?"

Mac heard a slight rustling in the background. He'd obviously woken her up, so he knew she was in bed. Listening to the sound of her limbs sliding over the fabric of her sheets had his heart pounding in his chest. And other parts stirring.

He could picture her lying there—hair spread out over her pillow, blanket resting just above her mounding breasts.

With almost more effort than he had, Mac pulled his thoughts back on track. "It's just been a long few days." He squinted his eyes closed and pinched the bridge of his nose.

"Anything I can do?" He heard genuine concern in her quiet tone.

Not unless you can turn back time to when you were still just Jace's little sister.

"I'll, ah, let you know," he stammered. He couldn't bring himself to end the conversation. Mac searched for something else to say. "How is it having Bri back?"

"It's so great." There was a smile in her voice now. "I've missed her so much."

"I heard she brought a daughter home with her."

"Min. She's two and so beautiful. Bri saw her in an orphanage and fell in love. That little girl couldn't have found a better mom."

Mac didn't say anything.

"I know you don't like her," her voice held a hint of exasperation, "but you don't know her. She's not the person she shows to the world."

"If you say so." He turned the topic back to the little girl. "How did she come to be alone?"

"That's Bri's story to tell. Not mine."

He understood her loyalty to her best friend. He remembered more than a few confidences he'd shared with Jace, sure in the fact they'd be safe.

He didn't want it to end, but it was after two in the morning. They both had busy and demanding careers that required their best.

"I guess I'd better let you get back to sleep," he said reluctantly.

"What about you? You said you haven't been."

Just hearing her voice and knowing she was safe made Mac feel more at ease than he had been in a long time. "I think I might be able to tonight."

"Well, goodnight then," Kaia murmured.

"Goodnight, Kaia." Mac hung up and set his phone aside. Tired beyond bearing, he settled down onto the couch. And slept, deep and dreamless.

<center>~~~</center>

He didn't stir until nearly six. Which gave him plenty of time to grab some coffee and a shower before heading to the office.

As usual, he was the first one in. But later, when he started to hear others arrive, he was surprised when Melissa didn't stick her head in to say her usual good morning. Another half-hour went by before he realized *no one* had spoken to him. With a frown, he went to see what was up.

Everyone in the room gave him a furtive glance and then got immediately back to work. The noise level dropped significantly.

He approached his assistant's desk. "What's going on?"

Melissa brought her gaze up to his and studied him. Whatever she saw there made her relax, and she smiled.

"Mornin', Sheriff."

"Why is it so quiet in here?"

Melissa grimaced. "We didn't want to disturb you."

"What? Why would that bother me?"

She looked guiltily up at him. "Well, for the last couple of days, you haven't been in the greatest of moods. We were giving you some space."

Mac hadn't realized his exhaustion and sour mood had spilled onto his entire staff.

"I'm sorry for that. I haven't been getting much sleep." Mac thought about his conversation with Kaia, and how just talking with her had settled him. "I was finally able to rest last night."

He paused, looking around. "Was I really that bad?"

Melissa gave a strained smile. "You look a lot better today."

He must have been, because she'd studiously avoided his question.

"If there's anything I can do," Melissa offered, "just let me know."

"I will. Thank you."

Mac went back to his desk, regretting that he'd treated his team so poorly. He'd have to remember to watch that next time. No one appreciated being dumped on for no reason.

He had plans to resume his hunt later today, but before that, he needed to follow up on a long shot. He wanted to run the name Ted Barnes through the system, the poacher Kaia had caught, to see if he had anybody he ran with regularly. And then afterwards, the names of all known poachers in Montana and the surrounding states.

Kaia's stalker had gotten here pretty soon after Barnes' press conference. So, he'd start by checking all of the nearby towns within a day's drive of Lost Creek. It would be a lot, but he had a feeling that somewhere in those names would be the one he was looking for.

After compiling all the necessary searches, he had a list of about three hundred names. Each one had either been arrested or convicted on a poaching-related offense, which covered a gamut of crimes from the ridiculous to the most severe.

This was way too many to tackle on his own. He'd have to split up the list among his guys and hope someone hit pay dirt.

After making several copies, Mac stepped out into the bullpen. "Can I have your attention, please?"

Six deputies and Melissa stopped what they were doing and swiveled his direction.

"For anyone who doesn't have something active they're working on, I need you to start eliminating the names on this list." He held the pages up. "On here are close to three hundred poaching offenders that need to be sorted out. Those who are in prison or dead can be checked off. For the ones still on the street, get a last-known address. We need to pinpoint each one's whereabouts. If they're documented elsewhere, that means they're not here, and therefore, not the one we're looking for. All right. Let's get busy."

As a step towards reparation, when lunch rolled around, Mac called in a delivery order from the diner down the street. Within twenty minutes, his guys were feeding their faces while they scoured the internet.

By the close of business, they'd been able to cross a third

off the list. Finding the whereabouts of these asshats wasn't easy—being on the wrong side of the law meant most didn't want to be found. But they'd stick with it and narrow down the pool of suspects.

Mac had to find this guy before he made another move on Kaia.

~~~

Just as Mac had starting his day hunting, so had Kaia. Only on a different level. After the middle-of-the-night phone call, she'd lain awake for hours. The news that they hadn't located the poacher yet troubled her.

He'd stalked her for days. She doubted he would just pack up and leave at the first sign of defeat, despite what she'd said to Mac. He was too focused on her. The close call would have only pissed him off. These men weren't known for quitting when things got tough.

They wanted their prize, and nothing would stop them from bagging it.

So, if he were still out there hiding, where could he be?

Kaia thought about what she knew of the forest. Her unique perspective gave her an advantage over the average person. She'd use that to isolate the places he could most likely remain undetected for long periods of time.

A few came to mind right away. But she wanted a more comprehensive list to work from.

Rolling over to glance at the clock, Kaia saw that it was almost four. If she left now, she could check one or two out before she had to get to work. She knew where Mac had been searching, so she'd concentrate her efforts in another direction. If she found anything, she'd call Mac and give him the location.

Decision made, she threw the covers aside and got to her feet.
~~~

Kaia stripped out of her tank and sleep shorts. Tugging on her robe, she padded out to the kitchen. Going directly to the sliding door, she flipped the lock and pulled it open. With her hands tucked into the pockets, she stepped down onto the deck and then into the dew-wet grass.

The moon gave plenty of light to see by as she made her way to the tree line. Once inside, she picked her way through until she was a couple hundred yards in. She'd started stashing a black duffle out here just for this purpose. Slipping out of her robe, she folded it up and tucked it into the bag with the change of clothes she kept there. Making sure it was out of sight again, Kaia let her cat rise.

The world opened to her. Sight, smell, hearing, and even the gentle brush of wind across her fur sent thousands of messages to her brain. All of which she'd use in her pursuit of this man.

She took off at a run, the sight of the large predator sending small nocturnal wildlife scurrying for safety amidst their nightly scavenging for food. But she paid them no heed. Tonight, man was the prey.

Kaia slowed as she neared the first site she'd chosen. It could barely be described as a cave, but it would give someone shelter if the weather was mild.

Choosing her footing carefully, she picked her way over rocks and around trees, always keeping an ear open for any sound that would indicate movement nearby.

At the outside of the entrance, Kaia stopped. Tipping her head, she listened for shuffling or breathing—anything that would give away the presence of someone inside.

But she heard nothing.

Taking a chance, she set one paw in front of the other and inched forward until she could see into the darkened interior.

Her round eyes gathered all the light she needed to see that it was empty. And had been for quite some time. No human had been here.

Wasting no time, Kaia sprinted off.

The second and third locations were also a bust. No visual indications or lingering scents to imply anyone had inhabited the areas recently. She was running out of time, but if she hurried, maybe she could check one more on her way back home.

As she neared the old hunting blind someone had left to rot, she knew she'd found the right place. Carefully scouting around, she caught the scent of old blood. She'd smelled that before. Kaia sniffed out its source and found it in a pile of leaves and brush at the rear of the shack. The evidence of his foul deeds had tainted the very earth. The traps weren't there now, but they had been. Was he out there right now, hunting for her? Setting the monstrous metal jaws to snare the unsuspecting?

He'd been hiding here. And not too long ago, the stench of death still lingering heavily in the air.

Pissed off and frustrated, Kaia swung around and ran for home.

Unearthing her robe, Kaia tucked it around her and jogged up the deck. She hustled to her bedroom and snatched up her cell phone, but before she could call Mac, it rang.

She was concerned when she saw Helen's name on her screen. Kaia answered immediately.

"Helen? What's wrong?"

"You need to come now. Something has spooked the horses. I'm worried it might be the cougar that man on the news was talking about."

Shit. How could she assure Helen there was no man-eating cat without giving away too much?

"I really don't think you have to worry about that. I'm sure it's nothing, but just to be safe, I'll be there in a few minutes to check everything out."

"Oh, good. I'll see you when you get here, dear."

The whole ride over, Kaia thought more about where the

poacher could have gone than what she'd find at the barn. Horses were sensitive and skittish creatures by nature. Anything could have set them off.

When she arrived, she took a moment to reassure Helen that everything would be fine, and then proceeded to where her charges were still restless and calling out.

"Hey. What's going on in here?" Kaia called as she walked in. Going to the first stall, she checked on Shorty.

"Hi, buddy." She inspected him all over to make sure he was in good shape before moving to the next and the next. Finishing up with Oscar, Kaia stepped back and looked up and down the row.

"All of you seem to be fine, but I'll make a lap outside to be sure."

The second she stepped out the rear doors, her cat went on alert, picking up a heavy male scent. Someone had just been here.

Was it the poacher? Had he somehow found his way this far? Thinking about the blind, Kaia realized that its position put it closer to the barn than to where she'd encountered him before. Could he have stumbled upon it, and the animals had sensed him?

Odds were, he was gone. Nothing here would have tempted him to stick around. But just to be safe, and to ease her own mind, Kaia thought she'd better give the area a thorough once-over.

Paying close attention to everything around her, Kaia walked the perimeter of the large building, even stopping to search the nearby out-buildings. All were as she'd left them, and nothing had been disturbed.

No one was there. She was sure of it. It was likely just as she'd thought—he'd stumbled upon it by accident, checked it out, and then left.

She had to call Mac anyway, so she'd fill him in on this

incident as well. Turning to walk back into the barn, she reached for her phone.

And realized it wasn't in her pocket.

Thinking that maybe she'd left it in the Jeep, Kaia jogged back down the aisle towards her car. After a quick search with no luck, she deduced she must have left her cell at home.

"Well, shit." If she waited until that evening to update Mac, he'd go ballistic. He'd probably go off on her anyway when she told him she'd been hunting, but waiting would only make it worse.

With no other choice, Kaia knew she would have to run home and grab her phone. She jumped in the Jeep and started out. As she neared Helen's house, she stopped.

Getting out, she walked up to the porch where Helen was sitting.

"Was everything okay?"

"Yeah," Kaia told her. "They probably just sensed an animal or something. I checked around the premises, but I didn't see anything. Whatever it was is gone now."

"Are you leaving?"

"Just for a few minutes. I forgot my phone at home, so I'm running back to grab it. I won't be gone too long, and then I'll get my work day started."

"Okay. I'm glad this ended up being a false alarm."

Not quite a false one, she thought, but at least one where nothing had happened. "Me too."

She made the drive home in record time. Leaving her Jeep running, she dashed in and found her phone lying on her bed.

Rushing out again, Kaia slid into the driver's seat. She took a second to connect her phone to the onboard Bluetooth and dialed Mac. She'd use the drive back to tell him what she'd found.

He answered on the second ring. "McNamara."

"Reid," Kaia shot back in the same no-nonsense tone.

Mac chuckled on the other end of the line. "Do I really sound that officious?"

Kaia smiled and eased out onto the road. "No. Just busy. You got a minute?"

"I've got a few. What do you need?" She could picture him leaning back in his chair, his long legs stretching out in front of him.

"I may have found another of the poacher's holes."

"Where?"

She told him about her hunting expedition that morning and what she'd found.

"Damn it, Kaia." She could hear the frustration in his voice and pictured him running his hand through his short dark hair. "I thought you were done going off on your own?"

"Do you want to catch this guy or not? I can help. I know the forest better, and I can get into places no one else can."

"Fuck." His tone held a note of defeat. "If he's abandoned that one too, he has to be on the move. Can you think of anywhere else he might go?" he asked grudgingly.

"I've got a few more ideas. Probably none as likely as the ones I visited today, but I'll check them out anyway." She paused. "One other thing. Helen called me early to tell me that something had spooked the horses. I scouted around but didn't see anything. Someone had definitely been there, though."

"Do you think it was our hunter?"

"That was my first thought, but I don't know. If it was him, he had to have just stumbled onto the barn as he was searching the woods. That blind isn't all that far from the farm." At least, that's what she hoped was the case.

"All right. I'll see what I can find out and let you know."

"Thanks." Kaia pulled to a stop in front of the barn. "I gotta go. I'm back at the barn and just wanted to let you know what was happening on this end."

"Okay. If you get the slightest feeling that someone is getting too close, call me."

"Will do. I'll keep a lookout."

"All right. Talk to you soon."

Kaia kept her senses open throughout the day and watched the horses for any signs of unease. But the day passed quietly, and at sundown, she headed home.

When she walked into her house, Bri and Min were sitting on the floor. They were playing a game she recognized from the sweet candy treats all over the board.

"Hey, that looks like fun." Kaia squatted down by them.

"Do you want to play with us?" Bri smiled at her daughter and then up at Kaia. "It helps with learning colors."

"I do. But let me get cleaned up first." Kaia looked over at Min. "Pick me out a player. I'll be right back."

She took the time to wash up and change her clothes. She was sitting on the edge of her bed when her cell rang. It was Mac.

"Hello?"

"Hey. Just wanted to let you know we checked out that old blind. Evidence showed someone had been there, but like you said, he was long gone. We had a team of dogs with us. They picked up a scent and tracked it for a while, but they ended up losing it. We worked them in the area for over an hour, but they were never able to pick it back up."

Bri called her name from the living room.

"Okay, keep me posted, and I'll do the same."

Kaia held her breath. Would he fight her? She'd just made it obvious she still planned to scour the park for this guy.

"Fine. Just please—be careful."

Kaia hung up and breathed out a sigh. Conversations with him were getting a little easier to have now. He didn't seem to treat her like an errant child any longer. While he may not agree with her on most things, he didn't scold her and piss her off like he used to.

Maybe he was seeing her more as an adult and equal. Maybe they *could* be friends.

An image of him making love to her flashed deliciously in her mind and heated her skin. But before she could think any further on that, Bri yelled her name again.

"I'm coming!" Kaia shook off the memory, determined to enjoy some simple play time with her best friend and her honorary niece.

12

For the next couple of days, Kaia patrolled the park by early morning, and Mac did his rounds in the evening. Each night they spoke on the phone to compare notes.

"I really don't like how this guy has disappeared on us."

"Maybe he *did* leave," Kaia offered. "I wouldn't have thought it possible, but who knows? It's too bad we couldn't have ID'd him before he took off."

"We might be getting close to having a suspect. I ran a search on known associates of Barnes and came up with a few names. So far, my guys have been able to eliminate all of them but one. We're still trying to run him down, but in the meantime, I've also got my team plowing through a list of convicted poachers. It's just slow going. We've dismissed all the ones that are dead or jailed. However," he blew out a frustrated breath, "that still leaves a lot of people to sort out and find."

"So, where do we go from here?"

"I'll stay on the list, and you keep your eyes open. If he didn't run for the hills, he could be waiting for us to let our guard down. So, stay on your toes and watch your back while you're out there."

"I will."

"Any other issues at the farm?"

"No. It's been quiet out there." The conversation ended with a quick goodbye, and they hung up.

Kaia didn't sleep well that night, and when she woke up the following morning, she felt restless. Even her morning run hadn't helped to lift her mood.

She pushed it back enough to get through the training she had scheduled for that day. But when she left, instead of going straight home, she headed into Anaconda. She thought a day like this called for ice cream sundaes.

A parking spot opened up not too far from the door of the supermarket. She pulled in and, juggling her purse and phone, slid from her Jeep. As she came out from between the cars, she had the strangest sensation. Like someone was watching her.

She slowed her pace, glancing around. There were people everywhere, but none looked as if they were paying undue attention to her.

The feeling persisted as she resumed her trek to the front of the store, and she almost changed her mind about going in. But she was in a very public place, and she refused to miss out on her fun evening with Bri and Min over a *feeling*. No one was going to mess with her here anyway.

When she drove home, she was extra vigilant, conscious of the vehicles near her and looking for anyone that could be following her. Turning onto her road, Kaia's eyes stayed glued to her mirrors, waiting to see if another car turned in behind her.

None did, and she heaved out the breath she'd been holding.

Was she being paranoid? There'd been no obvious sign that anyone was watching her. Maybe she'd just overreacted. The poacher wouldn't have been able to tie her to the cougar...

Her heart skipped a beat. Unless he'd somehow seen her shift.

She'd been so careful. Could he have followed and gotten an eyeful of her changing form? What would he do with that information? It really didn't bear thinking about, because if that were the case, her life would be over.

As her driveway neared, Kaia slowed and pulled in next to Bri's car. Grabbing the grocery sack, she hopped down from her seat, taking a moment to gauge whether or not the sensation was still there.

No heebie-jeebies. It must have been a false alarm at the store. Overactive imagination, maybe.

Calmer now, she let herself in. Bri came out of the hall just as she crossed into the kitchen.

"Hi," Kaia greeted as she set the bag on the counter. As soon as she started to dig the contents out, Bri came closer.

"Uh-oh. Rough day?" She picked up the pint of chocolate in one hand and the pistachio in the other. "You only go for two flavors if something is *really* bothering you."

"Nothing specific." Kaia shrugged. "Just an overall...blah. I didn't sleep very well."

"Not being able to find that poacher is getting to you," Bri guessed.

"Yeah." Kaia got down two bowls. "I just don't see him leaving, even with him almost getting caught. In my experience, that's just not how they're built. Which also means he's still out there somewhere."

Bri opened the drawer and pulled out two spoons. "Okay, so if he didn't leave, then where would he be?"

"That's just it—I don't know. We've checked every place in the park we can think of. Other than that old hunting blind I found and the one Mac located, we've never found a trace of him." Kaia took the ice cream scoop out of the crock on the counter and rammed it into the frozen treat. "This is driving me crazy."

Bri rubbed her arm reassuringly. "I have every faith that you'll find him. Between you and Mac, that guy doesn't stand a chance." Then, with a wicked grin and a much lighter note in her voice, she added, "Now, let's go make ourselves sick."

And they did. By the time Kaia had made her way through

the scoops of chocolate and pistachio ice cream covered in gooey syrup, she did feel a little ill. But it had been worth it. Sharing that time with her friend, and then Min, had pushed aside any lingering feelings of unease.

Seeing the look on Min's face when she came out and saw what they were eating was priceless. She'd had to have a bite out of each of their bowls, comparing and testing until she was a sticky, giggling mess.

Kaia let Bri take care of her daughter's bedtime routine while she cleaned up the ice cream catastrophe.

She was wiping down the counter when Bri found her. "I know you said it before, but please, *please* promise me you'll be careful. This whole situation seems to be getting more and more complicated."

Wrapping her arms around her best friend's neck, she hugged her tightly. "I promise."

~~~

He'd seen his tawny beauty again today. Watched her. Followed her.

She was magnificent. And meant to be his. He'd been biding his time, waiting for the right moment. When it came, he'd have her. No one would dare take her away from him again.

~~~

Kaia lounged on the warm rocks, idly flicking the end of her tail as she surveyed the forest below her. She'd been out here for about an hour just taking in the beauty. She knew she needed to get back, but the peacefulness of it all kept her in place.

She'd felt so unsettled lately, and the quiet splendor around her soothed.

While she might wish to spend the day here, she knew that wasn't an option. She had too much work to do.

Reluctantly, she got to her feet, her large, broad paws providing sure footing for the downward trip to the ground. Reaching the bottom, Kaia started off towards home. She'd only gone a few paces when she noticed the body of a small animal lying on the trail in front of her. It hadn't been there when she'd arrived, and she wondered where it had come from.

She cautiously eased forward and saw it was a rabbit. The absence of blood anywhere on it caused her some alarm. Rabbits just didn't die like this. And not in the middle of a trail.

Nudging it with a paw, the body rolled over, but the head twisted at an awkward angle. Its neck was broken.

What the hell?

Kaia glanced around but didn't see or smell anyone nearby.

Who could have left this here without me even noticing?

The unsettled feeling came back with a vengeance. She didn't like this. Not one bit.

Skirting around the rabbit, Kaia hauled ass for home.

Over the next few days, Kaia found more. Always near where she'd been, and always somewhere she'd find them. Different small game, all with their necks broken. Left for her, she'd come to believe, like presents.

Was the poacher trying to lure her in? Were they filled with poison? She hadn't smelled anything unusual on the carcasses, but it could be something she wouldn't be able to detect.

Did he expect the lioness to just chow down on these gifts he was leaving her? Only to roll toes up, ready to be carted off by him?

She didn't fucking think so.

When she got home from her run that morning, she called Mac.

"We've got a new problem," she led with first thing.

"What's that?"

"For the last three days, I've been finding dead animals in the park."

"What kind of animals? I haven't heard anything about this."

"The first was a rabbit, then a groundhog, and now a gopher."

"A rabbit, a groundhog…Kaia, those are prey for a lot of the predators we have in the park. Anything could have killed them."

He wasn't getting it. "I wouldn't have called you if they'd been killed by other animals. They've all had their necks broken, Mac. *And* they've all been left where I'll find them on my morning runs."

That had his attention. "What the hell?"

"That's exactly what I said the first time I saw one. The longer it's gone on, the more it's pissing me off. Does this bastard think I'm stupid enough to just blindly take what he's offering and say, 'Come and get me?'"

"He thinks you're a mountain lion, Kaia."

"I'm not anything he's ever seen before," she ranted.

"But *he* doesn't know that. To him, you're just another cougar. Have you ever seen him while you're out there?"

"No. And I've been looking."

"Is there anything about these animals that's off?"

"Besides their broken necks? I don't think so. They could be pumped full of poison or a sedative, but I haven't gotten close enough to find out. I just avoid them."

"We should bring one in and have it tested to find out for sure. I'd hate to have another animal take advantage and suffer."

Well, shit. She should have discarded the carcasses—not left them out for the next animal to pick up. She felt like a total idiot for not having thought of that before.

"How do you want to do this?" she asked.

"If you don't mind, I may tag along tomorrow morning."

"If he sees you out there—"

"He won't. Here's what we're going to do." They discussed the plan up, down, and sideways to make sure everything was clear.

This could work, Kaia thought. And maybe they could finally catch this asshole.

When Kaia left her house the following morning, she had a feeling of anticipation running through her. As she made the shift and took off into the park, she wondered if this would be over soon.

She could get back to her normal, uncomplicated life.

Kaia was careful to do everything she normally did. She ran and chased prey. Sauntered through the trees, and finally approached the section of woods they'd agreed upon.

Making the twelve-foot leap up onto the rocky ledge was nothing for her. Once there, she settled in and began to groom herself. After that, she dropped down onto her side and closed her eyes.

She didn't nap, but instead listened intently to any sound going on nearby. Would she be able to hear the poacher leaving her the treat?

As hard as she concentrated, though, she heard nothing.

After about thirty minutes, she stretched, rolled, and gradually got to her feet. She took a moment to survey her domain before descending to the ground.

Loping off, she kept her eyes peeled for the little present. She didn't see it right away. He'd placed it farther down the trail she'd come in on. She stopped and scanned the surrounding area.

Had he known Mac was there? Was that why he'd dropped this here, and not closer? But how could he have?

Approaching it slowly, she kept her senses attuned to everything around her. The primary objective was to catch him leaving it, but because of the way he ghosted in and out of situations, they knew they needed a contingency plan. In the event they didn't see him make the drop, she was to take whatever he left, and proceed to a second location.

Because she'd always left the offerings, Mac had thought if she took this one, it might spur the poacher into following her to see how she liked his present.

Mac would stay behind and hopefully apprehend him when he showed himself.

Kaia pawed at the dead fox and noted how the head wobbled separately from the body. It was definitely one of the hunter's gifts. Sniffing at it, she couldn't detect any scent on it other than the normal smell of the animal.

Gingerly, she picked it up by the tail, and started off down the trail.

The other spot they'd chosen was a good quarter mile away. They wanted to have plenty of time to see if she were followed.

When she reached her destination, Kaia lay down with the fox between her front feet. No way in hell was she going to nibble on any part of it, but she needed to put on a good show in case she was being watched.

About fifteen minutes later, she heard a rustling. She rose to a sitting position and swung her big head around to see Mac making his way out of the trees. Frustration was clear on his face.

"Nothing. I didn't see a goddamned thing. No sight of him leaving the carcass, and not a single rustle of leaves when you left. Did you sense *anything*?"

He looked over at Kaia as if he were expecting a response. He grimaced when he realized he'd been asking the cougar. "Crap."

She chuffed out a laugh.

"I don't suppose you saw anything?"

The cat swung her head from one side to the other.

"I'll never get used to this." Mac turned and scanned the area. "Well, this was a big fucking fail." He glanced down at the fox. "At least we still have that."

Kaia looked down at the dead fox at her feet.

Mac pulled an evidence bag from his pocket. Bending, he scooped the dead animal into it. "I'll get this back and find out for sure if anything dangerous has been added."

Before he could stand or move out of range, her cat took matters into her own paws. She prowled forward and rubbed her head against his thigh.

Oh no, no, no. You can't do this. You stop it right now!

She completely ignored her. The damned cat continued to molest Mac, dragging her body along his with such vigor that she knocked him off-balance and he fell to his backside. Sitting on his ass in the middle of the woods, he had a full-grown cougar in his lap, mauling him.

Kaia tried to talk some sense into her feline side, but no amount of coaxing worked. She was fully intent on getting as much of her scent on him as she possibly could. And his on her. Kaia was absolutely mortified and could think of only one way to stop this. Desperate times, and all that.

Besides, she was already embarrassed beyond measure at this point. A little more shouldn't hurt. Much.

They were alone out here so, calling to her human side, Kaia fought against the will of the lioness. She was set on claiming Mac as her own, but Kaia eventually won out. Barely. And found herself—completely naked—sprawled on top of Mac.

"Uh, hi," Mac stuttered, looking up into her face. This close, she could see the light gleaming in his short spiky hair, his hat behind him where it had been knocked off by the amorous cat.

"Sorry." Kaia tried not to think about being so exposed in front of him. Or how good his body felt against hers. "This was the only way I could think of to stop her from raping you. She's been acting very…out of character lately. I don't know what's wrong with her."

Kaia made a move to separate herself from Mac as gracefully

as possible. But his hands came to her bare hips and gripped tightly for a moment. Gazing directly into his eyes, she saw the dark striations in the blue of his irises. And watched as they flooded with heat.

Then before she knew what was going on, they were both on their feet. He was five feet away, and his back was to her. He bent to pick up his hat and settled it on his head again, keeping his face averted. He began unbuttoning the outer shirt he'd worn against the morning chill and reached back to hand it to her without looking.

Kaia slipped it on gratefully. The shirt enveloped her and reached to mid-thigh. She took a moment to soak in the warmth and scent of him.

Before she made it weird, she pulled herself back. "I'm good. You can turn around now."

"Do you want to tell me what the *hell* just happened?" he demanded as he pivoted on his heel. Any want or need that had been visible before was banked now.

She grimaced. "I'd rather not."

"Kaia." Stretched patience rang in his tone.

She so didn't want to have this conversation, but she should have known he wouldn't leave it alone. To his credit though, it wasn't every day you were on the receiving end of a mountain lion's affections. It had to be a little disconcerting to say the least.

As much as she hated to discuss it with him, she owed him some answers. So, with a fortifying breath, she began. "My cat...she, ah...she's been acting odd."

"No shit."

Kaia shifted her weight back and forth on her bare feet, not sure of the best way to put it. "I think...that is...I'm pretty sure she's...going into heat for the first time." The last words sped from her lips.

"Going into heat," he repeated, clearly stunned. He rubbed

his hand over the back of his neck. "First of all, how can that be? You're twenty-eight. I would have thought that happened a long time ago. And second, why is she all over me? I'm human. She's not."

"A part of her is. But to tell you the truth, I don't understand it myself. My mom sat me down when I was eleven and tried to explain it all, but I didn't really pay attention. I was young, and the last thing I wanted was to talk about sex and stuff with my mother." Kaia wrapped her arms around her middle. "What I *do* know, is that the animal side of a shifter matures much more slowly than the human does. We're not able to change form until we're around five years old. At that point, the animal is just a cub. It would be hard for the little ones to shift into full-grown cats."

"That makes sense."

Kaia nodded. "So, while *I* made that step towards womanhood when I was eleven, my cat is only just now having her first cycle. I didn't realize it would take *this* long, though. I guess I've been under the impression it had already happened, and I just hadn't noticed."

He studied her for a moment. "Should we put off this op until she's through this? I wouldn't want her to compromise a plan because she's frisky and there's a man nearby."

"That won't be a problem."

"How can you be sure?"

Kaia felt her cheeks flush and cleared her throat. "Because it only seems to be you she's interested in."

His face was a mask of shock. "Me?"

"Like I said, I'm not sure how this works. My mom died shortly after that one botched conversation. And I doubt Jace had a clue, even if he *could have* worked up the nerve to talk about that with me."

Understanding softened the lines around his eyes. "You have two grandmothers now you could talk to," Mac offered.

"I know," she sighed. "But that's not really a chat I want to have the first time I meet them. 'Hi, nice to meet you. Why does my cat try to hump my brother's best friend?' Yeah, I don't think so."

Kaia pushed her hair out of her face. "Estrous lasts a month. Thankfully, two weeks have already passed." She swallowed. "I just have to make sure to keep you and my cat separate. Especially during the eight days she's actually in heat. Which, unfortunately, should be soon. But don't worry. I can handle it."

"What is this doing to *you*?"

She deliberately played stupid. "What do you mean?"

He called her on it. "You know exactly what I mean."

Yeah, she did. But there was no way she'd tell him she thought of him every day. That she stayed hot and itchy all the time. That she'd had the most erotic dream of her life about him tying her up and making love to her.

"It's not…comfortable. But it's not anything I can't deal with." *As long as she didn't sprain a wrist in the process.*

"Uncomfortable how?"

"Mac. Do we really have to get into this?"

"I'd like to." There was something in his eyes she couldn't read. "How does your cat being in estrous affect *you*, Kaia?"

Keep it impersonal, she told herself. Basic. "She's more restless. I can feel her stirring, brushing against my skin. Which, in turn, makes *me* feel restless. She gets agitated easier. And like being near someone who's bitchy, it puts me off."

"And when she's amorous, as she was a bit ago?"

Her face hardened and she stared him down. "I'm not having this conversation in the middle of the woods while I'm in nothing but your shirt, Mac. I've embarrassed myself enough for one day. If you don't mind, I'd appreciate it if you'd take that fox away, so I can get out of here and get to work."

She turned to walk away, but he closed the distance between

them and grasped her arm.

"Kaia."

His gaze drilled into hers, holding her prisoner and making her stomach flutter. Her body started to heat, and the cat inside of her purred in response.

Before Kaia had to find an excuse that wouldn't cause even more questions, she heard a sudden growl fill the air.

She knew that sound.

13

Kaia spun around to see a massive cougar leaping for Mac. Going straight for his throat.

Only Mac's quick reflexes saved him from the killing bite, but the big cat still took him down. Without thought, she shifted in an instant, her cat taking over to protect her man. Mac's shirt fell to the ground in shreds, and as soon as she'd landed on all fours, she was on the move.

The cougar had Mac pinned to the ground, his arms raised and crossed like a shield, protecting his face and neck. Blood already coated his forearms from the cat's razor-sharp fang teeth as he fought off the vicious attack.

He took a blow when a large paw swiped out at him. Raking down the side of his head, it left a furrow near Mac's temple. Dark red blood instantly welled up and flowed.

With bunching muscles, Kaia sprang and hit the male mid-body, driving him off of Mac.

They tumbled together briefly before finding their feet again. The male crouched and braced, ears turned and flattened to his head. He snarled at her and then slid his focus to Mac somewhere behind her.

Not taking her eyes off the larger cat, Kaia stepped into his eye-line, drawing his attention away from his target and keeping it on her. He'd have to go through her before he got to Mac.

Angry, he struck out at her with his huge paws. She answered with her own growl and swiped back at him, letting him know she wouldn't back down. Mac needed time to get away. She had to keep him busy.

Unless he was hurt. Was he lying in the dirt, dying?

He was behind her, so she couldn't see him. No matter how hard she listened, she couldn't hear him either.

Her heart was racing, but her fears had to be pushed aside. This cat was skilled and strong and hell-bent on killing. She needed all of her wits about her to keep them both alive.

There were other cats in the park, but she'd never had one come into her territory. This big male must be new to the area, brought in by her being in estrous. Mountain lions were normally solitary animals. But when a female was in heat, males could scent the hormones from miles away.

He'd probably only come, thinking he'd find a receptive female to mate with. Instead, he'd found her.

Not going to happen, big guy.

It wasn't his fault he'd stumbled into the wrong situation. Now she just had to persuade him to move on. That he'd get no action here.

She hissed and charged at him, taking a couple more swipes for good measure—and making sure he knew she wasn't into him.

He backed off but tried circling around her. She cut off his route by rushing him again, letting him know, in no uncertain terms, to leave.

A scream of rage told her he wasn't happy at being denied. But the angry cougar finally seemed to give up, huffing as he finally retreated and ran off.

Mac.

Kaia spun on her paws to find him standing about ten feet behind her. He was battered and bloody, but the pistol was steady in his grip, obviously prepared to shoot if the newcomer hadn't taken the hint and left. She was glad it hadn't come to that.

"Thanks." He grimaced and brought the back of one hand to his head. He looked down at it and his arms. More blood than skin showed at this point. "Not too bad for going against an adult male cougar. We'll have to talk about what just happened here, but later. Let's get the hell out of here before he comes back."

Kaia's stomach roiled thinking how much worse he could have been hurt. Her female went to him. Sniffed at his injuries.

"I'm okay. It's not as bad as it looks. A lot of blood, but I don't think anything needs stitched up. Soap and water and I'll be good. Go ahead and go. I'll be right behind you."

She waited. Stared up at him.

"I'm fine, I promise. Go."

Sure that her suitor was gone, and with no choice but to take Mac at his word, Kaia darted off into the woods. And home.

She was way past flustered by everything that had just happened. But her thoughts couldn't help but return to the direction their conversation had taken before they'd been interrupted. She'd told Mac some very personal things. And between that and flaunting all her girlie bits in front of him, she needed some time alone to think.

Thankfully, she was able to get in, throw some clothes on, and leave again without seeing Bri. For probably the first time in her life, she hadn't wanted to see or talk to her best friend. There would be too many questions, and Kaia just didn't have the strength to deal with them right now.

~~~

Mac stayed where he was and watched her go. His head was still spinning over what had just happened. And his heart had yet to return to its normal rhythm.
~~~

He looked down at his arms again. Prodded at his head. Felt along the path the claw had taken. The wounds would need to be disinfected, but he'd come through pretty well, all things considered.

"Holy fuck." He'd survived a mountain lion attack with nothing more than cuts and bruises. Thanks to Kaia. She'd taken on a full-grown male that was easily twice as big as she was. He thought he'd been a goner when he'd felt the heat of that cougar's breath on his face.

And then she was fighting him. It was a loud and intense battle that had seemed to last a lot longer than it had.

Kaia had kept her own body between him and their visitor. Mac had had his gun out and was ready to use it, but he'd fervently hoped he wouldn't need to.

Mac found the remnants of his shirt Kaia had been wearing when she shifted. He took a few of the larger pieces and used them to clean himself up a bit. He tied a strip around one particularly deep gouge on his right wrist.

The only reason Mac could see for this attack, was that Kaia's cat was coming into heat. It must have drawn the male in. He was only obeying thousands of years of instinct. To breed and procreate. Mac couldn't hold that against him.

He would have hated to do it, but he would have shot if it looked like either of them were about to be hurt. He was just glad she'd been able to move him along.

He'd have to let the rangers know a new player was in the park. And to be on the lookout for cougars patrolling the area. Potentially aggressive ones at that.

Mac's mind switched to Kaia and the conversation they'd been having. He knew he'd pushed her and gotten too personal, but he'd needed answers.

He'd seen heat and need flare in her green eyes more than once. Including when she'd been laid out on top of him, naked. Were her responses to him only because of her feline coming of age?

And what about his reaction to her? Was she giving off some kind of pheromones right now? Did the fact that he was going crazy in his need for her stem from that?

He let out a sigh.

It would be a nice out, but Mac knew this wanting was all his. At some point, he'd stopped seeing Kaia as Jace's annoying little sister and discovered what a smart, independent, sexy-as-fuck woman she'd grown into.

Try as he might, fantasies about how her body would feel gliding over his tormented him daily. He'd had only a taste of the real thing, and he couldn't wipe the memory from his mind. He may not have known what to do with the lioness that had been all over him, but he'd certainly known what to do with the naked woman.

Before he'd been able to stop them, his hands had taken the supple flesh of her hips into them and squeezed.

Visions of what could have come next floated through his mind, but he pushed them aside. It had almost killed him, but he'd set her away from him and gotten to his feet. He'd even acted the gentleman and turned his back, offering her his clothes.

It hadn't only been a chivalrous act, though. It had also been an act of self-preservation. Because he knew if he'd looked at her another minute, he would have taken her then and there. In the state he'd been in for the last several days, he wouldn't have cared if the whole world had seen them. She was the only thing consuming his mind.

A sense of threat brought Mac abruptly out of his fantasies. The hair on the nape of his neck rose, telling him danger was near.

Had the male returned?

Instinct had Mac spinning around and dropping into a crouch. At the same time, the report of a rifle sounded.

So, the poacher had followed. And had upped his game.

His intuition had saved his life again. But fire still scorched a path over the back of his right shoulder as the bullet grazed him. He rolled for cover in case another shot was imminent and came to a stop up against the trunk of a large tree. Drawing his gun again and keeping his head down, he tried to get a bead on where the shot had originated.

The short duration between the discharge and the hit told Mac that the shooter wasn't very far away.

And not opposed to shooting someone in the fucking back.

Pussy ass cocksucker.

Mac flexed his shoulder. The path the bullet had scored through fabric and flesh throbbed and burned. He knew all his wounds would be full of dirt and dead leaves that had been picked up by his scramble to stay alive. But there was nothing to be done for that right now.

Instead he tried to ascertain if his would-be assassin was still there. Remaining completely motionless, Mac looked for any movement in the surrounding area that would give away his shooter's location.

Five minutes passed with no sign. Had he fled once the shot was fired? Did he think he'd hit his mark? Or was he out there now, waiting for a chance to finish him off? He still had to be pretty pissed that Mac had taken his prey away from him. Was this his retaliation?

Mac didn't know, but he wasn't going to let this bastard win. Coming slowly to a crouched position, Mac held it and listened. He cocked his head and concentrated on the sounds around him.

Birds, silenced by the shot, began to sing again. And the call of tree frogs echoed through the woods, indicating to Mac that the threat was gone.

Son of a bitch.

Mac could go after him, but if he'd learned anything in the

last few weeks, it was that this joker was adept at hiding out here. He would update the APB and the park guys, letting them all know that the poacher had just been upgraded to an attempted murderer.

He slowly got to his feet, his shoulder aching like a motherfucker. He'd head into the office, shower there, and have Melissa take a look at him.

Grabbing his hat again and the bagged evidence, Mac started out of the trees.

~~~

He raged.

From the moment he'd seen her, she'd been his. Destiny had decreed it so.

But when he'd seen her sidle up to that bastard, nuzzle him, offer herself to him, he'd felt a madness fill him. Did she not know she was disgracing herself—her species—by acting in such a way?

She was a spectacular and unique creature, and *he* was the one she belonged to. He'd searched long and hard for her. She was a match made only for him.

He'd spent time studying her, leaving her offerings to show her what she meant to him. To gain her trust. And then for her to do that—betray him this way—it could not be allowed to continue.

It was all *his* fault. That man had to be clouding her judgment. He was ruining everything the hunter had worked so hard for.

In the next moment, he'd stared transfixed as the unimaginable had happened. She'd changed. Right before his eyes. One moment she'd been the regal and magnificent mountain lion, and the next she'd been a long, lean, beautifully naked woman.
~~~

He'd gasped. Not believing what he'd seen.

When the shock of what she'd done had passed, he'd realized she was more than he could have ever envisioned. She'd enable him to attain everything he'd ever dreamed of.

Fury had grabbed him by the throat then as he'd witnessed what looked like a lover's embrace between them. She definitely hadn't seemed bothered that she was lying, naked, on top of that goddamned sheriff.

Had she screwed him? Sucked him off? The thought of that possibility pushed him over the slippery slope of reason.

When the rage cleared, he'd found himself back at his truck. One way or another, that fucking sheriff had to go. Seizing the opportunity, he grabbed his high-powered rifle. By the time he'd returned to where he'd left the betrayers, she'd been gone, but the man was still there.

Perfect.

He'd brought the scope level to his eye, sighted in on the sheriff's broad back, and had pulled the trigger. He'd seen the man go down and grinned.

Obstacle eliminated.

As quickly as he'd been able, he'd grabbed up his weapon and headed out. No need to be here if someone else showed up because of the echoing shot.

~~~

Kaia was finishing up at the barn later that day when Mac walked in. She'd worked so hard to put what had happened between them that morning out of her mind. And now, with just one look at him, it all came rushing back.

The shock and embarrassment, but mostly, the feel and scent of him.

She had hoped she'd have more time to settle herself before having to see him again. But that was not the case.
~~~

"Hey." She strove for casual as he approached. He didn't look too bad for having gone toe-to-toe with a cougar. His arms had been cleaned and treated. The side of his head had a couple of butterfly bandages holding the gouge together. But all in all, he looked good.

Really good.

He didn't bother with pleasantries. "The tests came back on the fox." Mac stopped just past Oscar's stall, tucked his hands into his pockets, and leaned his shoulder against the wall. "No drugs of any kind. I don't know why he's leaving you dead animals now, but he's not doing it to hurt you."

Before she could say anything, Oscar got up to his usual ornery self and head-butted Mac, hitting him in the back and pitching him forward.

His ripe curse, and the way he was clutching himself, alerted Kaia that Oscar must have hit one of his injuries from that morning.

"Mac?" Kaia reached out to lay a hand on his arm.

"I'm fine." He turned away from her to glare at the horse and she gasped. There was blood forming a jagged circle on his upper back.

"Did he bite you?" She didn't think; she just reached for the buttons on his shirt before he could answer. "I don't remember you having any bites or scratches back here. Let me see."

Mac shrugged out of her grip and took a step back. "He didn't bite me. It's nothing."

"It's not. Take that shirt off and let me see."

When he didn't move, Kaia put her hands on her hips, tilted her head, and stared at him. It took a full ten seconds.

"Oh, for fuck's sake." Mac's long fingers attacked the buttons.

Kaia tried not to notice how chiseled his chest and abs were as the shirt started to come off. It was impossible, though. She'd felt the hardness of them and smelled his intoxicating scent only a few hours earlier. Her mind could finally put an image to what she'd had pressed against her naked body that morning.

His shirt slid down his arms, and off. He fisted it in one hand. "I'll show you it's no big deal, and then we can move on."

As her brain had short-circuited at the sight of his gleaming torso, it took her a moment to remember what they'd been talking about. "Yeah. No problem."

Her mind cleared in an instant when he turned his back to her. There was a large white bandage just below the top of his shoulder. It was soaked with fresh blood. This may not have been caused by Oscar, but the grouchy stallion had definitely aggravated it.

"What the hell happened? This wasn't here before. Did the cougar do this?" Kaia stepped in close to him and lifted the corner away. Beneath the gauze, a gouge about four inches long scored his skin, a deep track of missing tissue.

"This needs to be redressed." She went to get her first-aid kit, calling back over her shoulder, "Sit down and tell me how this happened."

When she returned, he'd pulled an old stool over to sit on.

Kaia got to work cleaning away the new blood and checking to make sure no other damage had been done by the cantankerous horse. She felt around the edge and poked at the skin surrounding the gash.

"It looks all right. I don't think it needs stitches. You'll have a scar, but it'll heal."

"Yeah, that's what Melissa said."

So, his assistant had seen to it.

"She would know." Kaia knew Melissa had four rough-and-tumble boys at home, ranging in age from six to fourteen. From what she'd heard, they were always in some fight or another, and she was sure Melissa had seen her fair amount of blood and gore.

Kaia soaked a cotton ball with a wound care wash and

dabbed at it. "Are you going to tell me how you got this?"

The broad expanse of Mac's back rose and fell beneath her fingers. "After you left this morning, the poacher took a shot at me."

"*What?*" Kaia actually felt the blood drain from her face. It left her light-headed, and she went cold and clammy all over. Her heart was thumping madly in her chest. Her cat, sensitive to her moods, stirred and prowled in her mind—disturbed as well. She stepped out around the stool, so she could look Mac in the face. "He tried to kill you. Because of me." Her voice shook.

Mac stood in a rush. His long fingers pushed up into her hair and cradled her face in his large hands. His blue eyes were deep and earnest. "No. He shot me, because of me. *I* deprived him of his prize. *I* am the one dogging his every move. *I'm* the one who is going to take him down."

"But you wouldn't have even been there—" She hated the thought that she'd put him in danger.

He gripped her upper arms softly. "That's not the way this works, Kaia. Friends help friends. The only one to blame for any of this is him."

Kaia suddenly felt sick. Her gaze snapped to his. "Oh, God. He was there—watching us. He saw me shift, didn't he?"

The quick flash of shock in his eyes told her he hadn't considered that possibility. "I don't know. But it's probable."

"Oh, God," she repeated as she tried to turn away from him.

"Hey." He bent at the knees to meet her at eye level. His voice had softened to almost a whisper. "I won't let him hurt you. He won't get anywhere near you, I promise." His attention dropped to her mouth before coming back to her eyes.

The moment strung out, and a different kind of tension filled Kaia.

Ever so gradually, his head lowered towards her. Kaia found herself trapped in the blue depths of his gaze. A secret part of her didn't want to fight it. But then there was the part of her that remembered he was her brother's friend, first and foremost.

"Mac," she breathed, her lids drooping against her will. "We shouldn't—"

"Yes. We should. I can't fight it anymore. I want you."

Kaia was dying. His lips were so close to touching hers. His hot, steamy breath was washing over her, warming her. Making her heated blood flow.

She felt the very slightest brush of his mouth on hers. Her body leaned into him, anticipating, when a throat cleared from the doorway behind them.

14

Kaia jerked back and spun to see Bri, with Min on her hip, standing there with a shit-eating grin.

Behind her, Mac muttered a frustrated, *"Fuck!"*

"Sorry for the interruption. Min wanted to see the horses. And her Aunt Kai, of course."

"Of course she did." Kaia pasted on a smile, went to them, and took Min into her arms. Saved by the bell. Or toddler, as the case may be.

As she turned back to Mac, it was to see him shrugging back into his shirt. Suddenly, the reason he'd had it off came back to her.

"I still need to re-bandage that wound."

"It's fine. I'll see to it when I get home." Mac strode out, leaving them standing in the barn.

Bri gave her a sly look once Mac had driven off. "Damn. Should I even ask? He looks like hell."

"Later. Please." Kaia sent Bri a look that begged her to let it drop for now.

"You got it. I'll bring the adult beverages."

Kaia was grateful for the distraction for the next hour. Seeing everything through Min's eyes let her experience life's miracles all over again, taking her back to a simpler time and place. The little girl was so joyful and in wonder of everything around her. It brought a lightness to Kaia's conflicted spirit.

Later that evening, true to her word, Bri had the tall white bottle of creamy liqueur and two shot glasses ready. Having already put her daughter to bed, Kaia would have Bri's undivided attention.

And maybe she needed to get all this out. God knew she'd gotten nowhere with it on her own. She had no idea how to proceed from here, and she was confused and at odds with herself.

Bri handed her the small glass as soon as she sat down on the couch with her. And following tradition, they clinked glasses and tipped their heads back—swallowing it all at once.

"Talk." Bri took both, filled them again, and handed one back to Kaia. "You'll feel better."

They'd done this many, many times over the years. When either of them had had a problem, they'd drink, talk it out, and come up with a solution. Kaia hoped now wouldn't be any different.

"This entire situation is making me crazy."

Kaia told Bri everything that had happened, ending with the almost-kiss she'd interrupted.

Kaia sipped at this one instead of shooting it. "So, while part of me wanted to punch you in the face for coming in at that exact moment," Kaia grinned a little, "another part was glad you did."

"We'll come back to the danger in a moment. I think what has you most unbalanced has to do with Mac." Bri took her free hand. "It shouldn't be this hard, sweetie. If you have feelings for him, why wouldn't you explore them? You two have known each other longer than you and I have. It's clear as glass he feels something for you. What's the problem?"

Kaia sighed. "The problem is, I don't know if what I'm experiencing is me, or my cat being in heat. What if I'm only behaving this way because she's horny? And what about him not being a shifter? Both of my parents were, and so were their parents. I've always thought that's how it was meant to be."

She thought about the child in the other room. She wasn't ready for kids right now, but one day. "Would babies even be possible?"

"I think it says something that she seems to have chosen him. If a relationship between you wasn't possible, I don't think she'd have been interested. Isn't one of an animal's highest instincts to procreate?"

"Hmm. I didn't think about it that way." Kaia laid her head back. "I just wish I knew more."

"All of the answers are just a simple phone call away," Bri reminded her.

"I don't even know them. I'd feel ridiculous asking them about this."

"But talking with your grandmothers would clear up all these questions. Call them."

Kaia hedged for a moment and then reached for her phone.

"Will you stay?" she asked Bri when she made a move to stand.

She settled back in. "Of course."

Kaia dialed her grandmother on her mother's side. She'd raised a daughter, so she'd know best how to explain what was going on with Kaia's body.

And just to fortify her courage so she wouldn't change her mind at the last minute, she held Bri's gaze as it rang.

"Kaia," Jackie greeted sunnily. "I love that you're calling. How are you?"

"I'm good." Bri nodded at her for encouragement. Kaia steeled her nerve. "Do you have a minute? There're a few things I need to talk to you about."

"Absolutely! I've got all the time in the world for you, honey. What can I help you with?"

Okay. Here goes. "My cat recently went into estrous—"

"Oh, that's wonderful!"

"Um, yeah…but the thing is, she's kind of taken a liking to a friend of the family. And…he's not a shifter."

Jackie was silent for a moment. "And that's an issue for you?" Her voice carried a disapproving edge.

"I don't know. Should it be? I mean…I thought… Mom and Dad were both shifters. And I'm pretty sure she told me you and Patrick are too. Same with my dad's parents. I guess I just figured that's how it was supposed to be."

"No, darling." Jackie's tone softened. "Love is love. It's doesn't matter what form it takes."

"And, um, kids?"

"They'll be shifters. It's a dominant gene, so it's passed to the children, regardless of whether the other parent is a shifter or not." She paused. "What about you? Are you sweet on him too?"

"That's something else I wanted to ask you. Could her… amorous leanings…be affecting how I feel towards him?"

"No, honey. You each can feel what the other is experiencing, but neither can influence the other. You know, if she's chosen this man, you should consider yourself lucky."

That news surprised her. "Why?"

"Female cougars are very…particular."

"What do you mean?"

"A woman can go her entire life without her animal side bonding with the man she's chosen. She can fall in love, marry, have kids—all without her cat making that same connection. But when it does happen…When the feline half finds a male worthy of her—as it sounds like yours has—that man is a true life-mate."

"Life-mate?" Kaia wasn't sure she liked the sound of that.

"When our lionesses choose their mate, it's for life. It's not easy finding that one man that can rival the female, and there are a lot out there who never achieve that level of joining. When you do find it, it's special."

This was getting too heavy, and very permanent-sounding.

"What if I don't agree with her choice?" Kaia demanded, her voice a little sharp. Her life wasn't going to be dictated by anyone, not even the cat living inside of her.

"Do you?" Jackie asked her, point-blank. "They're usually pretty smart at finding that one man who can be exactly what you both need and want."

"He's not what *I* want," she argued, though her reasoning sounded desperate, even to her. "He's overbearing, obnoxious, and bossy."

"Well, maybe she's made a mistake." Jackie didn't believe that, and Kaia knew it. She was only placating her.

Kaia let out a breath. "I'm sorry. I've been kind of on-edge lately."

"That's understandable, dear," Jackie consoled. "You've had a lot of changes in the last few weeks."

"Thank you for answering my questions. With Mom gone, I haven't had anyone to talk to about any of this. I feel like I'm missing vital information about myself."

"Call any time. We're always here for you."

"Thank you."

When she hung up, Bri was watching her.

"I think I caught the gist of that. Your cat has decided Mac is your mate. What are you going to do?"

"I don't know." She dropped her phone onto the cushion beside her. "This is such a freaking mess."

"What did your grandmother say when you asked her about the cat's feelings affecting yours?"

"What I kind of already knew. That we can sense each other's emotions, but they won't change how the other one feels."

"You know what that means, don't you?" Bri wouldn't let her fall back on denial. It was one of the things she loved about her. She always called her on her bullshit and spoke the truth, no matter if it hurt to hear.

"Yeah. Damn it." She was falling for Mac. *Fuck.*

"So, what are we going to do about this asshole stalking you? Do you really think he saw you change form?"

"I have to assume he did." Kaia tried to take stock of what that meant. She had nothing to base it on. "I've never been in this position before. I've never been this exposed. Even when I told you about what I was, I knew I wasn't in any danger. But now…"

"Do you think he knows where you live?" There was a hint of distress in Bri's voice.

Kaia could understand her fears. There was an innocent child here that could get hurt if this guy showed up.

"I really don't think so. Even if he did see me shift, he wouldn't know who *I* was." Kaia paused. "But, if you feel you can't stay here, I completely understand. We have to think of Min first. Her safety is paramount."

"You're right. It is." Bri's face was creased in thought. "I'll hold off on making any decisions right now. But if there's any sign that he's coming here…"

"Definitely," Kaia said in agreement.

That night, Kaia began doing checks of her property. She walked the perimeter every morning before work, and in the evenings before she went to bed. It was two mornings later that she found what she'd been dreading. A dead raccoon at the edge of the forest, its neck broken.

"Son of a bitch!" Sick and scared, and mad too, Kaia took her phone from her pocket and dialed Mac.

"He's been here," she said as soon as he answered. "He's been to my home."

"I'm on my way." He hung up before she could say anything else.

Fifteen minutes went by before she heard the sound of his vehicle pulling in. A door slammed, and he came striding around the side of her house. As soon as he saw her standing on the back deck, he headed her direction.

"Where is it?" His face was set, and the shadows from his hat gave him a sinister edge. His already dark blue eyes looked like the sky as a horrible storm was rolling in. He was supremely pissed at this turn of events.

Kaia knew the feeling. She pointed. "There. Just beyond the tree line, at the base of a maple sapling."

Mac walked into the trees. It only took him a moment to find it. He squatted down next to the animal and studied it. Wordlessly, he turned his head and got the same unobstructed view of Kaia and the house, just as anyone would who'd stood there.

That jackass could have been sitting there, watching her—for who knew how long. It gave Kaia the creeps just thinking about it, and she rubbed her arms to ward off the chill.

Her attention was drawn back when Mac stood. He tipped his head in the direction of the house. Understanding his meaning, she turned and went inside.

Once he'd joined her and closed the door behind him, he turned to her with a stern look. "I'd rather not have you fight me on this, but I'm moving in here until we catch this guy."

She opened her mouth to protest, but he spoke over her.

"It's not only you and Bri out here, but that little girl too. This man has already gone from poaching animals to trying to kill me in just a few days. It's not safe here."

"Do you really think moving in here is a good idea? You'll become an even bigger target. I won't have you hurt again because of me, Mac."

"This is my job. I know what I'm doing."

"And that's all this is? A job?"

His gaze held steady on hers. "No."

She saw so much swirling in his eyes.

"Kaia?" Bri's voice held a note of trepidation. Her jeweled eyes skipped from Kaia, to Mac, and back. "What's going on?"

Kaia had so hoped she'd never have to say this. "He's been

here," was all she said.

Bri took that in and nodded. "I see."

"Mac wants to move in here."

"I think that's a great idea," Bri surprised her by saying. "He'll be here to protect you. And to make his job that much easier, I'm going to take Min and go see my parents for a while. We stopped briefly when we got back to the States, but I know they'd love a longer visit."

Kaia hated that this was driving her best friend away, but she got it. They'd already talked about Min's safety coming first. "I understand."

She went to Bri and wrapped her tight in a hug. "I love you."

"I love you too. We'll be back, though, so don't give away our room."

"I won't. And I'm holding you to that." Kaia smiled and released Bri to go pack.

Resigned to what would happen next, she slowly swung back around to face Mac. But she couldn't resist poking at him a little. "I took over my parents' room a long time ago, and because Jace's was the bigger of the two remaining, I gave it to Bri and Min. That means you're left with my old room."

She eyed his height and breadth critically. "It might be kind of cramped, but I'm sure you'll do great in my old twin-sized canopy bed. I hope the pink-striped bedding and wallpaper won't bother you too much."

Kaia could barely hold back the grin at his look of utter horror. She was sure he was remembering exactly what it had looked like when he'd hung out here with Jace. Little did he know, there was a queen-sized bed in there now. She'd redecorated it in white and water-color hues. There was no girly canopy in sight. Pity.

"I'm sure it'll be fine." His tone said he'd rather sleep outside. But of course, he wouldn't. "I don't suppose I can talk you out of working today?"

"Nope. The horses need to be fed, and I need to fulfill my contracts with their owners to train them."

He sucked in air and let it out. "I didn't think so. All right." He did some quick calculations. "I'm going to follow you to Helen's. I can't stay though—there're some things I need to clear off my desk first."

His gaze drilled into hers. "If you see or hear *anything* while you're working today, you call me. I think we have a little time before he moves again, but I don't want to take any chances. Promise me you'll call me."

Kaia nodded. "I will. If I sense anything weird at all, I'll call."

Mac took her at her word. "Okay. I'll take care of what I need to at the office, grab some gear, and meet you back here tonight. What time do you think you'll be back?"

"Usually around six."

"Okay, I'll see you tonight."

"Sure. Yeah."

Kaia had a feeling that nothing in her world would ever be the same again.

~~~

Mac had already experienced that epiphany the first time he'd kissed her. His world had altered, and it was never going back. No matter how hard he fought it.

Moving in with her wouldn't kill him, but it would damned well work every ounce of control he possessed. And he wouldn't have the buffer of Bri and her daughter there to help. They may not get along, but Mac had been counting on her to stand as sentinel to Kaia. The woman he wanted with every fiber of his being. He craved the taste of her, the smell of her, the feel of her. All day, every day.

When she'd shifted and ended up naked on top of him, he'd thought nothing could top that moment. Her softness fit to his
~~~

body as no other before her. Those wide, full lips had been mere inches from his mouth. All he'd had to do was raise his head, and he could have savored them.

He still remembered the glimpse he'd gotten of her full breasts, flat stomach, long toned legs, and nicely rounded ass. All wrapped in silky-smooth skin the color of milk chocolate. She was more beautiful than he ever could have imagined. He'd had to tear his gaze from her to give her the privacy she deserved, but the sight of her was etched for all time onto his soul.

But, damn it! He wanted more.

Mac's fingers actively itched to touch her again. He recalled clearly the feel of them sinking into her hips to hold her to him. He'd dreamed of gripping her just there as she rode him, her eyes boring into his as her breasts bounced with the movement.

In the heat of the moment in the barn, he'd told her he wanted her. And it was true. But he hadn't been so far gone to miss her hasty withdrawal when Bri had shown up. Or the fact that she'd not acknowledged his words at all afterward.

But he'd seen the flare of heat in her eyes. The need. He knew she was feeling the same, but why was she was so hesitant? If he were ever going to have her, he needed to rein it back and take it slower with her. Give her time.

Shifting in his office chair, Mac forcibly wrenched his thoughts away from the intoxicating beauty. If he hoped to get anything done today, he needed to concentrate on something else. It would be difficult enough later when they were both in the same house for hours at a time, sleeping only feet away from each other.

What the hell had he gotten himself into?

Mac rubbed his hand around the base of his neck for a moment and then got back to work.

By five, he had patrols set up to drive by Kaia's house every hour. The park crew had been updated and had promised to up their rounds as well, focusing on the areas closest to her house.

Everyone was on the lookout for this guy.

When he left for the evening, he reminded Melissa that he'd be at Kaia's and that he could be reached on his cell at any hour.

He drove home to get what he needed there. As soon as he walked into the house, he braced himself for the greeting from Moose. The hulking dog was a two-year-old Merle Great Dane. He weighed in at one hundred and eighty pounds. On his hind legs, as he was now, with his front paws draped over Mac's shoulders, Moose stood eye-to-eye with him.

"Hey, buddy." Mac scrubbed his fingers along Moose's jawline. "How was your day?"

Moose's large, wet tongue slid up one side of Mac's face from chin to brow.

"That good, huh? Did Duncan come over to feed you and play?" Duncan was the neighbor's seven-year-old son. He and Moose had become fast friends from the start. When Mac couldn't get home, he could always rely on Duncan to take care of Moose for him.

A deep and rumbling string of grumbles answered him. Moose was a very talkative dog. They'd carried on more than a few conversations.

"I'm glad you guys had fun today." He set Moose back on all fours and gave him three solid thumps on his side. "Are you up for an adventure?"

Moose sat, cocked his head to the side, and grumbled again.

"You're going to have to be on your best behavior."

Big brown eyes looked up at him, and Moose gave his reply.

"I know you're a gentleman, but this lady is different. We'll be staying in her house for a little while. She's in trouble and needs our help."

Floppy ears that hung down the side of Moose's large, broad head perked up. Garbled sounds followed.

"I'm glad you feel that way. Someone means to do her harm, and we can't let that happen. She's important to me, boy."

Moose studied him quietly. Then he lifted his butt off the floor and stood before him as if ready for battle.

"I knew I could count on you. Okay, let's pack up and head out."

15

As Kaia drove home a little after six, she didn't know if she'd be walking into an empty house. Bri and Min hadn't been there long, but she dreaded the silence that would meet her, now that they were gone.

She wasn't sure what time Mac would be arriving. His hours as sheriff were probably quite unpredictable. Did he even have set hours? Or was he on call at all times? That wasn't something she'd ever thought about. She'd never really given *him* much thought, and now here he was, dropping everything to come help her. Kaia didn't know how to feel about any of it.

Or about the fact that his SUV was sitting in her driveway when she pulled in. It was a good thing Bri had given him her key before she'd left.

Turning off her Jeep, Kaia sat and stared at her house. Knowing he was in there brought butterflies to life in her stomach. Could she do this? Could she live hip-to-hip with the man she may be falling for? That her cat had already claimed as theirs?

He'd said he wanted her. That he couldn't fight the pull any longer, but what did that really mean? Did he just need an itch scratched? She wouldn't have thought that of him. He'd made such a big deal about protecting her and watching out for her because of the promise he'd made to her brother. How did his wanting her coincide with that?

And what about her own feelings? Jace was definitely a large presence between them. Did she dare follow where her heart was taking her? Could this become meaningful? Her cat seemed to think so.

What she was experiencing with Mac was more intense than anything she'd ever felt before. Did she even want to battle it back herself?

It seemed her subconscious had already shown its hand there. Her dreams had been powerful and erotic when he'd been all the way across town. She was a little afraid of what they'd be like with him only feet away. She'd be sharing her personal space with him. Seeing him, smelling him. Feeling him. And to make this even more difficult, she was pretty sure her cat was in full-blown heat now, making her especially agitated and edgy.

How long could she keep her distance? How long could she deny what she really wanted?

Taking a bracing breath, Kaia got out. As soon as she opened the front door, she stopped and gasped while her cat spit and hissed. "What the hell is that?"

The biggest dog she had ever seen in her entire life was stalking towards her.

"Mac?" she called, unsure.

He stepped out of the kitchen wiping his hands on a towel. "Hey, you're home. That's Moose." He directed his attention to the animal watching her. "Moose, be a gentleman and say hi."

The pony-sized dog walked right up to her, slowly lowered his butt to the floor at her feet, and looked adoringly up at her with huge brown eyes. His long tongue was lolling out of one side of his mouth. It amazed her to realize the top of his head was even with her chest. He was enormous. And gorgeous.

The base of his coat was a silvery-gray. Over that were black splotches of varying shapes and sizes ranging over his entire body. Except for his chest. That had a bright white blaze right down the center.

"Moose, huh? That's definitely fitting." She took a step forward and held a hand out for him to smell. Animals could sense her cat. Some were okay with it once they understood there was no danger. But others couldn't get past the scent of the predator in her.

His large black nose sniffed along her hand and wrist for several seconds. His lips were so soft and velvety, it reminded her of her horses.

Despite the fact that she'd washed before she'd left the barn, he could probably still smell them, along with her lioness, who was also tentatively sniffing.

"Are you and I going to get along?" Kaia eyed him carefully. She was shocked when he let out the deepest vocalization she'd ever heard. And could have sworn somewhere in there it sounded like, "Yeah."

Her gaze shot to Mac who was still standing by the kitchen. "Did he just...?"

"Answer you? Yup," he chuckled. "Moose is one of a kind."

"I can see that." Kaia was running her hands all along his face and neck now. She'd never petted a dog she hadn't had to bend over to touch. "Great Dane?"

"That, or bulldozer."

Kaia had to grin when Moose turned his head and sent a look to Mac. His expression clearly said, "Really?"

"What's his coloring? I'm familiar with the harlequins and some solids, but I don't recognize this."

"He's a Merle. Which is the pattern—not so much the color," he explained. "And they're a lot more common than you think. But because it's not considered a desired, breed-standard color, you don't see them at shows or on TV. Basically, they're just pets."

"Well, either way," Kaia bent forward just a little and kissed his soft, floppy cheek, "you're very handsome."

His long whip-like tail thumped on the floor in response.

She straightened again and took in the sight of Mac. He'd come from the kitchen and had one of her hand towels thrown over his shoulder.

"What have you been up to?" She noticed a delicious scent wafting from the kitchen.

"Cooking dinner. I figure with me and Moose moving in, we need to pull our weight."

"Really." Kaia smiled at that. "If you're cooking, what will Moose be doing?"

"Guarding." Moose woofed in agreement.

She laid a hand on top of his wide head. "I feel safer already." Returning her gaze to the man standing before her, she asked, "So, what did you make?"

"Tortellini with shrimp and pesto. It's an easy throw-together thing that only takes about fifteen minutes."

Kaia started for the kitchen to check on dinner. "It smells wonderful."

Moose was hot on her heels, and she crossed right to the stove and lifted the cover off the pot. The smell of garlic, butter, and herbs hit her nose and made her mouth water.

"Oh, wow. This looks amazing."

"Well, have a seat, and I'll get it served up." He made a motion that shooed her towards the table.

She went, grateful he wasn't making this weird.

Mac scooped helpings into bowls and brought them over, taking the chair across from her.

"So, tell me more about Moose." Kaia thought that might be a safe topic. "Where did you get him?"

"I like to think I rescued him."

Kaia took a bite and nearly moaned. It was so good. She turned her attention back to Mac as she forked in another.

"I found him on one of those internet sale sites. We'd had a tip that someone was selling stolen goods on it, so I was searching the different categories, looking for certain items I knew to have been taken in a robbery the week prior."

He took a bite, chewed, and went on.

"For reasons I will never understand, one of those items was an aquarium. I was scrolling through all the posts in the pet section looking for it, when I saw this long-legged, gangly pup. He had the biggest, dopiest face and ears I'd ever seen."

They both glanced over at Moose. Kaia thought he must have grown into them, because there was nothing dopey about him now. He sat there almost regally.

"A guy was selling him. He'd bought him but then decided he didn't want him."

"I can't understand people like that." Kaia frowned, mad on Moose's behalf. "A pet, any pet, is a life-long commitment. Just to change your mind one day is so wrong."

"I agree completely," Mac told her. "It was evident right away he was only in it for the money. He even tried to get more by saying the pup was a 'rare' color. I knew enough about the breed to know that was bullshit. I called him on it, told him who and what I was, and wouldn't you know," the smile he gave her was cold, "he agreed to bring the price he was asking way down."

Mac's face softened when he looked over at his four-legged friend. "So, at four-and-a-half months old, he came home with me and became Moose. He passed all the health checks with flying colors and graduated from every obedience class I could get him into. He's turned into a perfect gentleman. Until I give him the order not to be."

"Do you think that guy originally planned to breed him? That he was hoping to make money off him that way?"

He brought his attention back to her. "I really hope not. With Moose being a Merle, it could have been dangerous."

That took Kaia by surprise. "What? Why?"

"Great Danes are a very complicated breed, and there are

irresponsible people out there who don't do their research. Or just don't care. Other than for the mighty dollar, of course. I had some general knowledge about the breed before, but since meeting this big guy here," Mac looked lovingly over at the huge dog, "I've learned so much more."

"Through a group on a social media site, I met this woman. Her name is Lauren England, and she's trying to educate people about what can happen when any of the spotted variations like Harlequins and Merles are bred. A Merle doesn't just come in black and gray. Any color a Dane comes in can produce a Merle, or Harlequin for that matter."

Kaia had no idea. She listened with rapt attention.

"She runs a page called 'The Legendary Lillith, A Double Merle,' with the express purpose of education. You see, both the Harlequin and the Merle carry the Merle gene. This gene causes a bleaching to the coat. With the Harlequins, it gives them that brilliant white base. With ones like Moose, it hasn't made it completely white, but that base is shades lighter than it would have been without the gene. That's why he has the spots."

She remembered what he'd said about it being potentially dangerous. "I take it it's this gene that causes all the trouble."

"It is. When uninformed breeders mate two dogs that both have this Merle gene, a quarter of the resulting pups can be blind, deaf, or both. These puppies are what's called Double Merle, because they've gotten a copy of the gene from both parents. They'll have a predominantly white, if not all-white coat, because they've essentially been bleached twice. Same with their eyes. They'll usually be a light blue or some other odd color.

"How the ears are affected is that these pigment cells play an important part of translating the mechanical vibrations of a sound wave into electrical impulses. Double Merles don't have those cells. That means the impulses can't travel to the brain, and the dog can't hear."

"That's horrible."

"And that's not even the half of it. These pups can suffer from numerous other forms of eye conditions that can rob them of their sight. Some so bad that the affected eye has to be removed. Lauren has three Double Merles right now. Lillith had to have one of hers removed and, unfortunately, is blind in the remaining one. Lane is deaf with limited sight. Lemon, her new little guy, is also deaf. People search her out to help with pups that they have. Lauren finds them homes with knowledgeable families. She's taken it upon herself to help these guys and give them the best lives she can. She's trained all of hers using a combination of hand and vocal commands. She's amazing in the work she does with these special-needs dogs."

"It sounds like it. I had no idea."

"Most don't. I didn't, until this guy came into my life. I'm just glad that I found him, and maybe saved some pups from a hard life."

Kaia couldn't believe how much Mac had dedicated himself to learning about his dog. She was coming to understand he really was one of the good guys.

They talked for a little longer, and then each went off to their respective rooms. Just before she closed her door, he spoke from the doorway of her old room.

"Canopy, huh?"

Kaia only grinned at him as she went in and shut the door.

~~~

He wasn't dead. The fucking sheriff had lived. He thought for sure he'd have her all to himself now, but here that bastard
~~~

was.

And to make this infinitely worse, he was obviously planning on staying here with her. This would not be tolerated. She was his and would always be his. This fucker needed to go.

He had to plan.

~~~

The next few days passed kind of awkwardly. They were very careful around each other, trying to ignore the tension that was rising between them.

She learned that Mac had taken a few personal days off from his office to watch over her and hopefully catch this guy. In a hard-won compromise, Kaia agreed she would vary the times that she ran in cat form. He would have preferred her to not go at all, but he understood the need. To ensure her safety as best he could, he patrolled her property and the surrounding woods every day, searching for signs that the poacher had been there.

They'd not found a "gift" since the day Mac had moved in. But they didn't make the mistake of believing he'd come to his senses and left. They knew he was still out there, watching her. Waiting.

For what, they didn't know. This particular poacher was behaving very oddly. Almost obsessive. But until he revealed his motive, all they could do was be vigilant and live life.

Which meant she still went to work. Mac would go with her but made himself scarce once they were there. Moose, though, became her constant companion.

Kaia and Mac went about their business, and neither said anything about the feelings that were developing between them. There was the occasional, accidental brush of skin or a lingering look. But they did their best to keep it platonic.

And because of that, Kaia was quickly approaching her breaking point. Thanks to her cat being in heat, she was extra
~~~

itchy and difficult to deal with, and therefore, so was she. If something didn't change soon...

When Kaia woke well before the sun four days after Mac had moved in, she felt especially on edge. And the dreams hadn't helped. As she'd feared, they'd taken on a whole new level of hot. And they were merciless.

She needed to burn off the excess energy. Mac had asked her not to go anywhere without telling him first, but she had to get out. She had to, or she didn't know what would happen.

Slipping on some loose clothes, she stepped softly down the hall past Mac's door. If she woke either him or Moose, all bets were off.

The sliding glass door made no sound as she pulled it open just enough to fit through. Closing it behind her, she walked across her backyard and into the trees.

Taking all the appropriate precautions, Kaia found the secluded spot where she kept her emergency bag. She stripped out of her clothes and stored them away. Once naked, she shifted and ran.

She kept at it until the cat was finally winded. Oh God, had she needed that. All this pent-up frustration was driving her mad. Frustration over the poacher, frustration over Mac, and frustration over what the hell she was going to do about both.

Long before she had any of it figured out though, she started back towards home. She knew he'd be pissed. But all had gone smoothly. She'd seen no sign of anyone, or anything.

As her cat approached the tree line that bordered her lawn, she could sense him. He was there. Watching for her return.

Mac.

She crept closer until she could make him out through the leaves. He was so fucking sexy standing there, gazing out, looking for her. Dressed only in jeans, his sharp features were dark. Ominous. The black brows over those blue eyes were drawn together. Her excellent vision could pick up the way his hands gripped the deck railing. So tightly, the skin over the knuckles was pulled taut. His entire body braced, ready for the hell he would rain down on her for taking off.

While the cat side of her observed him, she could feel the word *mine* pinging around in her brain. But the human side still struggled against the pull of him. Even knowing she was going to have to suffer through his raging, she still wanted him.

She could feel her convictions wavering as she stood in the shadows. Did she want it to happen? Ever since that kiss, the last few weeks had been building up to this. The heat, the strain on her nerves, the inadvertent touches that set her on fire, and the smoldering looks that made her knees go weak.

Could she take this last step? With *Mac*? She was almost afraid of what would happen if she didn't. She feared she might go crazy.

Kaia was so tired of taking care of the arousal he ignited in her by herself. She wanted someone else's hands on her body. She wanted Mac's hands. And his lips. Chest. Arms. Legs. She wanted every bit of him pressed against every bit of her.

She desperately needed one very specific part of him buried so deep inside of her that she wouldn't be able to think, or breathe, or exist.

There really was no choice to make.

The lioness stepped out of the woods and into the low light of early morning. As soon as her paw touched the grass, he spotted her. He never took his focus off of her as she padded across the yard.

16

When she neared the steps, she let the transformation take her over. One slender, bare human foot came down on the first tread.

Reaching the top, she stood before him, completely naked. Kaia saw his pupils constrict, and she thought she heard a soft grunt as if he'd been hit.

Her inner temptress preened, and the lioness rolled and purred. She licked her lips, and his gaze dropped to her mouth. Kaia had to take a secret breath in order to speak.

"Were you looking for me?"

"What are you doing, Kaia?" Mac's voice was gruff and raspy. She loved the sound of it.

Kaia let her body brush along his as she moved past him to the door. Now she knew why her cat loved doing it so much.

She had the pleasure of feeling him jolt at the contact like an arc of electricity had traveled between them.

She gripped the handle to slide it open but noticed Mac was still facing away from her. His wide shoulders rose and fell. Once, twice. Was he bracing himself? To face her? She grinned softly.

He finally turned to her. But his attention was immediately drawn down, his gaze following the long length of her naked body.

She finally addressed his question. "I'm coming in from a

run, Mac. What are *you* doing?" Kaia put her free hand on her hip, his eyes tracking the movement.

He didn't answer. And his complete concentration on her brought a delicious warmth coursing through her body.

To hide the shiver that overtook her, Kaia turned and walked into her house. She made it no farther than the kitchen when she heard the door slam and lock. A moment later, she was pulled roughly around and suddenly found herself lifted and placed on the countertop.

Mac immediately moved into the space between her legs, fitting his lower body snug against hers. She was reveling in the feel of his hardness when his hands went up and into her hair. He captured the sides of her face and looked deep into her eyes.

"You're playing with fire, Kai. Are you sure you want to do this?"

Oh, she was so sure. "Burn me up, Mac."

He crushed his mouth to hers and held her immobile for the onslaught that was his kiss. Mac possessed her mouth in a way no one ever had. In a way she'd never allowed anyone.

He was forceful and demanding, taking what he wanted and demanding a response.

Her hands found their way to his hips, and she curled her fingers into the belt loops, pulling him closer into her parted thighs. The heavy erection against her core told her she'd pushed him past the point of reason.

Mac's mouth found the curve of her neck and bit down. He laved it with his tongue, and Kaia gasped as need shot through her, soaking her center.

He took his time tasting and savoring her, trailing hot, wet kisses up and down her neck. Along the top of her shoulders. And down the valley between her breasts. As he tormented her stiff, sensitive nipples, Kaia's head fell back, causing her hair to tumble down in waves.

She couldn't catch her breath as he made his way upward. He sealed his mouth to hers again and stole what was left of her sanity. She'd started out the seducer, and he was utterly destroying her.

On a gasp, Kaia tore her lips from his. Not to be outdone, she dipped her head and concentrated on the rock-hard plane of his chest.

Her mouth blazed a trail from one muscled shoulder to the other as his hands were busy kneading and molding her ass and hips. When he pulled her closer to the edge of the counter, Kaia thought he'd fill her aching core and take her. But, instead, he knelt in front of her.

As he studied her neatly trimmed mound, his hands trailed up her inner thighs. Anticipation making her body thrum, Kaia braced her weight behind her with her hands. Her gaze stayed glued to his.

Kaia bit her bottom lip when he shifted closer and, using his fingers, opened her wide. The touch of his tongue on her sex had her eyes rolling up into her head and her arms nearly buckling. She fought to keep herself upright, so she could watch as he consumed her.

Seeing his head buried between her legs was the sexiest thing she'd ever seen. And what he was doing with that mouth should be illegal.

Kaia moaned, the sound low and long and sounding suspiciously like a purr. "Oh, fuck." Her hips rocked against his face, the abrasive stubble of his cheeks on her sensitive skin bringing her to new heights.

She knew she wouldn't last much longer, and when his lips found her clit, she was lost. Kaia drew breath in to scream, but it clogged in her throat when he speared two fingers into her. Her body clamped down on them as her climax rolled over her.

Before she could gasp air into her burning lungs, Mac stood, unhooked his fly, and pushed his jeans down and off. Taking a good firm grip on her ass, he thrust into her even as the last remnants of her orgasm still lingered.

Kaia wrapped her arms around his neck and held on as he pounded into her. Her body came roaring back to life in a rush, her need matching his. They were both panting and grunting—the sound of their bodies coming together loud in the otherwise quiet house.

She shattered again, and he kept thrusting in and out of her. Kaia's body was one big exposed nerve as he set out to take her even higher yet. He dipped his hips, changed the angle, and pushed deep. She didn't think it would be possible, but he had her on that thin edge once again, teetering to go over.

His grunts were expelled so close to her ear she could feel the hot breath wash over her face and neck. Kaia was floating in a haze of arousal when he demanded, "One more."

She forgot to breathe when a bigger, more powerful orgasm robbed her of all senses but touch. Her entire being narrowed down to the shaft moving in and out of her. Every pleasure sensor she possessed was sending messages to her brain until it overwhelmed her, and she almost blacked out.

Mac plundered her convulsing center, his hands winding underneath her arms to grab her shoulders from the back. He pressed down against them, pulling her further onto him as his speed increased. Kaia held on, grinding against him as he buried himself to the hilt and roared with his release.

When her fuzzy brain finally started to come back online, she was still clinging to him. Her arms and legs were locked around him, and they weren't releasing their hold without some outside help. Because her body was completely lost.

It now belonged to him.

Even her cat was still and sated for the first time in weeks. The rumbles of her purrs reverberated through Kaia's mind, and the sound of her contentment had Kaia nearly dozing.

As they sagged into each other, their breathing evened out

and eventually returned to normal. Kaia didn't want to move but knew she couldn't stay sitting on the counter naked.

"God, you piss me off to no end." The voice that emerged from between Mac's lips was guttural and raspy. He slowly unwound her arms from around him and then leaned back to stare at her. "What the hell did you think you were doing out there this morning?"

Kaia wasn't going to take a dressing-down while he was still buried deep inside of her. She pressed her hands into his chest, but he didn't retreat.

"Can you move, please? I'd like to get cleaned up before you yell at me."

"No." Mac slid his hands under her ass and picked her up, turning as he started to carry her through the house.

"What are you doing? I thought you were pissed off?"

"I am." He kicked her bedroom door open, strode across the room, and laid her out on the bed, never losing their intimate connection. "But I can multitask." Mac began to move inside of her, slower and more leisurely than before.

"Oh," Kaia gasped. "Good to know."

"We can fight it out when I'm finished with you."

"I'm not afraid of you," she panted, feeling his cock harden anew as her body ignited all over again.

He was braced on his arms above her, staring down into her face. "I know."

Mac pulled slowly out of her before deliciously sliding back in, his pelvis rocking against her swollen and sensitive center. Kaia moaned in response, pulling her knees up to give him better access.

His thick length filled her to bursting, and he shifted, pulling his own knees up underneath them to tilt upwards inside of her. Her breath came out in a gasp as he pumped in and out in short movements, hitting that sweet spot and pushing her over the precipice once more.

His lips came down on hers, swallowing her cry, his tongue pushing slow and deep as he made love to her mouth. Sucking in her bottom lip, he captured it with his teeth and tugged gently as he pulled away from her.

Raising to a kneeling position, he placed his hands on her knees and pushed outward, opening her up to watch as he moved in and out of her. The sight of him watching was so erotic, it brought her right back to the brink of orgasm. Moving his hands, he took each nipple between his fingers, rolling the nubs between his thumbs and forefingers.

The sensation shot straight to her core and she came, erupting violently around him as he continued his torturous pace.

He came back down to her, holding his weight on his elbows as he took her mouth again. Kaia rocked her hips upward, meeting each slow, luxurious thrust with one of her own. The strokes lengthened as he pulled farther out before plunging back in. The slow, controlled movement was almost excruciating, her body already so sensitive after all his ministrations.

Mac's breath came heavier, and the strokes deepened, pushing farther in every time they came back together. She wrapped her arms around his waist, cupping his ass and pulling him closer, trying to take even more of him.

"*Fuck*, Kaia." His body tightened and convulsed, his pelvis mashing against hers in release.

When they collapsed against each other this time, they both promptly fell asleep.

When Kaia awoke sometime later, the sun was fully in the sky, and Mac was wrapped around her. Her back was to his front, his breath fanning over her neck and shoulder. She took a moment to luxuriate in the feel of him, warm and strong behind her.

She ran her fingers lightly over the skin of his forearm where it lay around her middle. The dark hair over olive tones drew her to explore. She traced the veins that ran the length of his arm, pumping blood through that gorgeous body.

A body that had brought hers to life in the most glorious of ways. She had never, in all her life, been fucked so thoroughly. She'd given back as well as she'd gotten, but Mac had claimed her in a way she hadn't known was possible. Last night had been amazing, and it almost made her want to kick herself for having waited so damned long. She'd never thought it could be that way.

Behind her, his breathing changed.

She turned within his hold until she was facing him. "Before you find your mad again, I have something I need to say."

He looked at her suspiciously. "Okay."

"I didn't set out to piss you off this morning. I've already mentioned that my cat has been restless and unsettled lately, which in turn, makes it hard on me. The only thing that's been helping is when I let her out, so she can run it off. She runs until she's exhausted and nearing collapse, but it makes it a lot easier for me to deal with her."

He propped his head on his hand. "Is there something I can do? To help her? Or you?"

Oh, you've done plenty. Kaia felt a flush starting up her neck and hoped Mac didn't notice. "She's fine. There's nothing..." Kaia's gaze dropped to his chest, and she cleared her throat. "I actually think the problem has worked itself out. I don't think it'll be an issue anymore." Both she and her cat were sated for the time being, the latter being practically comatose at the moment.

Mac rose up to stare down at her and studied her for several heartbeats. "That day in the woods. You told me she was coming into heat and had chosen me." He sat up away from her. "Is that what this was about? Your cat went into heat and wanted me? And you were just along for the ride?"

The way he watched her said he didn't like the thought of

that.

Kaia sat up also. "No." She added emphasis to that one word. "Yes, she's gone into heat, but that has nothing to do with me or my feelings." What was the best way to explain this? "Her unease affects me, but only in the way that when someone around you is in a bad mood, it kind of puts you in a bad mood too. Although what we just did pleases her greatly, my actions are my own. And only mine."

His eyes searched her face. "I have to ask. Why…how did she pick me? I'm not like you. There's no mountain lion or anything else inside of me."

"I know. But that doesn't seem to matter to her. She's gotten it into her head that you're her…" God, she still had trouble with the word, "mate."

"Mate." That sat him back for a moment.

"Yeah. She's decided you're hers. For life."

Kaia couldn't tell how he was taking the news. His face held no expression.

"And what about you?"

"What about me?"

"Am I your mate as well?"

"I…haven't decided yet."

For some reason, that didn't seem to bother him. "Well, until you do…" He came back down to her and covered her body with his, sliding inside of her, "it looks like I have two demanding ladies to take care of."

Kaia grinned up at him. "Think you can handle it?"

"Oh, I've no doubt." His blue eyes sparked.

With only that, her system hummed. "Well, get to it then, Sheriff."

He pulled out, and thrust back in. Kaia let the purr she usually held in check rumble in her chest.

"Fuck. That is such a sexy sound." He pushed into her again. "I'll have to give you reasons to make it more often."

And he did. Many more times, until exhausted, they fell into a heap.

~~~

He was set. He knew what he had to do, and he knew when he could make his move. And after what he'd seen this morning, it couldn't happen fast enough. She'd gone to him. She'd changed, butt naked, and gone to him.

Once he was done, she'd never think twice about that fucking sheriff again. He'd have her all to himself. No one would claim her, but him.

~~~

It was close to noon by the time Kaia got to the barn. And heard about it from its occupants.

"I know. I'm sorry. It won't happen again." She got busy with her chores, and as was his usual, Mac had gone to do whatever he did while she worked. She didn't see him again until she was in the round pen with Daisy. He stood at the rail with Moose at his side, both of them watching the show.

Daisy was nearing the end of her stay at the facility, so she knew what she was doing. She moved around the fence without a line on. As Kaia gave her orders, the white filly responded perfectly.

Which meant that Kaia was able to split her focus between her pupil and Mac. She was observing him out of the corner of her eye when she saw him slip his phone from his pocket. He glanced at the screen and then moved away to take the call.

Even though he'd taken some time off to act as her babysitter, he was still the Sheriff. He'd need to be kept advised of what was going on. Kaia assumed something had come up that needed his attention.

He returned about ten minutes later as she was exiting the exercise pen.

"Everything all right?" she asked as he fell into step beside her.

"No. There's an issue that I have to see to. I've got to go."

"Go?" She stopped and turned towards him. "What is it? What's happened?"

He took a breath and let it out. "One of my deputies was responding to a call and was in an accident. It sounds serious. I need to go."

"Yes, of course you do." Kaia started into the barn. This had to be vitally important to pull him away from her. "Call me later and let me know how your deputy is doing."

"I put a call in to the station. A couple of my men will be here in a few minutes to stay with you."

She stopped and turned back to him. "Do you think that's necessary?"

"I do. This could be just as it seems—an accident." His expression was hard and unreadable. "Or it could be an elaborate ruse to leave you vulnerable."

Kaia felt the shock on her face. She hadn't even considered that. "What?"

"Accidents happen every day, I know. But I have to wonder, why now? He has to have seen us together. He knows I've moved in and must realize he can't get to you if I'm around. My guys are good at what they do and can handle pretty much anything that comes in. But if one of them is hurt... Let's just say there aren't many instances that could call me away from you right now. I'm thinking the timing of this is a little too convenient."

"You really think this could be a trap?" She absently rubbed the filly's neck.

"If I didn't take into account the possibility, then I don't deserve my badge." Mac stepped in close and cupped her cheek in his hand. "He won't come anywhere near you. I promise."

"But what about you? He's already proven he'll take you out if given the chance. He could be waiting out there for *you* to be alone."

"All the better." His eyes went icy, simmering with frigid anger. "He and I have a few things to talk about."

It came across loud and clear that she couldn't talk him out of this. "Please, be careful."

"I will. Johnson and Harvey should be here any minute. If I don't make it back before you're finished, they'll escort you and Moose home, and then keep watch over you."

Before she could protest more, Mac kissed her long and deep, fuzzing her brain. When they heard the sound of a car engine, they turned to see one of Anaconda's patrol cars pulling to a stop.

His blue eyes searched her face. "I'll see you later."

"You'd better. Or I'll hunt you down."

He nodded and swung around to walk out. He stopped and spoke briefly with the deputies, got nods in return, and then he was gone.

Kaia took a deep breath and cross-tied Daisy so she could brush her down. As much as this whole situation bothered her, there was still work to be done. And hopefully, that work would keep her mind off of what could be happening out there.

17

Mac hadn't called or returned by the time she was ready to leave. It had been hours, and Kaia was anxious to hear... something. Anything. Had his deputy been hurt as the report had stated? Was he okay? Was Mac okay? Not knowing was killing her.

With nothing more to do at the barn, she made sure everything was put away and the stall doors were secure. She looked down at Moose, who'd stuck to her like glue since Mac had gone.

"You ready to head out, handsome?"

He gave her a deep-throated garbled answer.

She laughed lightly. "I'll take that as a yes. Well, let's gather up our guards and go home."

She made the five-minute drive with the patrol car tailing her. When she pulled into her driveway, they came to a stop at the curb. Kaia waved to them and got one in return as she and Moose walked into the house.

"Are you hungry? We should probably eat something." Food didn't sound particularly appetizing at the moment, but she needed something to keep her hands busy. It would also keep her mind occupied, so she didn't think about what could be taking place.

Moose followed her into the kitchen.

Twenty minutes later, he parked at her side again when she

sat down at the table with her bowl of boxed mac and cheese.

She only got a few bites down before chucking the rest. Maybe a little TV would keep her brain engaged.

Kaia gave up a short while later. Nothing there could keep her attention. She was worried about Mac and, until she heard from him, there would be no relief. It didn't help that her cat was agitated as well. But that could just be her picking up on her own unease.

Or…it could mean something was very wrong.

Was her cat privy to trouble she wasn't? Could she know if Mac was in danger? She'd chosen him as her mate, but did that give her some kind of connection to him that Kaia didn't have, because she was still fighting it on some level?

Suddenly, the lioness roared in her head and demanded to be let out. She clawed and raked at Kaia's insides, pushing for the shift. She had never done anything like that before, and Kaia didn't think she could hold her cat much longer.

Oh, God. What's happened?

Not stopping to think, Kaia stripped there in the middle of her living room and ran for the back door. She skidded to a stop when Moose followed.

"You have to stay here, boy. I need to change to run and find him. I don't want her to hurt you. Or you her."

Moose growled and moved to block her from leaving.

"Moose! Move! I have to go!"

He didn't budge, and there was no way in hell she was physically moving him.

What do I do now?

She looked into his big brown eyes and saw the same determination she felt. "If I say you can come, will you let me go?"

The large Dane cleared her path.

"You and she had better get along," she bit out, "because we don't have time to take this introduction slow."

Kaia slid the door open, and with one more dubious glance at the dog, shifted.

They gave each other a cursory sniff, and then they tore out of the house together. Streaking across the darkening backyard, mountain lion and Great Dane were gone from sight before anyone even knew they were there.

Mac hadn't said where the accident happened, but it was obvious the feline knew something she didn't. So Kaia had to trust that her cat knew where to go. She just hoped that they got there in time.

~~~

Mac had been on the scene for hours. It had taken quite a while before the car his deputy had been driving could be recovered. And now the body of his friend and co-worker was being loaded into the ambulance to be taken to the morgue.

All around him, the site was being thoroughly processed. What evidence they could find was being tagged and logged. As Mac worked to evaluate and reconstruct the crash site, a picture was coming into focus.

The patrol car had been answering a call for assistance. Running lights and sirens, he was traveling over the speed limit, but not recklessly so. Every officer on the force was familiar with this corner and knew how to safely navigate it.

From what he could see here, he'd been midway into the turn when something catastrophic had happened. Skid marks revealed the car had lost control and swerved into the oncoming lane, where another car carrying a family of five was coming from the opposite direction. From there, evidence showed that, with no other choice, the deputy had made a split-second decision that had ended his own life, saving the others in the process.

Following the black marks on the roadway, Mac deduced
~~~

he'd somehow gotten his car in hand enough to change its trajectory. Instead of slamming into the other car, he'd sent his own in the direction of the guard rail.

Only it hadn't held. And he'd plummeted over the side.

This stretch of road was known for its vehicular casualties, the blind corner catching many drivers unaware. And the seventy-five-foot drop on the other side of the railing was cause for more than a few fatalities by those who'd misjudged their speed and capabilities.

But that wasn't the case this time. A good man had been murdered here.

As soon as he'd seen what was left of the car, the scene had become all too clear. And a cold, deadly rage had taken hold of Mac. It threatened to boil to the surface, but he held it in check while he put the rest of it together.

The gunman had chosen his ambush site well. And he'd probably counted on the tire shredding and destroying the evidence of what he'd done. There would have been nothing to prove this wasn't just a horrible accident.

But by some miracle, enough of the blown tire had remained intact to show them the grimly neat bullet hole in the sidewall. That alone told the tale of what had actually happened.

Had the fucker stuck around long enough to witness his handiwork? Or had he done as he'd done with Mac—taken the shot, and fled like a coward?

He could, even now, be making his way to Kaia.

The only problem with that theory was that his gut didn't think so.

It had never lied to him before, and right now, it told him that the asshole was still here. That Kaia had been right. *He* was the target, and the hunter was probably staring down his scope at Mac right now. Waiting for the scene to clear out so he could accomplish his main goal.

Under the guise of surveying the scene, Mac studied the

surrounding area. Taking into consideration the direction the car had been traveling and its approximate location when the bullet struck it, he extrapolated the most likely vantage point of the hunter.

With a course plotted, Mac moved off, using the vehicles to shelter his movements. With luck, he'd find the bastard with his eye still to the scope, searching for someone who wasn't there.

Once past all the activity, he broke into a run and moved as quickly and quietly as possible. He needed to cover as much ground as he could before the bustle at the scene slowed and the emergency crews left. When that happened, his absence would become obvious.

In his experience, poachers were skilled marksmen, but they weren't anywhere near trained snipers. There was a limit to how far they could accurately hit a moving target. As Mac approached that point, he slowed. Drawing his sidearm, he held it at the ready as he picked his way over downed trees and debris. His eyes scanned for any movement that would give away his opponent's position.

After close to half an hour of slow and painstaking searching, Mac began to rethink his certainty that the shooter had stuck around. Were his instincts wrong this time? Had he only waited here long enough to see him show up before doubling back to his intended target?

It made Mac's stomach clench when he thought about Kaia. Was this murdering bastard watching and waiting for his opportunity to grab her? Had he screwed up? Had he played right into his hands?

Mac was ready to race back to his truck when he heard it. Just the whisper of fabric rustling against fabric. A sound so foreign to the deep forest, Mac knew immediately what it meant. Moving only his eyes, he tracked the noise. And caught a glimpse of the end of a barrel sticking out from the crotch of a small tree. Only about two inches of the black steel showed, but it was enough to give it away.

Choosing his foot placement carefully, Mac started forward, gun raised and ready to fire.

Only to be hit from the side with a force that knocked him on his ass and expelled all the air from his lungs in a sudden rush. At the same time, a bullet hit the tree right where his head had been.

A dog's deep barking suddenly rent the air. Birds and squirrels sent up a ruckus as they were startled from their perches. With everything going on, Mac nearly missed the sound of someone crashing through the woods as they fled.

The dog's barking went into another level of frenzy as it followed.

Mac recognized it instantly. He also understood the tawny fur pinning him to the ground. "What the hell, Kaia?" He set his hands against her and pushed, scrambling to his feet as the barking escalated before suddenly going silent.

Shit. "Moose." Mac took off running. "Moose!" he yelled into the now-quiet forest. He waited, nearly frantic, but there was no response.

Fuck. Mac thundered through trees and low-lying brush, the cougar right behind him.

Knowing that Kaia had the better tracking ability between them, Mac allowed her to lead and tried to keep up as best he could. They hadn't gone very far when Mac heard the sound he'd been fearful of never hearing again. Moose's deep bark.

They ran a few more yards, and the wild yips grew louder. Mac knew they were moving in the right direction. Had Moose cornered the hunter? He scanned the terrain as he ran. The mottled pattern of his dog's fur made him difficult to see in the speckled sun and shadowed interior of the forest.

Following the sound, Mac and Kaia found him. He'd fallen into a deep gully. He seemed to be fine as he jumped, trying to reach freedom. But the ledge was just out of his reach. He stood at the bottom, barking like mad.

Mac glanced around, searching for any sign of the hunter. There was none. And no sound of him either. He'd evidently managed to outsmart Moose and get away.

Mac was abruptly brought out of his thoughts when Moose gave a disgusted woof. As if to say, "Hey, dumbass. Quit standing around, and get me out of here!"

"Sorry, bud. Hold on." He turned to Kaia. "I'm assuming the poacher is gone?"

She did a slow survey of the area, and then the cat's head went up and down.

With the all-clear, Mac maneuvered his way down to his dog. There would be no picking him up to carry him out—not when the dog weighed almost as much as he did. Instead, Mac got behind the Dane, set his shoulder into Moose's rump, and pushed. The going was slow, but they finally made it up to where Kaia waited.

Out of breath, Mac split his attention between the two animals. But got lost in the green of Kaia's eyes. It still struck him to see that distinctive color looking back at him from the body of a mountain lion.

Would he ever get used to it? Or the fact that the woman he loved could transform into this gorgeous creature?

That brought him up short. His heart gave a thump in his chest. Loved? *Holy shit.*

He studied the feeling. How it filled him to the brim and stripped him raw all at the same time. It sure as hell felt like love.

Shaking himself, he raised a finger and pointed at them accusingly. "One of you had better tell me what the hell you're even doing here." His glare settled on the only one who could answer him.

The cat gave him a look best described as haughty and began

to shift. Within seconds, there was a gorgeous naked woman standing in front of him. He ignored the sight of her, so he could get some answers.

"Saving your life, if I'm not mistaken." Her hands went to her slender, smooth hips. "My cat sensed something was wrong. I couldn't just wait at home, and Moose wouldn't let me leave the house without him."

"And it didn't occur to you to just stay there?"

"It's a good thing I didn't," her head tilted, and those green eyes heated, "or you'd be dead right now. That bullet would have killed you if I hadn't intervened."

Moose went on alert, his focus on something behind them. Mac began to hear voices shouting in the distance. They were drawing closer.

That gunshot must have alerted the men still at the accident scene.

"Son of a bitch." He hated to do it, but he couldn't risk anyone finding Kaia naked and out for a stroll through the woods with his dog—and her being in cougar form wouldn't have helped matters either. Too many questions and no way to answer them.

He turned to Kaia. "Shift back and get your asses home. I'll be there as soon as I can clear this up. And then we'll talk."

Kaia sent him a fulminating look, but she did as he asked.

Once dog and cat had run off, Mac started towards the men in the direction he'd come.

"Sir, we heard a shot. Is everything all right?" one deputy panted out.

"Yeah. I went to see if I could find where the shooter had set up, but he was still there, hunkered down somewhere in the trees. Before I could spot him, he took a shot at me. He took off, and I lost him."

"Do you want us to do a search?" the man asked.

"No." Mac shook his head. "Too few of us right now to cover

this area, and he's got the advantage. We'd be sitting ducks out here." Motioning back the way they'd come, he added, "If everything at the crash site is taken care of, head on out. I'll meet you back at the station."

~~~

It was close to eleven when Kaia heard Mac pull in. Although she hadn't felt like eating herself, she'd kept herself busy by cooking, guessing he hadn't gotten a chance to eat. She'd kept it warm for him, so it would be ready whenever he got there. Even if they argued over what she'd done, at least he could do it on a full stomach.

And, surprisingly, just the act of providing for him gave her a sense of peace. She hadn't had anyone to take care of for a long time, and it felt really good to see to someone else's needs.

The sight of him walking in the door made her glad she'd taken the effort. He looked completely worn out. And sad.

There hadn't been time to talk about it before, but she knew just by looking at him that his deputy had died.

"I'm so sorry," she told him, her tone thick with guilt. "He did this because of me, didn't he?"

"No. Not because of you. Because of him. None of this is your fault." Mac took his hat off and ran his hand through his disheveled hair. She could tell it was a gesture he'd made countless times over the last several hours.

"But my actions are what brought him here. If I hadn't tried to take justice into my own hands, none of this would have happened. You tried to warn me."

"I did. But there was no way any of us could have known the guy would develop this kind of fixation on you. Dealing with poachers is one thing. But this guy has gone completely off the rails. That's not something anyone could have predicted."

Mac scrubbed his hands over his face.
~~~

His weariness was so evident, it hurt her heart. Kaia reached out and took his hand. "Come on. I've kept a plate warm for you."

"I'm not really that hungry," he argued, but still he followed her.

Kaia nudged him towards the chair. "You still need to eat something."

"I'd rather have a shot of whiskey." He sent her a small, tired grin as he sat.

"I'll see what I can do." She leaned down to kiss his cheek.

Mac expelled a heavy breath as she turned to get his plate. Knowing the night he'd had, she brought him the drink, setting down the entire bottle at his elbow. She took a seat with him to keep him company while he picked at his food.

She kept up small chit-chat until he finally pushed the empty plate away from him.

Kaia took a deep breath. "Can you tell me what happened today? Out on the road?"

He took a moment to pour another drink. He threw it back quick and, with an exhale at the burn, relayed the day's events.

"He had a wife and two kids," Mac finished, his eyes full of grief. "Teenagers. I watched them reach for each other and fall apart at the news. Fucking hell." Mac pushed away from the table so suddenly, Kaia jumped and Moose rose to give a woof.

She followed him after a moment. He was standing at the front window, staring out into the darkness. She lifted her hand and rested it in the middle of his back in comfort.

"We'll get him, Mac. He'll pay for what he's done."

18

His plan had been working perfectly. The sheriff had been there, lured into coming to him. He'd expected the lawman to follow the trajectory of the shot and come to investigate. He'd been falling into his trap precisely as he'd planned.

A few more seconds, and the path to his tawny beauty would have been free of obstacles. And then, finally, he would go claim her.

He'd had the shot lined up from his blind a short distance away. He'd smiled gleefully when the ignorant fool had found the bait he'd planted. It had been an act of genius to prop a rifle in that tree, leaving just the end of the barrel sticking out to draw him in.

But then, as his finger had pulled the trigger, all hell had broken loose. His bullet had missed as his target had gone down under a flash of familiar blonde fur. And then suddenly, an enormous gray dog had burst through the foliage, jaws snapping as thunderous barks startled the shit out of him.

He'd only had a split second to react. With no time for another shot, he'd run, barely escaping with his life.

If not for that ditch, he wouldn't have made it out of there. He'd hoped the fall would kill the damned dog, or at least damage it enough that it wouldn't return. But he'd heard it barking its displeasure at having lost its quarry.

It was a set-back, but he wasn't one to give up. He wanted

her, and he would have her.

~~~

Kaia awoke the following morning with a new determination. What she'd told Mac the night before was true. This nut-job would pay for all the suffering he'd caused.

But they'd have to find him first. And that's exactly what she was going to do. She'd turn those damned acres upside down until there was no place else he could hide.

Formulating her argument, Kaia rolled out of bed and wrapped herself in her robe. As was his habit, Mac had gotten up a while ago. She knew she'd find him in the kitchen drinking coffee, looking at the news online until he could check in with his office.

When she walked in, he was staring at the laptop screen. Something wasn't right.

"Mac." She rushed the rest of the way in. "What is it? What's happened?"

All she could think was that someone else had gotten hurt. That the poacher had targeted someone else to get to her.

Oh, God. Helen.

Mac's blue eyes were grim when he shifted his attention up to her. "A body was found washed up at Georgetown Lake."

No. No. No. Her fears had come true, and her stomach pitched.

But wait. Georgetown was roughly twenty miles away. Not far, but out of the usual range of this douchebag. And Helen wouldn't have been in that area. "Was it someone you knew? A friend?"

"No. But reading the report gave me a bad feeling. I called an acquaintance on the police force there to get more information."

He held her gaze for a long moment. "It's the poacher."

What? He's dead? She didn't know how to process that.
~~~

Once the initial shock had worn off, Kaia started to come to terms with what Mac had said. Her first thought was that it was over. This whole mess was finished. She didn't have to worry about finding this guy and stopping him from hurting anyone else. She didn't have to agonize over whether he'd seen her shift form or not, and what that would mean for her.

He was dead. She didn't even care how it happened. She could have her life back.

The second thing her brain noticed was that Mac didn't seem to share her relief. His expression was still pensive.

"Why aren't you pleased? He's gone. Out of our lives. No more hunting, no more tracking, no more danger. We can forget about him and move on."

"His neck was broken, Kaia."

That bit of information put a hitch in her step, but she pushed it aside. "So, he fell. Or someone helped him to get that way. I don't care. He wasn't a good man and probably had lots of enemies. It wasn't you or me, so it doesn't really matter. Let Georgetown deal with that, and let's get on with our lives. It's over."

"No. It's not." He rose and came to her, taking both of her hands in his. "The coroner estimates he'd been in the water for seven to ten days."

Her mind buckled, struggling to do the math. And came up with an answer she didn't want to contemplate. That was about the time she'd started receiving gifts. Of animals, with *broken necks.*

Her brows drew together, and she shook her head. "This just doesn't make any sense. There's two? How can that be? And you're absolutely sure it was the poacher that was found? The one you saw who'd shot me with the tranq dart?" Her heart was thumping hard in her chest at the ramifications.

"I haven't seen the body in person, but yeah." Mac nodded. "From the details they gave me, he's the same height and build.

And from the description, the body was dressed in the same clothes I'd seen him in the day he shot you." He paused and emphasized his next words. "It's him, Kaia. I'm sure of it. And when they ID him, I have a feeling it's going to be the friend of Ted Barnes my men couldn't locate."

Her mind whirled. She didn't know what to think. Who could have killed him? And why? The most logical conclusion would be a competitor—someone else who'd come to town for the chase. Poachers were killers by nature. It wouldn't be too hard to imagine that one had killed another if the score was big enough.

"Competition?"

"It could be another poacher."

Kaia heard skepticism in his voice. "But you don't think that's the case."

He grew thoughtful. "I'm not certain. It's just a feeling. But what I am certain of, is this development answers a lot of questions. Like why normal poaching behavior suddenly became more obsessive in nature. And why we've had such a hard time tracking him. If the coroner is right about time of death, it's this new player we've been hunting all over hell and back. And the one who shot at me. Twice. Whoever he is, I don't think he's in it for the same reason as the first guy. The goal is still the same, and that's you. But whereas the original suspect was looking for a trophy for his wall, the second one seems to be taking this a lot more personally."

"If he came to track the cat and saw me shift," the thought of that sent a cold shiver down her spine, "that could explain his obsession. I'm nothing like he's ever seen before. That's a big draw for people like them."

"I'm just not convinced this one is here for a souvenir. It feels different to me. He's not tried to hurt you in any way. In fact, he's been leaving you offerings. His only strategy so far has been to remove any obstacles to you."

Confused and unsure, Kaia stepped in close to him and wrapped her arms around his waist. His wound around her back and squeezed.

She absorbed some of his strength for a minute to shore up her own defenses. Feeling a little better, she leaned back to look up into his face.

"So, what now?"

He released her and sat back down. Kaia followed suit, and once they were both comfortable, he relayed where they stood.

"Now, we start over and reexamine the situation through a different lens. We need to alter our search parameters since the timeline has shifted by a few weeks. And…now that we know this isn't the same guy, and may not just be your average poacher, we need to begin by looking at your personal life."

"My personal life?" She wasn't following his train of thought. "Why?"

"Was there anyone who didn't take a breakup well? Someone who showed an interest in you, but you didn't return the sentiment? Has there been anyone else you've told your secret to?"

"No. The only ones I've ever shared that with is Bri and you."

"What about exes?"

"I haven't dated anyone since before Jace died. After, I just focused on building my business."

"How was the last breakup?"

"Mutual. We had some fun, but both of us knew it wouldn't last."

"I still want you to think back. Try to remember if anyone ever gave you a bad vibe or felt off in any way. It may not come to anything, but we still need to check it out."

Mac scrubbed his hands through his short black hair and then glanced at his watch. "Shit. I need to meet with my guys to go over this new information and coordinate the new search."

"Go." She held a hand up when he opened his mouth to argue.

"You said yourself you don't think his goal is to showcase my pelt on his wall. If he's not here to hurt me, I should be fine to go to work."

"He may not be out to kill you, but he still wants you badly enough to take out anyone in his way."

"I'm a shifter, Mac. He's just a man. I think I can protect myself from the likes of him. And the farm is my turf. It sits all by itself out there. I'll be able to see him coming from every direction. And if he does come…he'll get a surprise he won't soon forget."

Before he could mount any further objections, she went on.

"I'm tired of hiding, Mac. It's just not in my nature. I've done it your way. Now, I'm going to try it my way."

"By going out and putting yourself in danger?" he demanded.

She knew he'd fight her on this. She kept her voice even but firm. "No. By living my life. And staying prepared. He'll make his move—I have no doubt about that. But I'll be ready for it. You keep forgetting what I am, Mac. I'm faster, and stronger, and I have better senses than most."

"That's where you're wrong. I forget nothing when it comes to you. Especially the sight of you lying motionless on the forest floor. You may have nine lives, but I'd like to keep the one I have. And seeing you like that took years off of mine. I don't ever want to go through that again. I won't lose you, Kaia. Not now, not ever. I love you."

Her breath hitched, and she went warm all over. "Oh, Mac."

"I didn't say that to put you on the spot. I know you're still trying to come to terms with a lot. I only wanted to make sure you know that. Know that I think the world of you, and I want to make sure we have a long time to drive each other nuts."

Kaia quit fighting. She stopped finding reasons to back away. Stopped pretending she didn't already love him. With everything she was.

"You're not putting me on the spot, Mac. I love you too."

She leaned across the table and threaded her fingers into his hair, her mouth coming down on top of his. He grabbed her by the waist, pulling her into his lap. His hand snaked up to wrap around the base of her neck, pulling her closer and deepening the kiss.

When they broke apart, they were breathing heavily.

"Shit. I wish I didn't have to go." Mac's blue eyes were deep and smoky with arousal. "I'd love nothing better than to take you back to bed right now."

She vaguely wondered if this steady need would always tug at her, even when her cat was no longer in heat. Mac seemed to be the only one who could completely sate her, but he was right—they didn't have time for that right now.

"And I'd love nothing better than to let you." She grinned. "And I will, but later. We both have places we need to be."

Kaia leaned in again. When their lips met, she allowed the embers to ignite a fire that would torment them both throughout the rest of the day.

She shivered just thinking about it.

<div align="center">~~~</div>

Kaia spent the majority of the day thinking about how to track this new guy down. He'd been able to stay out of reach and out of sight as he stalked and hunted them. If Mac was right and his motives weren't those of the garden-variety poacher, then what did he want?

Her obviously, but why?

Well, that was kind of a no-brainer. He'd come for a mountain lion and found more than he'd bargained for. What was his endgame, though? Take her and cage her? Study her? Sell her to the highest bidder?

Kaia was so tired of not having the answers to go with her questions. And she knew Mac was too.

But until they uncovered more information, they were at an impasse.

Full of frustration, she poured it all into her work. Mucking stalls went a long way to burning it off, and she was feeling steadier when she became aware she was no longer alone.

It was his scent that reached her first. She recognized it. It was the same one she'd caught the morning Helen had called to tell her the horses were acting up.

Why was he here? What was his game?

Kaia turned slowly—pitchfork still in hand. This was the man they'd been looking for. If she played it right, maybe she could get the evidence they needed.

"Can I help you?"

He was an older man, maybe late- to mid-sixties. A little on the elderly side for a poacher, she thought, but he seemed to be in pretty good shape. Maybe that's what had allowed him to stick with it this long.

Kaia took in the rest of him and memorized everything, filing it away so she could relay it back to Mac. Six-foot, lean build. No scars or tattoos she could see. His hair was salt and pepper, trimmed short, though not as short as Mac's.

Well-dressed, which seemed odd for someone who spent the majority of his time skulking around the woods. Something else she found strange was that he carried himself with an air of... arrogance, like he thought himself better than everyone else around him. It was a quality she'd seen often in her wealthy CEO clients.

When he started forward, Kaia tightened her grip on the wood shaft in her hand.

"I don't know what you think you'll find here, but you'd best back the fuck off," she warned.

"I've come for you." His smile hinged on the insane, and his eyes gleamed with madness. "And now, no one will keep us apart."

"I'm not going anywhere with you." Kaia brought the long-tined fork up in front of her.

"Oh, but you are." He stalked forward another step. "I've waited a lifetime for an extraordinary creature like you. You *will* come with me. And you *will* obey me."

Kaia almost guffawed. "Not in this lifetime, asshole," Kaia spat with as much venom as she could muster. A whisper of fear had her heart pounding, but she reminded herself he was just a man. She was a shifter, for Christ's sake.

But that was no match for the handgun he suddenly leveled at her. "I really don't want to shoot you and mar all of that beautiful skin. But I will. Non-fatally, of course," he added as an aside, as if that made a difference.

"You're going to *have* to shoot me, because I'm not leaving here with you willingly."

"I think you will, because if you don't, that interfering sheriff you seem so fond of will die."

Kaia's breathing and heart stopped. She felt the color drain from her face.

He grinned at her reaction. "I wasn't too worried about mortally wounding him when I saw him this morning."

"You're lying." Kaia bore down to stop her hands from shaking where she held her weapon.

"I'm afraid not." He moved closer. "He came through the park after he left your house—I'm guessing to try to track me down. And I was finally able to get my shot since, luckily, you weren't there to protect him this time." His head tilted slightly. "Unfortunately for him, he didn't die right away. But no matter—I've got him bound somewhere out there." He gestured over her shoulder, out into the vastness of the state park. "Last I saw him though, he was bleeding pretty heavily. In fact, he probably won't last much longer."

Kaia didn't know what to believe. Mac had said he was going into the office. But had he stopped at the park on his way in, like the guy said? Was this lunatic lying, or was Mac out there, right this very minute, dying? If he'd never made it to work, would they have called her when he hadn't shown up?

No. They hadn't known he was on his way. As far as they knew, he was still watching over her. They didn't know the case had taken a giant turn. He'd wanted to talk to his men face-to-face to fill them in.

Oh, God. Mac.

If this guy was telling the truth, she couldn't leave the man she loved to die. She had to find him. If she went with him now, maybe she could talk him into taking her to Mac. Once there, she could shift and rip this fucker apart.

Her stalker moved to the side and motioned with the gun for her to walk past him. Out the doors and most likely into a car he had waiting.

"And don't even think of shifting," he warned, as though reading her mind. "It won't do you any good."

She had no choice. She had to go.

Kaia let go of the pitchfork, ignoring it as it dropped to the ground.

"Good girl. Now move." He waved the gun again.

As she neared him, he grabbed her by the arm, but she viciously shook it off. "Don't. Fucking. Touch. Me."

His eyes said she'd pay for that defiance, but he didn't lay a hand on her again. The barrel of the gun, however, came up to press against the side of her head.

"Move."

They'd just cleared the doors when Moose came out of nowhere. He plowed into her captor and took him down.

The furious sounds of snapping jaws and feral snarls said Moose was out for blood. He was in full attack mode, and nothing was going to stop him from killing the threat against her.

"Moose! Stop!"

Kaia needed the poacher alive. She had to know where he was holding Mac.

She jumped in and tried to wrestle the almost two-hundred-pound dog from him. But it amounted to nothing. The dog was too big and strong, fueled by adrenaline and the instinct to protect. She couldn't give up though. If Moose killed him, she'd never know how to save Mac.

Finally, she grabbed his thick leather collar with both hands. And, using all of her body weight, Kaia was able to pull Moose back a couple of feet.

But while she only barely held the dog in check, her assailant took his chance and bolted. He was in his car and speeding away before Kaia could catch her breath.

"No, no, no!" she yelled. Releasing Moose, she searched frantically for her phone.

With trembling fingers, she dialed Mac's cell. "Please answer. Please answer."

The call connected on the second ring. "McNamara."

"Mac," she breathed out. The tears she'd been holding back spilled over her lashes, and she sobbed uncontrollably into the receiver.

Weak with relief and trying to pull herself together, Kaia slumped to the ground. Moose, still taking his protection detail seriously, stood guard over her.

"Kaia, honey? What's wrong?"

Blubbering into the phone, she said in a rush, "He said you were hurt. That he'd shot you." Her voice hitched. "And you were dying."

"Who did?"

When she couldn't catch her breath to answer him, he swore.

"Fuck! The poacher was *there*? Are you still at the barn?" She pulled air deeply into her lungs, held it for a second, and released it. When she spoke again, her voice was nearly steady.

"Yes. He said he'd shot you this morning, and that you were

bleeding to death somewhere, and that if I didn't go with him, he'd let you die. He said he'd come for me—that I had to go with him or he'd shoot me too."

"Motherfucker!" Mac shouted into the phone. There was a moment's silence. "Okay," he seemed to gather himself, "is he still there? Are you safe? Where's Moose?"

"We're both here. Moose saved the day. The poacher's gone."

"I want you to lock yourself in somewhere. I'm on my way."

Kaia was still so rattled at the thought of losing Mac, she didn't even argue. She rose, grasped Moose's collar, and together they walked back into the barn. She went to a clean stall, stepped in with her Sir Galahad by her side, and rolled the door closed.

She walked to the farthest corner, sat down, and urged Moose down next to her. He draped himself over her legs, and there they waited for Mac to come.

In her mind, she knew he was okay. But her heart wouldn't settle until she saw him for herself. Felt the reality of him.

Moose heard him first. His ears went on alert, and his posture came to attention. The sound of Mac's voice calling her name drew her up like nothing else could have.

"We're here." She'd gotten some of her balance back as they'd sat together in the quiet barn. She still remembered the paralyzing fear she'd felt when he'd said Mac was hurt. But it didn't consume her as it had. She reached for the door and threw it open.

Mac rushed to her and scooped her up into his long, muscled arms like a boa constrictor.

He felt wonderful and, finally, she sagged with relief. He was really here, and he was fine.

"I'm not hurt. I'm okay." Kaia clung to him, not wanting to let go.

"I'm not." Mac turned his head and buried his face in her hair. He breathed her in for a moment before finally releasing her.

"Now tell me what happened."

She did. Every detail. She also broached something she'd been thinking about while hiding in the horse stall.

"We need help, Mac. Someone who could cover a lot more ground than men in trucks or on horseback. Someone who's dealt with this kind of issue before."

His brows dipped towards center. "We've got a forest full of cops and park rangers looking for him. None have been able to find him."

"They haven't been the right kind of people."

"And just what kind would get the job done?"

"Shifters. My family, specifically. Chances are, they've run across poachers before. They probably know exactly how to track and deal with them. Think about it. Who can move faster through dense woods than cats? And with enough of them in the forest, there won't be anywhere left for him to hide."

Some of the sadness and anger lifted from his face as he considered her words. "That just might work. Do you think they'll come?"

"We won't know until we ask."

19

An hour later, Kaia and Mac sat at the kitchen table. She laid her cell between them.

"Having second thoughts?" he asked when she didn't immediately dial.

Kaia shook her head. "No, it's just weird."

"What is?"

"Knowing that with this one phone call, a group of people I've never met could be dropping everything to come here."

"Are you worried they won't?"

"No. I think if either of my grandmothers has a say, the entire clan will come." Kaia gave a small laugh. "Especially Jackie. I've only spoken to her a couple of times, but she seems like a real force of nature."

"For what it's worth, I think this plan of yours is a good one. Like you said, they've probably dealt with this before."

Still, she hesitated picking up the phone.

"Is there something else?"

Kaia looked up into his deep blue eyes. "I don't want anyone else to get hurt because of this monster. He's already shot you, killed a friend of yours, and has my best friend in fear for her daughter's safety. These people will be coming here and putting themselves in danger to protect someone they don't even know."

"They're family. I don't think it'll matter if they know you or not. You're a shifter, just as they are. I'm sure they know what they're getting into, but I'd still be up front with them from the beginning. Tell them exactly what they'll be facing—that way they'll have a better chance at making this work. Forewarned is forearmed, and all that. And don't forget, they all have a secret weapon. Each person coming here to hunt this asshole down has a scary-as-hell cougar coming with them. This poacher will be no match for a large group of mountain lions."

Kaia felt some of the pressure in her back and shoulders ease. "You're right."

Reaching out, she dialed Jackie Logan. Once the connection was made, she put it on speaker.

They both listened as the line rang. On the third, Jackie's voice came through, clear and happy.

"Kaia, sweetie."

"I hope I'm not calling at a bad time."

"It's never a bad time to hear from you," Jackie assured her.

"I have you on speaker. A friend of mine is here too. His name is Mac, and he's the Sheriff here in Anaconda."

"Well, hello, Mac. It's nice to meet you."

"Same here, Ma'am. Kaia has told me all about you."

"Sheriff, huh? Is there a problem?"

"I'll let Kaia tell you that."

Jackie paused briefly. "That doesn't sound good. Kaia, hon, are you okay?"

"I'm fine. I promise. But we have a situation here that we need help with."

"What kind of situation?" Her tone took on a protective hardness.

Kaia took a breath and told her everything. "Over the last few weeks, he's been leaving me these…gifts. Small game. They've all had their necks broken. He always leaves them on the trail near where I've been that day." She paused a moment. "And today, he confronted me and tried to abduct me at gunpoint."

Jackie gasped. "Oh my God. He didn't hurt you, did he? Please tell me he didn't hurt you."

"He didn't." Kaia tried to soothe her grandmother. "Not a scratch. More scared than anything."

They heard Jackie let out a breath. "Oh, thank God. I don't know what I'd do if I lost you too."

Mac stepped in then. "He's becoming bolder, and he has to be stopped. But until we can find him, he's free to try for her again. We've had men from the police department and National Park Services scouring Lost Creek, but we've found nothing. We don't know how, but he's eluded us at every step. We're looking for more feet on the ground. People who have the advantage of traveling fast and getting into places a truck or horse can't go."

Jackie was silent for a few long beats. When she finally spoke, there was something in her voice. Something more than worry for her granddaughter.

"Yes. Yes. That's smart. We're more than happy to help. Give me some time to work out the logistics on this end. I'll call you back with the details. Don't worry, baby," she said, addressing Kaia directly, "help is coming."

"Thank you, Jackie," Kaia said. "I'll talk to you soon."

Hanging up, Kaia glanced over at Mac. "I know I don't know her very well, but I get the feeling she was holding something back."

"Yeah," Mac's blue eyes held hers, "I got that impression too."

"Any clue as to what it could be?"

"No, but there's no sense in stressing about it right now. Let's see what she says when she calls back."

Forty minutes later, as they ate dinner, her phone rang.

She hit the speaker button. "Hello?"

"Everything is all set," Jackie responded. "We'll be leaving within the hour."

"We?" Kaia should have expected her grandmother would

come.

"Yes. Four of your cousins and myself," she clarified. "But here's what we'll need to do."

They talked for another few minutes before winding up the call.

"I don't know how to thank you."

"None needed, sweetheart. We're family."

Which was pretty much what Mac had told her too.

Mac glanced at his watch as Kaia disconnected the call. "If I'm not mistaken, Colorado is a twelve-hour drive. If they're leaving within the hour, that'll put them here about seven tomorrow morning."

"Okay." Kaia was suddenly nervous. She'd be meeting several of her family members for the first time in a few hours.

Mac grasped her hand on the table. "Are you all right?"

"Yeah. It's just a bit daunting to think about meeting so many of my extended family. All at once, and for something like this. I'd imagined a happier occasion."

"I'll be right here with you."

"I know." She thought again of what her grandmother had told her. "What do you think about this plan of theirs?"

"I can see the merit in it. If he's watching, having a bunch of people come in and hang around may spook him. It makes more sense for them to split off. And Helen's will be the perfect place to hide the other vehicle while your grandmother stays here. The others making their way here through the woods will keep our poacher from knowing about their presence, while still allowing them to get familiar with the area. Once they've had a chance to scout around, they can wait until full dark before coming in."

"It just seems like overkill to me. But I guess they know what they're doing." She needed to get her mind off of everything that had happened and would be happening over the next few days. And she thought she knew of a way for both of them to relax tonight.

After dinner, they did the dishes together. When the last cup was put away, she turned to Mac. "Go take a shower. I've got a surprise for you."

"Oh, yeah?" He wrapped his arms around her waist and drew her in, giving her a soft kiss. "What did you have in mind?"

"You'll see." She stepped out of his embrace. "Go. While you're getting cleaned up, I'll take care of the rest."

When he'd gone, Kaia went to her bedroom, changed into the tank and shorts she normally slept in, and set up a few other things. When he joined her, all he wore was a towel slung low on his hips. Kaia urged him to lay face down on the bed. While he did that, she retrieved the bottle of oil she'd set on the nightstand. Once he was settled, she climbed up on the bed and straddled his hips.

Popping the top, she squeezed a handful out. She closed it again one-handed and set it beside her leg. Rubbing her hands together to warm the oil, she leaned forward and ran her slick palms down the middle of his back.

He groaned under her touch and then mumbled into the pillow, "You're the one who needs to be relaxing. I should be doing this for you."

"We both need this. And touching you, being with you, gives me all I need."

He sighed again when she pressed her thumbs into the tight muscles in his lower back.

Kaia spent several minutes working the tension out of his body, digging her knuckles in deep until the flesh softened and gave him some relief.

"Oh, God, that's amazing."

Just wait, she thought with a secret smile.

She worked her way over his sexy form—back, arms, thighs, calves, butt. He was a puddle when she told him to roll over.

"I don't think I can." His voice was garbled through the

bedding still smashed against his face.

"It'll be worth it, trust me."

She lifted herself above him far enough for him to roll. The towel around his waist came dislodged as he moved, but neither bothered to replace it. She settled back over him.

"Mmm, I like this better already." He grinned up at her.

Kaia chuckled. "Relax, killer."

More oil, and then she started on his chest, running her slick hands over his pecs before moving lower. Using her thumbs again, she dug a path up the center, starting from his belly button. Up and over his shoulders, and down his arms. She picked up one of his hands and concentrated on the firm, coarse palm, pulling and squeezing his fingers from the base to the tips. He sighed in contentment when she switched to the other hand.

She gradually made her way down his body, sliding hers further down as she went, not stopping until she'd also given his feet the same treatment.

Glancing up at him, his eyes were closed, and his breathing was deep and even. He wasn't sleeping, but he was drifting. She remembered that blissful place well from the last time she'd gone to the spa.

As she started back up his long length, Kaia stopped at the one area she'd deliberately avoided as she'd kneaded and soothed him. He'd come to attention long ago under her ministrations, but not fully. He was semi-aroused but tranquil.

Until Kaia wrapped her oiled hand around him and squeezed.

He drew in a breath and moaned.

His length grew within her grip. Holding him at the base, she opened her mouth and took him in. Her tongue swirled and licked along his shaft, flicking at the underside of the head.

His breathing shuddered, and his hand rose to rest on the back of her head. He didn't force her movements, only held onto her, fisting his hand in her hair.

Kaia relaxed and let him slide in as far as he could go. As she pulled back, she sucked hard, working him with her tongue and teeth.

"Oh, fuck, Kai." His hips rose and fell in small, jerky movements.

She knew he was getting close. His breathing was short and choppy, and his hand gripped her hair with more force. It wasn't painful—it just let her know he was enjoying her gift.

"Kaia. Oh, God." On a hoarse curse, Mac found his release. She didn't stop until he was spent and sated, taking all he had into her.

When he relaxed back, she slid up his body to snuggle in beside him.

He roused enough to look over at her. "You're wearing too many clothes."

She smiled. "And what are you going to do about it?"

Mac showed her exactly. And hours later, they lay naked, pressed together, sleeping.

~~~

At eight the next morning, Kaia and Mac were standing at her front window, waiting for their guests to arrive.

They had already been to the barn early that morning to get whatever they could done, well before her family was due in. Since the poacher was likely still watching, they gave him plenty of time to follow them back to Kaia's house, thereby leaving Helen's free and clear for the others to enter the forest in secret.

Kaia would have to return later to put in her day with the horses, but that could wait until after this meeting.

When a large SUV pulled in, Mac came over to stand right behind her. His arms went around her waist and hugged her tightly.
~~~

"Is Moose okay in my room?" They'd discussed it and, not wanting the dog to become overwhelmed by more shifters in the house, they agreed to close him in the bedroom for this first meeting. Later, they could make the introductions one-on-one.

She knew worrying about him kept her mind from stressing about who was here. And why.

"He's fine." Mac gave her a reassuring squeeze. "Let's go meet your grandmother."

Kaia nodded, Mac right by her side.

As they stepped out onto the porch, the vehicle came to a stop and parked. Kaia and Mac waited as the car doors opened. Her grandmother got out on one side, and a tall blond man emerged from the driver's side.

Kaia started down the steps and bee-lined to her grandmother. Jackie grinned hugely, opened her arms, and Kaia walked into them.

Her grandmother held her so tightly, Kaia didn't think she'd ever breathe normally again. But she was okay with that. She'd stay in this embrace as long as she could. It had been so long since she'd had a woman's love.

Silent tears fell down her cheeks. When she sniffled, Jackie leaned back. She reached up and cupped Kaia's face in her hands, wiping at the moisture with her thumbs. "Everything is all right now, baby girl."

Kaia didn't trust her voice. All she could do was nod at the reassuring words.

"Let's take this into the house." Mac helped with the suitcases and showed the newcomers in.

Once they were inside, Kaia turned to Jackie. "You found Helen's okay? The others were able to make it into the woods there?"

Jackie smiled. "Yes. Your directions were perfect, and everything went smoothly. We were able to split off there without incident." She paused for a moment. "That's some place over there. You must be so proud of the work you're doing. I'm a little embarrassed to say it, but I Googled you. You've made quite the name for yourself. That has to feel amazing, and I'm so very proud of you."

Talking about what she loved most went a long way to making Kaia feel more at ease. "It really does. I still have to pinch myself sometimes just to remind myself it's all real."

"You've done so well, baby."

"Thank you. I just wish Mom and Dad and Jace could have seen it."

"I know, sweetie." Sadness swam in the older woman's eyes. "But they know, and they are so proud of you too."

Kaia's throat and nose burned with emotion, but she nodded and smiled, happy to have her grandmother there with her.

"Now, as to the other reason we're here." Jackie indicated to the man who'd been silent until now. "This is Erik. He's your cousin on your dad's side. He's a Reid too. As far as the others, I'll wait until they get here later to introduce them."

"I want to thank you for coming here," Kaia began, glancing at Erik. "You don't know me from Adam, yet here you are. I wanted to make sure you know how much I appreciate this."

"When family needs help," he told her, "you drop everything and go."

Kaia gestured to Mac. "This is Sheriff Lucas McNamara. He's a good friend and has been helping me."

"Please, call me Mac. Everyone does," he added, holding out his hand to shake with her cousin. "I know you and the others are shifters like Kaia. I'm hoping that, because of your abilities, you'll have better luck at tracking this bastard. I don't know how he's doing it, but he's managing to stay a step—hell, three steps—ahead of us at all times."

"There's something I need to tell you about that," Jackie began, pulling Kaia and Mac's attention back. Her lightly lined face had turned serious. "I'm afraid it's not good news."

Kaia sat forward in her seat. Jackie's voice had taken on that same tone she'd heard over the phone. That she knew something she wasn't telling them.

"What is it?"

"We have reason to believe your poacher isn't really a poacher at all."

"What do you mean by that?" Mac was clearly suspicious, unsettled by this news.

Jackie looked first at Erik and then back to Kaia. "I didn't want to say anything until I knew for sure, but I did some checking after I hung up with you last night, and it seems..." It was easy to see she dreaded telling the next part. "It seems Gerald, the man who was obsessed with your mother all those years ago, has learned of your existence. But worse than that, is that he hasn't been seen in weeks."

Kaia's stomach pitched. "What? How?"

Jackie took a breath and let it out audibly. "We're not sure. We'd kept in contact with his father for a long time after your parents left, just to make sure he was being controlled. After a few years, he seemed to forget about her and move on. There hadn't been any issues with him for a very long time. Eventually, we stopped checking in on him and just got on with our lives as best we could.

"Gerald's father passed away a little over a year ago. We held our breaths, waiting for him to make some kind of move, but he never did. He stepped into the role of leader for his clan, and everything was good."

She paused for a moment. "We think now that he's had people spying for him all along, waiting for any word of your family. When you finally made contact with us, someone must have leaked that information. After your phone call yesterday, when you said he was much older, I needed to know for sure. I called a friend in his clan and learned he'd gone AWOL. I appealed to his next-in-command. He'd been around then, back when this all started, and knew Gerald's history. As a favor to me, he searched Gerald's house, and it turned up a picture of you. It was one you had sent to Elva and me. Somehow, he'd gotten his hands on it." Regret clouded Jackie's eyes. "Like I said, you look an awful lot like your mother. My only guess is that, when he saw it, it triggered something in him. I don't know if he's just lost it completely and thinks you're her, or if he's transferred that old obsession to you. Either way, there's no telling what's in his mind."

"Are you sure?" Kaia thought back to when she'd seen him. "I didn't sense a cat in him. I can feel all of yours. If that was Gerald that came to the barn, why didn't I notice his cougar? Maybe this is someone else."

Kaia didn't want to think about the possibility of this man being here. Watching her. For so many years, they'd lived in secret, protected from this animal. And now, with one email, Jackie thought she'd become his target, just as much as her mother had been.

"I don't have an explanation for that. Maybe he found some way of blocking it. But it *is* him—I know that for a fact. It was the animals he left for you," Jackie said in a weary tone. "He'd exhibited that same behavior before with your mom, trying to win her over by proving he could provide for her."

Mac was sitting silently beside her. She brought her head around now to look at him.

He held Kaia's gaze while he spoke. "When we found out we were dealing with two separate people, and this new one seemed more obsessive, we began looking into Kaia's past relationships, searching for anyone who could have developed this fixation on her. Nothing made sense, because there was no one. But this answers a lot of the questions we had. It wasn't a new threat, but a really old one."

"I'm sure you've already connected these dots, but Gerald most likely killed the poacher you'd been hunting in the beginning," Jackie said grimly. "He wouldn't tolerate anyone standing in his way."

Mac subtly rotated his shoulder, but Kaia saw it. He had to be thinking about being ambushed by this freak. "Yeah. We got that loud and clear. And you're right. When the body was found with a broken neck, it wasn't hard to follow the evidence back to whomever was leaving the game for Kaia."

"Son of a bitch." Mac shook his head. "It's no wonder we could never catch sight of him. All he had to do was shift, and he'd be gone."

Jackie nodded. "Unfortunately, that's correct. You, alone, couldn't have found him."

"But we can." Erik spoke for only the second time. "And we will." His tone was confident and strong. "You two go about your normal business and let us deal with him." Erik's decree didn't welcome any argument.

But he sure as hell got one.

"No." Kaia told him unequivocally. "I'm going to help you bring him down. He cost my parents their families, and me and my brother the chance to grow up knowing all of you. I won't sit by and let you all handle this on your own. I'm a cat too, and these are my woods. My home."

On a roll, she turned to pin Mac with a look. "And don't think you can talk me out of this either."

"I had no intention of trying. As a matter of fact, you stole my argument before I could give it." Turning his attention back to Jackie and Erik, he continued. "I'm the law here, so it's my job to see this killer brought to justice. But don't think I'm not fully invested in removing this threat against Kaia in any way possible. He's been allowed to torment your family for far too long. So, while *I* can't step outside the law of man, I won't stand in the way of your authority as shifters to deal with a shifter issue. *But*," he stressed the word, "I won't be locked out of this. I intend to help in any way I can."

"So, you'll let us do what we must?" Erik clarified, with a little bit of an edge.

"Yes," Mac affirmed. "But you're going to need us. He's had weeks to familiarize himself with the area. You'll be going in blind. Like Kaia said, this is our home. We know this park better than any of you. And Kaia more so than I."

"I think we can all agree," Jackie broke in before Erik could speak again, "that working together on this is the best way. Yes, Gerald has been an issue for this family for a long time. He should have been dealt with years ago, but because of who his father was, he was allowed to slide by. And because of that, I lost my daughter, son-in-law, and grandchildren. He has to be stopped, here and now. I don't care who does it or by what means. I just want what's left of my family back, damn it."

Kaia grasped Jackie's hand across the table and nodded to Mac.

Clearing his throat, he met the eyes of Kaia's family. "So, what's the plan?"

20

Aside from the few hours Kaia needed to finish her work with the horses, the day was spent getting to know one another.

Jackie took over the kitchen and began cooking the most delicious-smelling food Kaia had ever experienced. Erik ended up being a lot more personable than she'd first thought, his autocratic tone from earlier having set poorly with her.

But once they'd sat down and talked, she found that, besides being gorgeous, he was also funny and smart. The man looked like he'd just stepped off the cover of some sports magazine. Tall, blond, tan—he was the stereotypical surfer dude. How that was even possible, she had no clue, given she was pretty sure Colorado didn't have surfing beaches.

She found out that his sister was also a part of the group in the woods. They were her dad's brother's kids.

The rest she wouldn't meet for a few more hours, and those were Paul and Hank, who were related to her through Jackie.

She'd not seen or sensed any of them, but Erik assured her they were out there right now. Keeping watch over her, perched up high in the trees to avoid detection from the ground.

It seemed weird to know that three mountain lions were lying in wait around her property, protecting her from the same threat that had ruined her mother's life.

Dinner was a lively event. Jackie regaled her with tales of her mom and dad. Kaia laughed and cried and grew to know the parents that were taken from her far too soon.

Moose had been introduced to Jackie and Erik with no issues, and he lay at Kaia's feet now while they ate, still acting as sentry.

After dinner, they gathered in the living room. Jackie had rolled one of the suitcases she'd brought into the kitchen. As she left the room, she'd turned off the lights. As soon as it was dark, the others would make their way into the house by the rear sliding door. Once there, they would don their clothes and join the rest of the group.

It was nearly ten when Kaia heard the door open for the first time. Her stomach jumped. Sensing her nerves, Mac grasped her hand.

A few minutes later, a huge man walked in. Well over six foot, his shoulders were massive—so wide and muscled, Kaia wasn't sure how he managed to find shirts that fit. His hair was a flat brown with eyes to match, and his features were just as ordinary. As far as Kaia could tell, he seemed to be older than Erik by a few years.

"Kaia," Jackie began, "this is Hank. He's my youngest brother's son."

"Nice to meet you," Kaia told him.

Hank nodded at her.

The next one in had to be Erik's sister. Another blonde-haired model-type. Once again, Jackie made the introductions. "This is Jayme, Erik's sister."

Kaia laughed. "Yeah, I can definitely tell."

Both siblings were so beautiful, she could almost hate them on appearance alone. But the openness and sincerity she saw in their faces told her these were good people.

Five minutes later, the last one came in. A lean man of average height with extraordinarily red hair.

"Paul," Jackie smiled, "is your cousin on my side too. My sister's grandson."

"It's no nice to meet all of you." Kaia ran through every trick she could think of to commit names to faces. "I said this before, but I want to make sure to say it to all of you. Thank you for doing this. I can't tell you what it means to know I'm not alone anymore. That I have others like me I can turn to."

~~~

They fell into bed only a few hours before dawn. Mac held Kaia close to him and listened to her breathing. She was sound asleep, her back tucked into the curve of his body, and had been since the moment her head hit the pillow.

He couldn't imagine the toll the last few weeks had taken on her. She'd had so many upheavals in such a short time. Being targeted by a poacher and tranquilized, finding out the boogie man that had haunted her family her entire life was not only here, but had transferred his sick obsession to her. Dealing with the feelings that had developed between them and finding their balance. And finally, reuniting with so many new family members under less-than-ideal circumstances.

That was enough to overwhelm anyone—emotionally and physically.

Mac didn't personally expect to be getting much sleep tonight. Too many things were going on in his mind for it to rest, the most consuming of which was how to keep the woman he loved safe.

She wanted to be a part of this. And he understood that need to pull her own weight and do her fair share, especially when her family being here meant they could also be in danger. But at the same time, he would do *every damned thing* within his power to keep her from getting hurt. Over his dead body would this sick fuck touch even one hair on her head. His two generations of terror were over, and he'd pay for everything he'd done. Not only to Kaia, but to her parents and family as
~~~

well.

She stirred in his arms, groaning lightly in her sleep.

He hated that this was hurting her. She'd tried so hard to act as though it wasn't affecting her, but she hadn't been her usual hard-headed, get-in-your-face Kaia for a while now. He caught glimpses of the old Kaia every so often, but then another hit would land, and that side of her would get tucked away again.

As Mac thought back, he could pinpoint exactly when she'd changed, when something inside of her had shut down. It was when he'd been shot—when it had become clear that the adversary they faced would stop at nothing to get to her. Even if it meant killing Mac.

Kaia was entitled to whatever freak-out she needed, but if she intended to join in this hunt, she was going to need to find that take-no-shit attitude again. She couldn't go out there if she wasn't at a hundred percent. Any fear or hesitation would get her or the others hurt. Or worse.

Mac hadn't realized until it wasn't there anymore that the boldness she'd worn like a suit of armor—the same one that had driven him nuts for so many years—was a big part of why he'd fallen for her. It was who she was. She knew her mind, did what needed to be done, and fuck anyone who told her she couldn't. She was strong, smart, hard-working, and she never gave up.

She'd need all of those qualities, and more, to get through this.

When she made another sound of distress, Mac pulled her in close. He bent his head to hers and murmured soothing words into her ear. Instead of drifting off again though, she woke and turned in his arms.

"Time is it?" she mumbled into his chest.

"Still early," he whispered. "Go back to sleep."

She burrowed in closer, rubbing her face against his skin, much like her cat had done. "Why are you awake?"

"Just thinking." He loved the feel of her breath washing over him and the sound of her sleep-roughened voice. He kissed the top of her head. "Try to get some rest."

Kaia shook her head and made a negative sound.

"Dreams?"

She nodded.

"Want to talk about them?"

"Not right now." Kaia laid her soft, warm lips on his chest. "I'd rather have you."

Mac placed a finger beneath her chin and raised her head. When those dusky pink, pout-worthy lips were only inches from his, he leaned down and took them.

Already warm and soft from sleep, she melted into him. He brought a hand up to palm one of her breasts, brushing over the nipple and causing her to moan.

In return, hers found him and squeezed. Now it was his turn to groan.

They loved each other slowly. Neither in a hurry.

To the sounds of their heavy breathing, Mac trailed his fingers along her body from shoulder to knee. There, he grasped her leg and raised it to rest at his waist, opening her for him.

Still lying on their sides, facing each other, Mac slid easily into her.

The pace they set was languorous. Long, leisurely strokes in and out that were meant to stoke a slow, all-consuming passion. When allowed to burn gradually, some embers created a subtler heat that burned so much hotter than the initial blaze.

Mac could attest to that. Every cell in his body was searing for the woman in his arms. And if the mewling sounds whispering from her parted lips were any indication, she was feeling it too.

He didn't know how much longer he could hang on, though. He'd been balanced on that sweet edge of oblivion from the moment he'd entered her. But he refused to fall without her.

"Let go, baby."

His murmured words seemed to push her over the precipice, her channel constricting around him like a fist. Mac withdrew, almost to the point of leaving her, and then thrust one final time, her pulsing walls detonating an orgasm more powerful than any he'd ever felt before.

It drained him completely, and just before he dropped into sleep, he heard Kaia's breathing deepen, their lovemaking having done the same for her. Snuggling her close, he wished her sweet dreams.

~~~

When Kaia and Mac walked into the kitchen later that morning, her grandmother was already there.

"Good morning." Jackie turned from the stove where she was frying something and smiled at them both.

"Hi." Kaia wandered right to the brewing machine and popped in a tea pod. She'd felt a little self-conscious at first, having her grandmother know she was sleeping with Mac. But Jackie hadn't seemed too scandalized by it. She'd seemed rather pleased, actually. "Did you sleep okay?" Kaia asked.

Jackie had taken her old room, since Mac had moved into the master with her. Her bright smile faltered. "Well enough. I'll sleep better once this is finally over."

"We all will," Mac agreed, stepping up to the sliding door to look out. "Have you heard anything from the others this morning?"

"Just like we planned, Erik left early this morning, making a big show to call out from the car that he'd be back in a few weeks, whenever I was ready to go home. Then he went back to Helen's, stashed the SUV, and joined the others in the woods. He texted to say that they're all good, and there was no sign of anyone last night."

Jackie brought plates full of food to the table, encouraging
~~~

them to sit and eat.

Kaia looked bewildered. "How are cougars even texting?"

Jackie laughed as she took her own seat. "One of them is designated to carry a small backpack with anything they'll need—one of those items being a cell phone. Once they get posted up high enough in a tree, they stash the pack in some branches, near enough to hear it if it vibrates. Once they've ensured the coast is clear, they shift, take care of the message, and then promptly shift back. It may sound a bit complicated, but they're all very well-trained, and they've got it down to a science—all while remaining undetected."

Kaia was pretty sure that her eyes were bulging out of her head. She looked to Mac, who just shrugged and dove into his plate.

As they enjoyed their breakfast together, Kaia thought back to the previous night. She began to wonder about their ease and knowledge with what was needed in this situation.

"What exactly do they do back in Colorado? You said they were well-trained?" she asked around bites of fluffy scrambled eggs.

"The four of them are a part of an elite group within the clan." Jackie took a sip of her coffee and then set it back down. "There are about sixteen members in total, I think. They're in charge of keeping the peace within the community and ensuring we're safe from outside forces."

"Kind of like your own police force." Kaia glanced at Mac.

Jackie nodded. "Sort of, yeah."

Kaia glanced out the window. "Have they eaten?"

Jackie smiled. "They have plenty of provisions in their pack. And if they end up needing to hunt, they'll go on a rotation. They're used to this. But more importantly, they're *good* at it."

After their meeting last night, her four cousins had set up their perimeter again, finding hidden vantage points to observe from and keep watch. If Gerald happened to show up, they would send word. And the hunt would be on.

In keeping with their original plan, all comings and goings were to be kept as discreet and inconspicuous as possible. The sooner Gerald found out about Kaia's family being in town, the sooner he'd change his tactics, making it even more difficult to track and capture him. Right now, he thought he was only dealing with Mac as her bodyguard. And they needed to keep it that way for as long as they could.

Even if he did find out about Jackie, he wouldn't consider her a threat, due to her advanced years. He'd make decisions based on an incorrect assumption, and that would be his downfall. It was keeping the others hidden that was most important.

"I think there's something we need to revisit from last night." Jackie looked from Kaia to Mac.

Kaia knew what Jackie wanted to talk about. And by the set of Mac's jaw, so did he.

"We could spend the next, who knows how many, days running the woods looking for Gerald. We'd find him, but it would take time. Or…we can let him come to us and set a trap for him."

Mac set his fork aside. "And use Kaia as bait?" He shook his head. "I said it last night, and I'll say it again. That's not an option."

"Mac…" Kaia began to argue, but her grandmother cut in.

"We love her too, Mac. Very much. We won't let anything happen to her," Jackie assured him. "We're all going to be watching her very closely, and there's no way he's getting by all of us." She paused. "This could be our best chance of taking him down."

Kaia had been thinking about it, and she agreed with her grandmother. This could work. And she was sure Mac would see it too—if he could just get past the idea that she'd be put in the crosshairs. He was a great cop. His mind was quick and agile; building strategies and planning complicated ops is what he did. They could do this. *If* he agreed.

She had a feeling if it were anyone else acting as bait, he wouldn't hesitate. But it wasn't. It was her.

"Mac, can I talk to you for a second?" Kaia pushed away from the table and stood.

He rose silently and followed her back to her bedroom. When the door was closed and they were alone, she went to him, taking his large hands in hers. His blue eyes were shuttered, telling her he was ready for any argument she could wage.

"I love you. I didn't want to, but I do. And I have it on pretty good authority that you love me too."

"Kaia—" he started, his tone holding a note of annoyance.

"Let me finish." She waited him out and got a reluctant nod.

"You know this relationship wasn't an easy choice for me. There was a lot working against you."

Her comment broke through his icy control enough for him to send her a cocked eyebrow in return.

"But what *did* work in your favor was that you'd stopped treating me like a child. You started seeing me as an adult and your equal. Your partner. I happen to think we work pretty damned well together. Let's not lose that now. I know you're worried about me getting hurt. But, that goes both ways. He's tried to kill you, Mac. Twice that we know of, and maybe more that we don't. Do you think it's easy for me when *you* go out there every day?"

"Damn it, Kaia. It's different for me. It's my *job* to go out there. To put myself on the line. I've been trained for circumstances like this, and it's all I've ever known. It comes naturally to me, *because* I've been doing it for so long. It's not the same as when you do it." Mac sighed heavily. "We agreed to work together, Kaia. Not for you to use yourself as bait for this bastard."

"I'll do anything I have to do to rid him from our lives."

His shoulders rose and fell on a deep breath. He muttered something that sounded like, "Be careful what you wish for."

Kaia wasn't sure what that meant. "Mac?"

"Just a note to myself." He gathered her up again and wrapped his arms around her middle. His demeanor wasn't quite so adversarial now. "I was watching you sleep last night, angry that this is causing you so much pain, and realizing that you haven't been yourself for weeks now. That hard-headed, opinionated, knows-what-needs-to-be-done, fearless woman I fell in love with, has been missing a lot of the time. I never thought I'd hear myself say this," he sent her a smirk, "but I've missed the part of you that planned to take on any poacher who dared cross her borders. I thought I'd have to remind you of her, because you're going to need her to get through this. But more than that, *I* need her. And yet here she is, arguing with me."

She smiled softly now. "I did lose her for a while. I know that. But she doesn't stay down for long. She's here now, and she's here to stay." Kaia grinned wickedly as she tilted her head. "So…you're saying you love it when I bust your balls?"

"I wouldn't go that far," he chuckled and then turned serious. "But I've hated how this has made you question your instincts."

Kaia rested her head in the middle of his chest. "I've hated it too. So much was thrown at me, I kind of lost my footing." She leaned back and looked up at him. "But as long as I have you beside me, I'll never lose my way again."

He kissed her gently and threaded his fingers with hers. "Well, that's good. Because I'm not going anywhere."

And with that, they returned to the kitchen to discuss a new plan.

21

An hour later, Mac was getting into his car and driving off, lights and sirens blaring as if he'd been called out on an emergency.

And he fucking despised having to do it.

Leaving her here with her grandmother just didn't sit right with him. Even with the four additional bodyguards hiding in the woods, he would have felt better had it been him with her.

But to draw this asshole out, he had to follow along. He had to make himself scarce to give Gerald his opportunity to make a move on Kaia. He'd agreed the set-up was a good one, but he'd drawn a hard line on one item. One he wouldn't be swayed on. He was going home to her every night.

He might have to get through each day with her out of his sight, but by God, he'd watch over her each night. He'd sleep in bed beside her, and guard her with his life if this bastard got too close.

Being sidelined didn't mean he couldn't do his job, though. And that job was to investigate. So that's what he'd do. He'd learn every goddamned thing he could about the man who was tormenting the woman he loved. And by the time he was done, Mac would know what kind of toilet paper that motherfucker used to wipe his ass.

After a quick hello to his team, Mac closed himself in his office. He worked for hours, following every lead he could dig up. Some took him down blind alleys, but others connected him to something new and gave him another line to pull.

The information he was finding was pointing him in a direction that made his blood run cold.

Over the last twenty years, a number of women had gone missing in and around areas of Colorado where Gerald had lived. And after gathering the case files and seeing photos of the women, Mac knew their stalker was the culprit. All of the women bore a striking resemblance to Kaia. Or rather, to her mother.

They were all in their mid- to late-twenties, mocha-skinned with curly or wavy hair similar to Kaia's shade. The reports covered several jurisdictions, but thanks to national databases, they'd been connected to each other. According to what he'd read, no evidence could be found tying the disappearances to anyone in particular.

But then, Mac had knowledge the other cops didn't.

Mac sat and let the new details come together in his mind. The picture it formed was one of murder and depravity. This guy was fucked in the head, so obsessed with one woman that he looked for her in others. When they didn't, or couldn't, return his feelings, he killed them.

If Kaia's parents hadn't been smart and moved away, taking such extreme measures to conceal their location even from their own families, he would have eventually killed Cori. And most likely Nate too, because he'd been in the way.

Mac's conscience was at war. On one hand, the cop in him wanted this perp to pay for his crimes by living out the rest of his days in a cage. On the other, Mac wanted his own hands wrapped around his fucking neck for what he'd done to Kaia, her family, and all his other countless victims.

He knew he shouldn't think that way. As an officer of the law, he'd vowed to uphold that law. And he would. But the thought of just removing scum like this from the earth was more tempting than he ever could have imagined.

~~~

He watched the house through the rifle scope.

So, the mother had come. One more person to pay for keeping his tawny beauty from him for so long.

He'd wanted, for so many years, to make his father pay for taking their side. For not standing with his only son. As leader of his clan, he should have demanded they give her to him, despite the other clan's objections. Instead, he'd kept his own son bound under his thumb for years. Gerald's hands had been tied, because his father ruled with an iron fist. No one questioned him, and no one went against him.

Until his father had found out about the others. He'd been going to send Gerald away. He'd overhead his father talking with his lieutenant about him. Ashamed of his own son, they'd been discussing how best to remove him from their community and what to do with him.

Gerald couldn't allow that to happen. He couldn't permit his father to strip him of his status. He had to maintain his authority within the clan.

Better yet, he needed to elevate that status. And in order to do that, his father needed to die.

Well into his eighties, Gerald's father was still a stout and hearty man. He could still rule for many years to come and wield enough power to ensure Gerald was never seen again.

But if Gerald stepped into his father's seat, all that power would be his. He could allocate more men to the search of his mate. And no one could stop him.

His plan had worked perfectly, and at fifty-two years old, he'd become the ruling clan leader. And with a stroke of luck, shortly after that, news had come that she'd been found. A sign from the universe telling him that what he'd done had been
~~~

right. It was finally all falling into place.

And now, here he was, so close to obtaining his goal. No one could stop him. Not his father, not some human sheriff, and certainly not an old, decrepit woman. He'd have his chosen mate, and she would learn her place by his side. Or suffer the consequences.

He'd learned on his phone that the body of that low-life poacher had been found. That hadn't been much of a loss to the world—only a vile poacher who'd had the nerve to hunt his lioness. If he had caused her any damage, Gerald would have made his death that much more painful. As it was, he'd been merciful and delivered a quick death.

Which wasn't what he wanted for that fucking sheriff. When he'd seen them together in the woods, he'd become so angry he'd lost control. Gerald prided himself on his restraint. It had been drummed into his brain by his father for all of his life. But when he'd witnessed the tryst between his mate and the human, that hard-won control had been lost.

The shift had taken him before he'd known it, and his cat had challenged him, intent on ripping the skin from his bones. Only to have his woman defend that piece of shit.

That was a mistake she would learn never to repeat. He'd make damned sure of that.

Movement down below caught his attention and brought his mind back to the present.

What the hell?

Gerald watched as the sheriff came hurriedly out of the house and crossed to his dark SUV. Lights and sirens blasted within seconds, and it sped off.

He was obviously racing to a call, leaving Kaia behind. Did they think she was safe with only the old woman to guard her?

Gerald raised from the scope and smiled.

Fate was telling him that now was the time. She was there. Unprotected. *Go get her. Make her yours.*

Approaching the house would be too difficult, though. Too much openness all around it.

They knew what he looked like. If they spotted him coming before he got to his mate, he'd be screwed.

He needed more cover. Someplace he could ambush them.

~~~

Kaia watched Mac drive off and felt a little fissure of unease. It wasn't that she was unsure of her ability to take care of herself. Or even that Mac could take care of himself. But with a psychotic mind like Gerald's out there, anything could happen.

She looked deep and figured out the root of her apprehension. It stemmed from the fear that she might lose Mac when she'd only just found him. He'd been in her life forever, but only now did she understand what life without him would be like.

And that would be unbearable.

Her grandmother stepped up behind her and put her arm around Kaia's waist. "It's going to be okay."

"I know." Kaia patted her grandmother's hand and squeezed it in appreciation.

"So, it seems you agree with your cat now." Jackie smiled knowingly. "No more second-guessing her choice?"

Kaia grinned and turned to face her. "I'll have to give her that one. She knew, even when I didn't."

"They're pretty smart that way." Jackie pressed her hand to Kaia's cheek. "I'm so glad you found your true mate."

Kaia tipped her head into her grandmother's hand. "Me too." She straightened and narrowed her eyes. "But that doesn't mean I'm going to make his life easy. In the least."

An unholy gleam lit Jackie's eyes. "And I wouldn't expect you to. What's the fun in that? We women have to keep our men on their toes."

They laughed, sharing a hug.
~~~

When Kaia left a short while later, Jackie went with her. She'd been so excited at the prospect of seeing Kaia at work and learning about what she loved.

As they got into her Jeep, Kaia cast a glance to the woods behind her house. Her cousins were out there, keeping watch. But there was no way for them to follow her to work without being seen. They'd have to cross through the forest to meet her at Helen's.

She'd be out of their sight briefly, but the drive to the barn was less than five minutes. And then she'd be under their protection again.

Kaia looked over at her grandmother. "Ready?"

Jackie snapped her seatbelt and smiled. "I can't wait."

Returning the smile, Kaia pulled out onto the road.

They'd only gone a couple of miles when a loud explosion sounded, and her Jeep veered suddenly to the left.

She took a death grip on the steering wheel and hit the brake pedal with both feet. When she brought the Jeep safely to a stop, she had to take a deep breath. Her whole body was shaking.

"What the hell was that?" Jackie asked.

Kaia turned to her. "It sounded like a tire blew. Are you okay?"

"Yeah. I'm good."

Kaia's brow furrowed. "That's bizarre. They're not even that old. Maybe I hit something in the road."

She reached for the door handle to inspect the damage. But stilled when Jackie laid a hand on her arm.

She spun to look at her and saw fear and anger etched over her face. Kaia swung her gaze to peer in the direction her grandmother was looking. And saw Gerald emerging from the trees.

He held a gun pointed directly at them as he approached the Jeep. He walked right up to the passenger side door, glaring at

Jackie before switching his focus to Kaia.

"Get out of the car, Corinne." He shifted the barrel until it was aimed at Jackie. "Or I'll shoot her."

Kaia and Jackie exchanged a look of alarm, but before Kaia's brain could catch up, Jackie flung the door wide with as much force as she could. Hitting Gerald squarely in the torso, he flew backwards off balance and landed on his ass.

Jackie was out of the car faster than Kaia could have thought possible. By the time Kaia scrambled out and ran around the front of the Jeep, Jackie was on top of him, pounding him with fists fueled by hatred and revenge for all she'd lost because of him.

His nose was already bloodied, and she was still whaling on him.

Kaia saw his gun lying on the ground a few feet away and dove to pick it up.

"Jackie! Stop! Back away from him."

It took a moment, but Jackie finally stilled and pushed off of Gerald. Just as she was getting to her feet, he struck out at her with a wild blow. As Jackie went sprawling to the roadway, Gerald shifted and ran for the trees.

Kaia raised the gun and fired.

A pain-filled scream rent the air. She'd hit him, but not bad enough to stop him. She could still hear the sound of him crashing through the thick foliage.

Giving chase by herself was stupid. And she was worried about Jackie. Crouching down to the older woman still on the ground, she asked, "Are you hurt?" Kaia looked her over, checking for signs of injury or blood.

"No. Madder than hell but not hurt. Not much anyway. My hands smart some." She flexed her fingers and examined the scuffed and red knuckles.

"I imagine they do." Kaia grinned. "You really let him have it."

"Oh, God, that felt good. I've wanted to take that bastard's head off for years."

"He won't soon forget you, that's for sure." Kaia wrapped an arm around her shoulders and helped pull her to her feet. "Come on. Let's get this tire changed and get out of here. I've got some liniment I can put on those hands."

"We need to call everyone and tell them what happened." Jackie walked to the rear of the Jeep with her.

"Go ahead. I'll call Mac once we get to the barn, but I need to get this tire fixed." Kaia set to repairing her vehicle while Jackie sent out a quick text, warning the others that Gerald was injured and to keep a lookout in the woods. With a promise to explain more later, she told them to meet her in the tree line at Helen's.

Upon arriving, Kaia saw Helen sitting on the porch. She glanced over at Jackie.

"You up to meeting a friend of mine?"

"I'm fine, sweetie. And I'd love to meet anyone you consider a friend."

Kaia pulled to a stop and then parked. It seemed only right that these two special women, so very important to her, should meet. She was slightly worried that maybe they wouldn't like each other, but her concern was for nothing—they got along at first sight.

They talked briefly, and after a promise to Helen to chat later, Jackie followed Kaia back to the Jeep.

"She loves you," Jackie said easily.

Kaia smiled warmly. "I love her too. None of what I've accomplished in the last two years would have been possible without her. She gave me free reign to use her place. If I would've had to build all this myself, it would have taken a lot longer to make something of it. Our arrangement has benefitted both of us."

"And given you a family." Jackie reached out and touched

Kaia's hand on the gear shift.

"Yeah. It has."

"So, show me everything you do here."

First on the agenda was to clean and tend to Jackie's hands. And then, while Kaia put a call in to Mac, Jackie walked out back to meet up with the others.

He answered on the first ring, and she got right to it. "We're both fine. But Gerald tried to ambush Jackie and me on the way to the barn."

"What happened?" The words sounded like they were being pushed past a clenched jaw. And they probably were.

She recounted the events of the morning, ending with Gerald disappearing into the woods.

"And Jackie's all right?"

"She's good. I put some salve on her knuckles. But *man*," Kaia said in awe, "I gotta tell you—she was vicious."

"Can't say I blame her. He's put her and her family through hell." He paused. "The shot you got off. Are you sure you hit him?"

"Yeah. No mistaking it. I just don't know how bad."

"I'll send some of my guys in there to see what they can find. Hopefully, his dead, rotting corpse."

After hanging up, Kaia finally got to work. Over the next few hours, Jackie insisted on helping wherever she could. By the time Kaia stopped to take a break, Jackie was a sweaty, dirty mess, but her smile was radiant, and she seemed genuinely pleased to have been included.

"You do this every day?" Jackie drank greedily from the water bottle Kaia offered.

"Yup. Every day."

"You must either be Superwoman, or I'm just remarkably out of shape." Jackie sat on a hay bale and huffed out a breath.

Kaia chuckled. "I'm definitely not Superwoman. I've just been at this a lot longer. You're using muscles you probably forgot you had."

"I know that's right." Her grandmother put a hand on her lower back.

Kaia suddenly felt guilty. Jackie wasn't a young woman anymore, and she'd had a knock-down-drag-out fight earlier. Should she be doing work like this? "Are you okay? I shouldn't have let you do so much."

Now Jackie laughed. "I'm perfectly fine, dear. I'm not so old yet. And I keep in good physical shape. But you're right—jogging isn't quite the same as pitching hay. I'll be sore, but it's the good kind, and I promise I won't keel over."

She took her at her word, but Kaia mentally rearranged the activities for the rest of the day. "Well, it's a good thing we're moving on to the training now. I'll get set up, and you can come out when you're ready."

Kaia went to gather what she needed before Jackie could say anything else. Line in hand, Kaia went to Oscar's stall.

"Are you going to be good in front of my grandmother?"

When he stomped and threw his head, she got his answer loud and clear.

"So, it's the hard way today, huh? Okay then, let's get it out of your system."

"Is he mean?" Jackie stood a safe distance behind Kaia.

"No. He's just living up to his name and being a grouch." Kaia leaned against the stall opening and waited for the big bay to fire up his temper tantrum.

"The only one he's ever been a gentleman for is my friend's daughter. Min is two, and I think he fell in love with her instantly."

At the sound of the name, Oscar stopped and stuck his head over Kaia's shoulder to look down the hall.

"No, she's not here, you big goof." Kaia scrubbed a hand over his forehead. "But now that you're finished with your snit, how about we show Jackie what you've got?"

Kaia clipped the lead line to his halter and guided him out of the barn and to the round pen. After closing the gate, she moved to the middle and set Oscar in motion.

An hour later, she brought the lesson to an end. Turning, she saw Jackie standing at the rail.

She beamed at the large stud. "He's gorgeous."

Kaia patted his neck. "He is, but I don't tell him that too often, or it'll go to his head. He's hard enough to deal with as it is."

Jackie grinned. "One of those, huh?"

"Oh, yeah."

Kaia led Oscar to the cross ties and clipped him in. She handed Jackie a brush and guided her in what to do. They chatted as they washed him down until his coat gleamed red-brown, even in the shadowed interior of the barn.

She was cleaning up when Jackie approached her. "I haven't wanted to say anything for fear of upsetting you. But..." She halted, obviously hesitant to continue. At Kaia's encouragement, Jackie took a deep breath and nodded. "Would you mind taking me to where my daughter is buried?"

Kaia was a little ashamed she hadn't thought of that before now.

"Oh, Jackie. Not at all. We can go right now. It's not too far from here." Kaia stopped and grasped Jackie's hand. "And it won't make me upset. I always feel sad when I go, because I miss them all so much. But then I always feel better when I do. I'm sorry I didn't think to offer that sooner."

"It's okay, sweetie." Jackie cupped her face in her hand. "It's understandable. You've had a lot on your mind."

Kaia tipped her cheek into Jackie's palm and soaked in the love. She smiled when she stood. "We should probably let our guard-cats know we're taking a side trip."

"You finish up what you need to do, and I'll get word to them."

Jackie stepped back into the barn five minutes later. Behind her stalked a large, handsome mountain lion.

Kaia switched her gaze between her grandmother and the cat. "What's going on?" She wasn't sure which of her cousins it was—she'd never seen any of them in their animal forms.

Jackie sent the cat an exasperated look. "Erik is going with us."

"What do you mean he's going with us? How? People will talk if I'm seen with a cougar in my backseat."

Jackie sighed. "He's going to stay out of sight, but it's non-negotiable. Believe me, I tried."

Kaia shrugged. "I guess after what Gerald pulled this morning, I can see the need for caution." She dusted off her hands and reached for her keys. "In that case, let's get loaded up."

Fifteen minutes later, Kaia pulled into the old cemetery. She glanced up in her rearview mirror and shook her head at Erik's cat lounging across the full width of her backseat. Returning her attention out the front, she followed the road around to the large oak and parked.

As the women exited the vehicle, Kaia opened the back door to let Erik step out. Without hesitation, he scaled the towering tree, disappearing into the branches to look out over the dotted greenery and the stone monuments raised in places of tribute.

Kaia and Jackie walked side-by-side over the lush grass. With every step, her grandmother's grip grew tighter. Concern had Kaia bringing their clasped hands up where she placed a small kiss on Jackie's knuckles.

"It's right over here." Kaia pointed to the two stone markers ahead of them.

When they reached them, Kaia stood silently on the sun-warmed lawn while her grandmother gathered herself as she looked tearfully at the granite tombstones.

Jackie knelt and placed a trembling hand over her daughter's name.

"Oh, my sweet Corinne. I'm so sorry."

Kaia backed up a few steps and just let them be, averting her eyes and focusing instead on some wildflowers that grew nearby. She'd cried her fair share here too, in this place that held the last remnants of her family. She couldn't deny Jackie that same closure—the opportunity to say her goodbyes to the woman who was her child, a child she'd birthed and lost.

She couldn't imagine what Jackie had gone through. What any of her grandparents had suffered. Kaia had lost her parents, but they'd lost their children. Although they'd been taken way too early and far too young, children somewhat expected to lose their parents at some point in their lives. Parents, however, were never prepared to lose the child they'd grown within their bodies and loved so deeply from the moment of their existence.

Kaia would give her as much time as she needed.

A while later, Jackie turned. "I'm sorry. That hit me a lot harder than I thought it would. Seeing her here. Seeing them all." She cast her gaze over the second name on the dual stone, and the smaller one beside it that was Jace's.

Kaia went to her. "You have nothing to apologize for. I've been here dozens of times, and it still gets me sometimes." She lowered down next to Jackie. "How about we just sit here for a bit? We can talk if you want. Or we can just absorb the quiet."

"I'd like that." Tears still choked Jackie's voice.

They ended up staying for well over an hour longer. They told each other stories about the years they'd missed with both Cori and Nate. Kaia told her all about Jace—how well he'd taken care of her, stepping into both roles as mom and dad. About him joining her for impromptu teenage dance parties in her room, and how he'd always managed to make her laugh when she was upset. All while teaching her about her cat, and how they worked together.

And through these memories, Jackie got to know her grandson, laughing at some things, and shaking her head at some of the others.

After piling everyone back into the car and arriving back at the house, Erik slunk surreptitiously into the trees. Kaia and Jackie were both ready for a shower and something to eat.

And, Kaia thought, something she knew Jackie would enjoy immensely.

Refreshed and dressed a short while later, they met up in the kitchen to start dinner. Mac had texted her to say that if nothing else came up, he'd be there by six.

While they chopped and stirred, Kaia told her grandmother what she'd done.

"I pulled out all of our old photo albums and scrapbooks. I thought after dinner, we could go through them together."

Tears sprang into Jackie's eyes. "I would love that."

"And how about, in the morning, we go for a run? I really want to show you my park."

Kaia could see the spark in Jackie's eyes, but it was quickly overshadowed by caution and concern.

"Hey," Kaia said gently, "the idea is to tempt him to make a move. I ran every morning until this mess started, and I've felt like a caged animal ever since. My cat needs this, and I'd be willing to bet that yours does too." She grinned. "Besides, we'll have several bodyguards watching over us."

Jackie nodded and smiled then. "You're right. When your mom was young, we used to spend our mornings out running and exploring."

"She did the same with Jace and me," Kaia shared.

"All right, then. I'll text Hank and let them know what the plan is, so they'll be ready."

Mac wasn't so keen on the idea when Kaia told him about it over dinner. He was quiet for a long time, obviously waging a war inside his head over how to handle this.

When he released a tired sigh, she knew he'd reached his decision. "I know it's useless to try and talk you out of this. Just please promise me you'll be careful out there. That you'll both be careful."

Kaia's eyes widened in shock. She knew how big of a concession he was making, especially where it concerned her safety. She rose and went to him, cupping his cheeks in her hands and placing a light kiss on his lips.

"Thank you. And we will. Just as I'm sure my cousins will be while they're watching over us."

22

The next morning, Kaia and Jackie stood on the back deck in the crisp, pre-dawn morning. Each was dressed in cotton pants and a loose tee. After a quick grin, they strolled barefoot over the dewy grass. Once inside the tree line, Kaia took her to the spot where they could hide their clothes until they returned.

Both stripped and made the swift change.

In their feline forms, Jackie was smaller and leaner than Kaia, and she didn't have as much black shadowing on her face. Her eyes were more hazel, whereas Kaia's were a startling greenish-gray.

But to Kaia, she was beautiful. This was her family, her blood—a piece of herself that had been missing since the day her parents had been killed, and later, when Jace was taken. She'd missed having this connection with someone else for so long.

Here was another person like her, with her same abilities. Someone who could experience the world in the same way she did, and who could enjoy the freedom of running, leaping, and hunting through the forest with the same extended sight, range of hearing, and sense of smell. The world was richer, more vibrant, more *real* than any human would ever know.

Only another shifter could appreciate all it entailed, and she finally had that back. She had others like her again.

She wasn't alone anymore.

Kaia and Jackie bolted off, racing and weaving around trees and stone. Jackie tackled her and they rolled, playing like cubs as Kaia had with her parents and brother so long ago.

But while they teased and tumbled, they kept a vigilant eye out. Both knew the four other cats were somewhere nearby, but each watched for anything worrisome.

Gerald was still out here and could strike at any moment. But he didn't this day. And as far as they knew, he hadn't been spotted anywhere in the area.

Winded and relaxed, Kaia and her grandmother slipped back into the house. Mac was standing at the kitchen counter, drinking his cup of coffee.

Kaia immediately brewed a mug of tea for Jackie and grabbed another for herself.

"Any issues?" Mac asked.

"Not a one." Kaia blew across the top of her tea before taking a tentative sip. "We'll have to ask Hank and the others, but I'm pretty sure we were alone out there today."

She looked to her grandmother for confirmation.

Jackie nodded. "I didn't see any sign or get any feelings that he was watching us."

Mac contemplated that for a minute. "I don't know if I like that or not. Hopefully it means that he's injured and laid up dying somewhere. I just wish I knew for sure."

"My guess is he'll probably be out of commission for a bit," Kaia speculated. "Once he recovers, he'll make his move." She narrowed her eyes. "And then he's going down."

The pace of the last two days became their unofficial routine. Kaia and Jackie would have their morning runs. And then, while Mac went off to work, Jackie would accompany Kaia to the barn to help out there. They easily developed a working rhythm, and the next three days passed quickly and without incident.

But the longer it went on, the more on edge everyone became.

It was like right before a rainstorm when the air thickened, the weight of it pressing heavily against them while they waited for the bottom to fall out. They needed Gerald to show himself, to bring this tension to a head.

Kaia was in the round pen with Oscar on the fourth day, when suddenly, she knew.

He was here somewhere. He was watching her.

His wicked stare felt cold and disgusting, making the hair on the nape of her neck stand up. Her cat came to full alert, sensing danger was near.

Oscar, ever the troublemaker, noticed her distraction and threw his head, jerking her arm. Kaia gathered his lead to return him to his stall, when she saw Jackie step out of the rear door of the barn at the same time a shot rang out. Kaia saw Jackie pitch forward and land hard in the dirt, a bright red bloom growing beneath her head.

"No!" Kaia screamed, only vaguely aware of the answering squeal from the horse behind her. For the first time since they'd begun working together, Kaia ignored him and bolted out of the pen towards her grandmother.

But before she could reach her side, Gerald walked out of the barn. He was holding a rifle and smiling at her.

"At last. You are mine."

Gerald stood over Jackie's downed body, not paying one bit of attention to the woman he'd just murdered.

Kaia's voice was sharp as a blade and just as deadly. "I am going to kill you, you sick son of a bitch." Kaia stalked towards him, her only focus the demented man standing just feet away. "I will rip your head from your body and shred the rest to pieces."

He must have read his death in her eyes, because he gave a start and raised the barrel. It pointed directly at her, but she didn't care. This piece of shit would never leave here alive.

Something behind her drew his notice. His face went through

wave after wave of expressions. The slight fear she'd prompted in him was replaced with confusion, then shock, and finally rage.

Now it was his turn to shout. "No! Impossible!"

Her cousins were coming. Kaia turned just enough to see four mountain lions racing across the open pasture of land, screaming their fury. They vaulted the split-rail fence as if it were nothing. She had seconds to finish this bastard before they reached him and did the job for her.

But while she'd been focused on her family, Gerald had shifted and now stood in a tattered pile of shredded clothing, hissing and snarling as if readying for battle.

Kaia wasted no time in following his lead. Within a heartbeat, she was transformed.

Faced with five cats meaning to kill him, Gerald hesitated, and then bolted the opposite direction.

Kaia was right on his tail as he streaked through the barn and out the front side. He made a wide turn and headed back around the corner, his only option the woods as a means of escape.

No way in hell was she going to let that happen.

Kaia pushed for more speed and hit the tree line seconds behind Gerald. She raced through the forest in pursuit of the killer. The others were right behind her, closing in fast. But she'd had a head start, and she knew these woods better than they did. Her cat stretched with maximum reach each stride to cover the most ground and eat up the distance between them.

But then, so did the cat in front of her. He was larger, longer, and faster, but she wouldn't give up. She was going to take him down. One way or another, Gerald had signed his death warrant the moment he'd shot her grandmother. His reign of terror ended now. Today. And she'd be the one to finish it.

She blocked out the image of Jackie lying motionless and bleeding. But she'd use the rage it conjured to fuel her legs.

He fled through the trees, darting this way and that. He'd done well to familiarize himself with the area, but she'd grown up playing here. She could navigate this forest with her eyes closed.

They'd run close to half a mile when she saw him dart around the corner of a rocky outcropping. She followed with no other thought than not losing sight of him. There were multiple trails that led off from here when it opened up around the bend.

With a powerful shift of muscle, a flip of her strong tail, she'd just made the turn when she was hit by something heavy. Dropping down on her from above, the weight of it knocked her flat, driving her into the dirt, and the air from her lungs.

Kaia fought wildly against the mass holding her. Her cat screamed out it's frustration at being tricked. And then screamed again, this time in pain as claws raked across her stomach and side. Her chest heaved in and out as she tried to breathe through the searing burn.

Rough hands gripped her around the throat. It took her a moment to get past the pain enough to realize her attacker had let go of his cat and was now just a man, far more vulnerable to her sharp, talon-like claws. In desperation, she struck, swiping at him wildly, trying to land blow after blow.

But he was more cunning, and he'd planned his landing well. Stronger than she'd expected, he pinned her from behind, using his massive weight to battle off her attack with ease. He bent naked over her, his face close to her muzzle but still far enough away to spare him from being bitten.

"Shift. Now." His tone brooked no argument, and his fingers closed so tightly around her throat, she thought she might pass out. Her cat roared in protest, and she struggled against his hold anew.

They could both hear the others coming. Kaia wanted to grin and tell him to kiss his ass goodbye. But his next words froze her heart.

"Shift now, or your whole family will die. Do you think no one knows where I am? If I don't return, those loyal to me have been instructed to hunt down every member of your bloodline one by one, until they are extinct. So do as I say. Now."

Her cat lay still, panting. She thought of Jackie, lying in her own pool of blood. Of the cousins she had just met. Of the countless others she had yet to meet. And the innocent children her grandmother had already told her so much about. She couldn't allow any more of her family to be hurt. The look in his eyes promised to deliver on his threats, and he was crazy enough to do it. He would kill them all.

With no other option, she did as he commanded.

The open wounds on her chest, stomach, and side burned like hellfire as she made the change. Once the transformation was complete, the pain hit her full force and made her light-headed. She glanced down at herself and saw four parallel claw marks bisecting her torso. From left shoulder, across her breasts, and ending at the ribs on the right side. Another started at her right hip and extended to her belly button.

Gerald had known exactly how much force to use to not mortally wound her. She would heal, but the scars would forever remain.

Just then, Erik came barreling onto the tableau. Gerald hauled her up, pulling her roughly back against his naked chest, effectively using her as a shield should Erik, or anyone else, try to launch at them.

"That's far enough!" Gerald shouted. "Take another step, and I'll snap her neck!"

Erik's large male cat stopped in his tracks. Kaia watched as he shifted, becoming a tall, broad-shouldered man. As he glared at Gerald, three more mountain lions entered the picture. Without command, Hank, Jayme, and Paul fanned out, forming a half-circle around Gerald and leaving Erik to try and defuse the situation.

"If anyone makes a move, she's dead," her captor warned, eyeing the group carefully.

Erik, seemingly unbothered by his or anyone else's nudity, pulled Gerald's attention back to himself. "You'll never get out of here. Just let her go, and we won't kill you."

The sound of pounding hoof beats distracted them all for a moment.

Bareback, Mac flew onto the scene. He instantly pulled back on the black flowing mane and skidded Oscar to a halt when he came upon them unexpectedly.

What the hell was he doing here? How had he found them? Kaia fought back tears as she watched him.

Shrewd eyes took in the scene in a split second. Mac threw his leg over Oscar's neck and slid from the horse's back. At the same time, he drew his gun in one smooth and practiced motion. It may have been gripped and ready, but Kaia knew he wouldn't take a shot if there were any chance she'd be hit.

Ice dripped from Mac's words. "Do as he says and back away from her, Gerald."

Shock, and then intense relief, slapped Kaia in the face as another cougar silently padded in behind Mac. There was blood on the side of the tawny face, but there was no mistaking who this feline was. Jackie.

Kaia blinked, trying to clear her eyes. She'd seen her die.

Her thoughts were interrupted when Gerald gripped her tighter and spoke. "She's mine. She was always *meant* to be mine." At his declaration, Kaia gasped when the fingers at her throat shifted into claws. Since she could still feel the hard shape of him behind her, she knew the rest of him had stayed fully human. How was that even possible?

Her musings were jerked back to the present when he flexed the muscles in his arm, and the claws dug into her tender skin. At the same time, the other banded forcefully around her. It lay just beneath her bare breasts, directly over the rake marks he'd inflicted earlier. She drew in a sharp breath as pain lanced through her. Her wounds throbbed, and a steady stream of blood flowed as he kept her pressed against his body.

"No one will stand in my way this time. She was meant to be my mate—bear my children. She should have always been mine." His voice rose. "No one denies me!"

Kaia felt, more than saw, the other cougars edging closer in response to his madness. Gerald must also have seen, because his claws dug deeper into her throat.

Enough to make her whimper. The sound of her distress had Mac's face hardening, his hands gripping tighter on the gun. The muscle flexing in his jaw said he was using every ounce of self-control not to strike out at the monster holding her.

"Not another inch, or I'll rip her throat out." Gerald tipped her head back forcefully, showing them all how exposed she was. "I will kill her before I lose her again. She and I are leaving here, and none of you will follow."

She could hear the irrational tone in his voice. He was completely deranged.

"Gerald." Jackie stepped forward into the tense silence. The red staining her face and neck was a sharp contrast to her pale skin.

"You have to stop this, Gerald. Corinne wasn't yours. And neither is Kaia. You've ruined lives with your obsession. It has to end."

"I've waited years for my mate to come back to me. And now that I have her, no one will take her away from me again."

"That's not Cori, Gerald," Jackie said gently, trying to talk him down. "That's her daughter. And you're hurting her. You know Cori wouldn't want that."

"You lie!" he shouted. "You've hidden her from me all this time. Well, I've finally found her. And I am taking her with me."

It was evident he couldn't be reasoned with. There was no

telling how many would be hurt if Kaia didn't do something.

Swallowing around the pressure at her neck, Kaia cleared her throat. "I have to go with him. He has men on standby, waiting to hunt down our entire family line if Gerald doesn't come back. I can't let anyone else die because of this obsession. I have to end this."

Jackie's eyes met hers. "No. This ends here and now, because he has no one."

Kaia heard the truth in Jackie's words. Gerald had manipulated her again, and for that alone, she wanted to rip him to shreds with her own claws. But without shifting, that wasn't an option.

Wait. Could she do as he'd done? And transform only a part of herself? The hand that was only inches away from the most vulnerable part of a man. Could she do it?

Hell yes she could.

Barely even hearing the conversation as it continued, Kaia closed her eyes and concentrated on her right hand. She called to her cat and explained what she needed. She fought her a little—the hostile female wanted her own revenge on the monster that had hurt her. Kaia promised her if she did this one thing, when they were free, she would have her chance.

The lioness agreed.

It took Kaia's full focus to limit the shift to just that one hand. But she did it. Her eyes opened, and her gaze darted to Mac. His expression didn't give anything away, but she thought she saw a glimmer of satisfaction in his eyes. His body tensed, the hold he had on his weapon firmed. He gave her an almost imperceptible nod. He was ready when she was.

Gritting her teeth, Kaia let loose a growl. Simultaneously, she sunk her claws into Gerald's thigh and sliced upward over his cock and ball sack.

He screamed and jumped back as bright red blood spurted down his leg. In his surprise, he'd released her, but before she could strike at him again, he shifted. Catching motion out of the corner of her eye, she noticed Erik had make the change also. He and the others all crowded in to subdue Gerald and had him surrounded when she spoke.

"No. He's mine."

"Kaia..." Mac started.

She met his worried eyes as her body straightened, already assuming the role that was hers to play. "I need to do this, Mac. He's cost us enough."

He held her gaze for a moment and then gritted his teeth as he gave an abrupt nod. "Then get it done."

His confidence in her pushed any lingering doubt from her mind. She slid her glance to her grandmother. Jackie solemnly nodded.

Gerald's cat stared at her with murder in his eyes. He stood in the center of the circle made by her four cousins. He didn't dare try to run.

Kaia walked to the edge of the ring and stopped between two of the tawny bodies. Looking down at the rest of her family, she got a look from each of them that said, "Finish him, or we will." They were giving her the chance to find the justice she needed.

She let the change wash over her and felt power and strength fill her as bones and muscle reformed into one pissed-off feline. She gave a loud roar and then stalked past the line of her family and into the arena where only one of them would be coming out alive.

Kaia watched him closely, following what Jace had taught her so long ago. She could almost hear his voice whispering to her as his spirit joined hers in battle. *Don't focus on any one thing. Let your eyes see it all. When he gives the signal, be ready.*

The bunching of the muscles in his hind legs gave her an inner smile. *Gotcha.*

It was her only warning before he sprang. With a mighty leap, he crossed the distance between them in a blink. But she was one step ahead, dodging to the side. She swiped out with her paw to leave a trail of blood down his flank.

Before he had a chance to recover, she was on him. They tore at each other with claws and teeth, trying to find every soft and exposed spot. Growls and hisses filled the air as they fought. Kaia smelled blood—his and hers.

Along with the new gouges she'd inflicted, the wound to his groin was still bleeding heavily. He was losing a lot of blood, but then again, so was she. Her own fur was slick and matted, both new and old wounds flowing freely.

They broke apart, both heaving breaths in and out. They circled around each other, looking for the best way to strike. With a flurry of swiping paws, they came together again, rearing up on their hind legs.

Kaia ducked a blow meant to take her head from her shoulders and saw her opening. With deadly precision, she used her cat's balance and agility to twist around. She darted in, and her jaws clamped down on his throat, cutting off all oxygen.

Her long, deadly fang teeth penetrated deeply into veins and tissue. Blood was hot and thick in her mouth as she held him securely. He fought to free himself, raking at her ineffectually with his claws, but he was dead—he just didn't know it yet.

Injured and sore, she gathered the remaining strength she had left, and bit down, crushing his airway and ending it. Ending him. She heard the snap as she felt his neck break.

His body went limp underneath her, and she released her grip to slip out of the circle of her family.

Aching, tired, and limping, she padded her way to Mac. He held his uniform shirt in his strong, capable hands. This was the second time he'd taken the clothing off his own back for her.

The transformation back to human hurt beyond anything she'd ever known. So much so, she couldn't keep her feet and collapsed into Mac's arms. He wrapped the stiff cotton around her as her grandmother rushed over, tears in her eyes.

She stroked a hand over Kaia's hair and smiled. "You're going to be all right, sweetheart. We'll get you fixed up." She looked over at Mac. "Let's get her back to the house."

"How...?" Kaia trailed off.

Jackie smiled down at her. "I'll explain later."

Mac lifted her off her feet and cradled her against his chest. As he began to turn, Erik strode over. "We'll take care of the rest of it."

"Thank you," Kaia rasped, the pain still overwhelming.

Erik touched her arm. "You did good, cousin."

Kaia could only nod. She could feel the breakdown coming, and she wanted to be away from everyone when it happened.

She was able to stand long enough for Mac to mount the horse. He braced his foot for her to use as a stirrup. With help from Erik and Mac, they fit her across his lap. Mac held her all the way back to the barn. Once he'd gotten her settled inside the cruiser, he slid into the driver's seat. He started the car and pulled out on the road, headed back to her place. She snuggled in close beside him and finally let the tears flow.

The torrent had passed by the time the others made it back. Mac set about cleaning all of her wounds while the others saw to her grandmother.

Mac brought her some hot tea a little later. She drank it gratefully and then slipped into sweet oblivion.

<div align="center">~~~</div>

She awoke sometime later, confused. She couldn't remember falling asleep, let alone being tucked into bed. It took a few minutes to figure out that there must have been something in her tea. She couldn't be too mad about it, though, because she actually did feel a lot better.

Throwing the covers aside, Kaia looked down at her naked

chest and stomach. The slash marks were already healing. A big benefit of being a shifter was faster healing abilities. She would always carry the scars from today, but in no time, the worst of it would be gone.

Finding some loose clothes, she made her way to the kitchen. Mac was sitting at the table drinking coffee. It reminded her of another time he'd held vigil for her to wake from being drugged.

She went directly to him. When he saw her and sat back, she curled herself into his lap.

"How are you feeling?" His voice was soft, as were the hands that wound gingerly around her waist in an effort not to hurt her.

"Still a little beat up, but not nearly as sore." She grinned and lifted one eyebrow. "So, which one of you spiked my tea?"

He looked a little sheepish. "That would have been your grandmother. She didn't warn me she was going to do it, so I might have freaked out a bit when you went under."

"I would have loved to see that." Kaia kissed his cheek and then rested her head on his shoulder.

"She assured me all you needed was some sleep, and that it would make all the difference in the world."

"She was right." Looking around, a frown creased her forehead. "Speaking of…Where is everyone?"

Using one hand, Mac pressed her head back to his shoulder. "One car load already left, but Jackie, Erik, and Jayme stayed behind. You didn't sleep as long as they thought you would—they figured they had enough time to go and grab something to eat. They'll be back in a while."

She sat up. "Oh, my God. What about Jackie? How is she? How is she even alive? I thought…" She couldn't finish the sentence.

"She's fine. She has a big gash on the side of her head. And probably a concussion, but she'll be okay. It was just a graze."

"But the blood." She could still see it. "There was so much

blood."

Mac pulled her back in close to his body. "I saw it when I got there. But head wounds bleed a lot. Which I guess is a good thing, because along with you, it made Gerald think he'd killed her."

"How were *you* even there?" Kaia replayed the moment he'd come tearing in on Oscar. He'd looked like one of the Four Horsemen, come to deal out some death.

"I'd had a bad feeling all day. I couldn't shake it, so I followed my instincts and drove out to the farm. I must've gotten there soon after the rest of you had chased after Gerald. Jackie was just coming around and told me what had happened and where you'd gone. Oscar was already there, so I just grabbed him and took off. He's a fucking bullet, Kai. Holy shit, I couldn't believe how fast he caught up. I think he knew you were in danger and wanted to get to you. I had no problem at all with him fighting me."

Kaia took a deep breath and sobered. "Am I going to be in any trouble for killing Gerald? I know he's from an important family. His father was the leader of their clan, and so was he."

Mac's arms tightened around her reassuringly. "No. You won't be facing any kind of charges or repercussions from either clan. Before they left to go eat, I asked Jackie the same thing. Apparently, while I was getting you cleaned up, she'd already called to let them know what had happened here. She explained that the clans have always been aware of Gerald's history. They've all known he was unstable, which is why his father kept such a close watch over him. As far as they're concerned, you acted in self-defense, and you have the right to protect yourself and your loved ones."

Kaia took a deep breath and released it. "I'm just glad it's finally over. Not only for us, but for my family. I think my parents can rest easier now, knowing that the threat is gone. And my grandparents can have some measure of closure knowing that we finally got the bastard in the end."

The sound of the front door opening drew Kaia and Mac's attention. She thought it must be her grandmother and cousins returning. But the voice that greeted her wasn't theirs.

"We're home," the voice said in a sing-song way.

Kaia jumped up, wincing a little. "*Bri?*"

They came together in the living room and hugged fiercely. Finally letting go of her friend, Kaia bent down to gather Min up into her arms.

"Hi, sweet girl. I've missed you guys."

"Orsey?" Min demanded.

Kaia and Bri both laughed.

"Yes. We'll go see the horses," Kaia answered with a smile, pushing the fear and sadness away. Now wasn't the time for that. Now was for celebrating.

She turned back to Bri. "What are you doing back here so soon?"

"Mac called a few hours ago and said the coast was clear."

Kaia pivoted around slowly to stare dumbfounded at the man standing behind her. "You called her?

Mac gave her a nonchalant shrug.

He may not care for Bri—a fact that Kaia was bound and determined to change—but he knew she'd missed having her best friend there.

In three steps, she was toe-to-toe with him. She grabbed the front of his shirt in one hand and pulled him down to her. Just before her lips met his, she whispered, "I love you."

"And I love *you.*"

Kaia lifted on tip-toe and planted a kiss on Mac's lips. Min squealed in delight, bouncing in Kaia's arms. The adults all laughed, and Kaia handed the little girl back to her mother.

They moved as a group to the sofa. While Min played with blocks on the floor, Kaia and Mac recounted the recent events to Bri.

She sat stunned for a moment, her amber eyes wide. "This is all so unbelievable."

She looked like she was going to say more but was interrupted by the return of Kaia's family. Kaia was excited for her best friend to meet her remarkable grandmother.

She rose to make the introductions.

"Bri, I'd like you to meet my grandmother, Jackie Logan. Jackie, this is my best friend, Brianna Calladega."

Jackie came forward as Bri stood. "It's so great to meet you." Jackie took Bri's hand in hers. "I'm so glad my girl has had people around her who love her as much as we do."

Bri smiled brightly. "She definitely has that. She and I have been friends since elementary school." She turned and grinned at Kaia. "At this point, we're more sisters than mere friends."

"I'm so happy to hear that." Jackie motioned to the others behind her. "These are two of Kaia's cousins, Erik and Jayme Reid."

Bri smiled in greeting at Jayme. Then slid her gaze to Erik's. Kaia actually felt the moment their eyes connected.

There was a wave of...something—attraction, need, lust, combustibility—that exploded throughout the room. She was surprised it hadn't knocked both of them on their asses. The only outward sign from Bri and Erik that anything had happened was Bri's quick intake of breath and Erik's pupils expanding.

Kaia mentally rubbed her hands together in glee. *Oh, this is going to be good.*

Misha McKenzie has been an avid reader since learning how at four years old. Countless books later, she still loves to immerse herself into the lives of the people within those pages. After graduating high school, she went on to earn a degree in Business Administration, married her high school sweetheart, and had two beautiful boys. At thirty years old, while working as an office manager for a construction company, a family of witches began to brew, and The Magic of the Heart Series was born.

www.ingramcontent.com/pod-product-compliance
Lightning Source LLC
Chambersburg PA
CBHW051653180726
48284CB00006B/1986